Frank Rosewater

Utopia: A Romance of Today

A Solution of the Labor Problem, a New God & a New Religion

Frank Rosewater

Utopia: A Romance of Today
A Solution of the Labor Problem, a New God & a New Religion

ISBN/EAN: 9783743422179

Manufactured in Europe, USA, Canada, Australia, Japa

Cover: Foto ©Andreas Hilbeck / pixelio.de

Manufactured and distributed by brebook publishing software (www.brebook.com)

Frank Rosewater

Utopia: A Romance of Today

UTOPIA

A romance of today

PRESENTING

A SOLUTION OF THE LABOR PROBLEM, A NEW GOD & A NEW RELIGION.

by

FRANK ROSEWATER

F. TENNYSON NEELY
PUBLISHER

LONDON   NEW YORK

CONTENTS.

CHAPTER I.

My story begins with a blotch.

It was a huge spot, intensely black and shapeless, with a glaring bull's-eye in the center.

It appeared clad with a distinct personality and its look was so fixed and penetrative it went direct to my brain like an arrow.

It irritated that organ just as if the cold steel of an auger had been driving through the sensitive tissue.

That I ever survived the torture seems a miracle now, but at the time I must have been on the verge of madness.

That I did survive goes far to corroborate the oft-repeated assertion of my friend Dr. Giniwig that facts are the greatest of all miracles. "Facts" he says "are tangible miracles." Facts are common and that is the reason we have long ago ceased to open our mouths in wonder at them. Still they are wonders, and greater wonders by far than the intangible miracles of old. Miracles were fashionable in those days when nothing was worth thinking of unless it seemed impossible and the more utterly impossible it seemed the more it was regarded; and fashionable people are just that way to this day. Mark how our beautiful mock diamonds are snubbed as vulgar by Dame Grundy to whom only the costly gem is "proper," all going to show that

It's dollars, not beauty; it's wonder, not truth
Still catches the eye of the vulgar uncouth.

To return to the blotch, the thing was full of evil forboding and seemed possessed of a malignant spirit.

The apparition was irrepressible, clinging to my vision as if riveted to the eye. If I turned my head it would wheel around in a circle, never for a moment relaxing its incessant gaze. I tried lying on my back, but when it looked down plumb from the ceiling the torture became unendurable. I tried muffling my face in a pillow; I covered it with my hands, but all in vain.

There was no escape from the thing. The blotch with the evil eye was ever visible and the cold auger kept turning on, as if boring into my brain.

Was I mad?

Possibly; but before saying more let me explain its origin, for I know all about the blotch and can remember the very day it began to look so at me.

We were to celebrate our nuptials on Saturday next, Violet Murdock and I, and it was now Wednesday.

That was July the 12th in the dreadful year of the Columbian panic. We had a Columbian Fair the same year, but the panic was an outside exhibit to show the world our skill in finance.

Violet Murdock was a charming little bud of American womanhood with a mingling of dash and discretion and a pair of dark, bewitching eyes singularly entrancing. Her youth had been spent at a frontier fort within view of the snowy crests of the Sierras and here, unhampered by the conventionalities of city society she grew up a living embodiment of art in form and action. Truth was the fountain of her heart and spontaneity was her life.

In Paris she was adored and worshiped, her naive manner and sparkling vivacity infusing a fresh and piquant interest into the finished formalism of the salon.

She had become the flower of fashionable Paris, and when the whole world was at her feet it was not at all remarkable I should be among her admirers.

I was the senior member of a Chicago firm, rated at a cool million, and it seemed as if fortune were showering all her favors upon me when this charming woman yielded her consent to share my life.

On the Wednesday morning alluded to a cablegram was placed in my hand. The writing was peculiar but I had no difficulty making out the message, which read:

Chicago, July 12, 1893.

To Ross ALLISON, Paris:

Everything lost. Business completely gutted. Schuyler did it working ticker. Suicided. Awful, but brace up, Ross and God help you. WILLARD STOKES.

Never was a man more dumbfounded.

As the significance of the unwelcome message began to dawn upon me I fell back in my chair and supporting my head on both elbows, sat poring over the lines of that cablegram.

I remember sitting there in a dazed condition staring at the horrid message until the lines began to waver and thicken, slowly becoming more and more indistinct, and then the whole sheet gradually became one mass of black.

There it was, turning blacker and blacker—intensely black, and then the bull's-eye began to glisten and the thing began to lose its shape, and then its light poured into my brain and it became rigid like a tool, boring and boring away—and that kept right on.

The blotch, I tell you, started from nothing but that cablegram.

My world that morning consisted of just two things, myself and the blotch. Under my window was the liveliest boulevard in Paris but my vision was for all that complete in that mass of black, the evil-eyed blotch.

A hand on my shoulder startled me.

Turning around I was still more startled to be confronted only by the blotch.

Had I been touched by a spirit hand?

I was not a believer in spiritualism and inwardly laughed at the idea. I was sure I *felt* the touch, and had anyone been there he must have been incorporeal.

It made me feel strange until a voice broke the silence.

"Don't be alarmed, Ross; it's only me!" the voice said and I recognized it as soon as it struck my ear.

It was the voice of my friend, Dr. Giniwig—"Dr. Jacob Giniwig (first g soft, second g hard)" as his stationery invariably reads ever since a wag some years ago distorted the name into guinea pig.

"Bz–z—z——z——"

The hissing noise proceeded from the blotch, now assuming a definite form with a little blaze rising from a lower corner. It also gave forth an odor of smoke, and in the light I could read the very words of the cablegram.

In a few moments the whole thing had gone up. The next thing I saw Dr. Giniwig flinging away the remnant of a match.

"There's no cure for melancholia like prevention," he dryly remarked with a professional air of authority.

"You have destroyed my cablegram. What made you do that?" I ejaculated, displeased at his apparent audacity.

"Your cablegram—why Ross, my boy, you mean your hallucination. Be seated a moment and calm yourself. I will tell you all about it."

After a pause he continued:

"First of all let me tell you, Ross, you never had a cablegram. What you really saw was only a dream—an hallucination—a peculiar state of the mind or rather the nerves. The trouble was purely nervous and came from worry over your American investments."

Drawing out his cigar case he then compelled me to join him in a smoke and when our Havanas were lit he resumed:

"I was in your room a full hour before I realized you were laboring under an hallucination, and from some of your remarks I concluded it had begun with an imaginary cablegram. I had to reach the cablegram in order to dispel the illusion. So with a little study I finaly hit upon a plan, and after burning a whole bunch of matches I struck the objective location of the blotch, as you called it. At once the flame caught your eye and your tendency to illusion enlarged the flame, wiped out the blotch, destroyed the cablegram and presto, brought you to your normal senses. It was a magnificent case of *similia similibus curantur.*"

No one can imagine what a depressing effect that imaginary boring had, and I did not even myself realize it until relief had come. When the Doctor had finished his narrative therefore I was overjoyed, and never was a happier man than I, after being convinced that the cablegram had been only an illusion.

CHAPTER II.

"Ever been up in a balloon?" Dr. Giniwig en quired of me the next morning.

"No, I never have," I responded.

"I thought as much," he resumed, and after a moment's pause he continued, in his quiet, decisive way "to-morrow then you will make your first ascent."

I put in a vigorous protest but my professional friend insisted I was still in his charge and until I left Hotel Giniwig, his establishment, completely restored, I must submit to his regimen.

"Everything is arranged for 2 p. m. sharp;" he said, "today is Thursday—that will be Friday, and your wedding is to be Saturday. Humph! You'll be just in time, and I guarantee you will come back another man. A jolly quartet we will make with the Bacelle brothers to manipulate our air-ship! You've heard of the brothers—the most skilled balloonists in France and gymnasts of the first rank! There will be no danger whatever in their care, and the Sky Chariot is as sound a bag as ever held gas!"

"I expect to enjoy the sport; it will be capital!" I exclaimed, finally becoming elated at the idea.

"I knew you'd be delighted with it, Ross; but here I have something will *astound* you" he exclaimed, producing a pair of long wide-necked bottles and then he began pouring from one into the other a glittering liquid.

I had never seen anything but diamonds that sparkled like this liquid, and yet this was in broad daylight.

"Pretty, isn't it?" the Doctor asked, chuckling. "You wouldn't think this liquid can be crystalized so that the product became such perfect diamonds they couldn't be detected from the real gems even by an expert? It is a fact though, and it costs less than five francs to make a pound of the crystals. What do you think of that?"

There must have been an awful look of amazement upon my face for the Doctor immediately added:

"I've better use for it, my friend, than manufacturing diamonds! Now this is no halluciation; it is a great discovery—will revolutionize the world!"

His last words were spoken in a semi-whisper, and accompanying them he placed one of the bottles in my hand, label toward me and there I read the words "Dr. Giniwig's Shampoo" with the usual pronouncing directions underneath.

Putting aside the bottle he stationed himself in an easy chair almost opposite me, and cocking his feet on the desk before him began to address me in a style as if delivering a lecture to students:

"Someone, I believe it was Carlyle, has described man as the tool-making animal. This suggested to me the fact that a tool is an extension of the hands provided by nature. Nature furnishes animals with organs similar to those given to man but to man she has given ideas by the use of which he extends the organs, thereby greatly enlarging their scope and power.

"The telescope is only an extension of the eye, and so is the microscope. The telephone is an extension of the ear, and the phonograph extends the voice.

The wagon and the railway car are extensions of the feet, and so are the steamboat, the balloon and the bicycle.

"Our greatest achievements I recognized were extensions of the primary faculties and organs, and this led me to ask why, if the eye and ear can be so remarkably extended, could not the brain also be extended by artificial appliances.

"Eye and ear are but petty nerve centers in comparison with the brain, which is the greater eye that sees the relations things bear to each other and which, translating its views to language, is limited to the wordy process called reasoning. But the mind really sees; it does not reason, that being a lame process necessary in communicating its views. Memory is one form of its vision.

"But to the point. Years ago I had come to the conclusion that as we could at will move backward and forward in space and return to the same spot after years of absence, so the field of time must likewise be an open expanse awaiting only a better knowledge before we might be permitted to come and go, roaming backward or forward at will, returning to a condition of childhood and then advancing again toward riper maturity. All it required was to be able to reverse the order of development. Control the direction of growth and we may then grow younger or older as we like.

"I am not ready to claim complete success in my discovery, but I have so far succeeded that by acting upon the cellular corpuscles of the brain I transpose my patients back ten, twenty, nay fifty years in time, making the old become young and the sick return to primitive health. During the transformation they remain in a cataleptic state from which they recover only after the shampoo has expended its force.

"Why the shampoo has this peculiar effect" he explained in answer to one of my inquiries "I cannot tell. No one knows why strange things occur in life, but we all know they do occur. Why does fire burn and why does electricity produce such marvellous results? We may trace effects from one cause to the next but soon we arrive at a point whence no further answer comes and for final answer the existence of a fact is as good an explanation as any that can be made."

"A very good hoax, Doctor; but I am not subject to illusions today," I said in a jocular way after listening attentively to his wonderful tale.

"A hoax! Ha! Ha! Ha! Ha!" the Doctor retorted with a burst of laughter so violent that it tore a button from his vest. "I dare say I expected as much," he resumed, "for no one was more surprised that myself at the success of the experiment!"

"When the time comes, my dear boy, I'll verify my words by an *army of patients* that have been snatched from the jaws of death—cases embracing everything from a slight fever to consumption. The cure is so simple! All I have to do is to apply the shampoo, set them back to a period anteceding the disease and then simply let them start life over under altered surroundings, a different atmosphere for breathing and a change of water for drinking, and ninety-nine chances out of a hundred their troubles will never recur.

"One elderly lady I treated became so young and beautiful that her husband actually got to be roaring jealous, so that in order to maintain peace in the family I had to treat him to a shampoo gratis, and there never was a spoonier couple than this pair in their newly purchased second childhood!"

"Your story sounds plausible Doc, but for the silence of the newspapers. You couldn't muzzle the press if the story were true; yet I must say I admire it very much,'' I remarked with an air of triumphant incredulity.

"Yes, and it's as true as it is good," responded the imperturable Giniwig. "Why muzzle the press, my dear boy, when I could easier muzzle my patients! My terms have invariably been cash in advance and a bond to bind the patient to secrecy or else no treatment."

"In a short time my shampoo will become so commonplace," the Doctor continued, "no one will regard it with wonder and it will pass into the ranks of despised facts—too near us to be justly appreciated. You see the mind has its perspective as well as the eye, only it is just the reverse. A bird in the bush always looks as big as two in the hand, and the apple on the tree is sweeter by far than the best fruit on the table."

By this time the Doctor's blood was stirred, and rising from his chair he began to pace the room, rubbing his hands with evident glee till his eyes sparkled almost as bright as his wonderful liquid. Finally he got back into his chair again and once more began to speak.

"When I tell you my shampoo is a never-failing universal cure-all and a practical life-renewer, having the power to prolong life indefinitely I have only *begun* to enumerate its virtues.

"Of what avail would it be to live forever if we led wretched lives surrounded by hopeless poverty? If it were merely for the purpose of deluding mortals into extending the period of their sufferings I had better hide the discovery from the world and sink the shampoo into oblivion!"

"You might at least acquire a fortune with it,

Doc !" I said "and such a fortune, too, as would make the Vanderbilts and the Rothschilds beggars in comparison !"

"True, very true ;" retorted my friend "but I hope I shall never resort to quackery for the sake of paltry gold, be the sum large or small! I do intend to make a fortune, but I dare say I shall not take so much that conscience will turn it to a curse. I told you the liquid would preserve men in a cataleptic state—that is the pure liquid—and that puts one back a whole year in less that a day, but I have since discovered that a very weak dilution prolongs the cataleptic state almost indefinitely and scarcely alters one's condition.

"In the dilution its power will eventually free labor from the tyranny of capital, for it will furnish the workingman with a weapon that will render him simply invincible in future strikes."

"As a medical remedy, Doc," I said "I am perfectly ready to subscribe to your shampoo, but when you propose to put capitalists in a cataleptic state so as to get the better of them, I protest——"

I did not finish the sentence for I was interrupted by another of the Doctor's great laughing fits.

"My dear Ross !" he said on regaining his breath, "you have placed the cart before the horse this time, sure enough. The shampoo, my dear fellow, is to be used upon *workingmen*—not on capitalists. The liquid will put the poor fellows and their families all to sleep whenever the provider is out of employment ; and thus, placed safely beyond the reach of hunger and cold, famine will no longer be able to terrorize them into submission to the terms dictated by capital !

"It would be a jolly affair if some day there were to be a universal strike and everyone who worked with head or hand, together with their families would go into a cataleptic state and thus remain while the moss and rust of time settled upon every human structure on the face of the globe. Then when the finger of truth was at last pointed at the false creed of wealth and its perishable nature was exposed in contrast with the iniquitous terms it exacts—a continuous income besides the repairs necessary to its perpetuation—all out of the product of labor, men will ask why things are thus. Then it will be seen this power was due to its freedom to ignore the workingman's place in the social order where division of labor prevailed but distribution of labor was left to chance and in the bad distribution a vast army of unemployed was used as a cudgel over the heads of all who worked,—a cudgel that came down here and there in the shape of starvation and despair often leading to suicide and outrages that but for the intervention of charity would long ago have exposed the cursed mark of Cain upon the brow of the capitalist."

I was thunderstruck on hearing my friend's remarks. Judging from his attitude toward capital I should have assumed he had become an anarchist, but coming after my experience·with the blotch the day previous, it led me to doubt my own senses.

"What do you think of the shampoo? Wonderful, isn't it? Well sir, I tell you Dr. Giniwig's shampoo will some day conquer the world! It will be simply irresistible! Capital—the real root of evil, and even death will be vanquished by the power of this charming liquid!"

"If your shampoo is half you claim for it it will revolutionize society," I replied in a tone of approval.

"Revolutionize society!" the Doctor ejaculated. "It will create society! it will revolutionize the anarchy of existing commerce and the semi-lawlessness of the present civil government. But by the way, a shampoo treatment would be a splendid thing to afford you rest until the hour for the ascension tomorrow. What say you to giving it a trial?"

"As long as I am in your hands, Doc," said I "I will submit to any treatment you recommend."

"Very well, then; we will now go to luncheon" my eccentric friend replied, at the same time rising, "and on your return you shall be anointed with the only *genuine* elixir of life, Dr. Giniwig's Shampoo!"

CHAPTER III.

Early in the year 1850 a party of eighteen men and women were trudging wearily along in the deep gloom of one of those vast forest caves that abound in the heart of the African continent. Overhead an impenetrable canopy of leaves hid from view the celestial worlds, sunlight and starlight, floating cloud and the infinite dome of blue. No breath of air stirred to cool their throbbing temples. No sound relieved the painful stillness, save their own footsteps and the shrill screaming or gutteral roaring of the animal creation. Fever-breeding marshes lay in their path and treacherous lagoons blinked from the dark, low grounds. Massive trees were dimly visible, and now and then some beast would rush by utterly oblivious of their presence.

The wanderers represented the sole remnant of a party of adventurers who had embarked at Calcutta bound for the California gold fields and wrecked upon the rocks of the East African coast, had been driven inland by unfriendly savages. Forty-two persons had started from the coast, but one by one disease and exhaustion had reduced their ranks to eighteen, five of whom were women.

They were rapidly growing disheartened and day by day the journey seemed to become more and more hopeless. Whither they were going no one knew. No compass guided their footsteps and for all the wan-

derers could tell they might have been moving in a
circle without the slightest chance of ever seeing daylight again.

Their leader, Capt. James Bartlett, was a veteran
seaman of undaunted spirit, but for whose constant
urging they would before this have sunk in despair
and utter abandonment.

Waking from their slumber one time the Captain
thought he espied a glimmer of light in the forest.
All immediately turned their eyes in the direction of
the supposed light, and after gazing eagerly a few
moments the majority arrived at the same conclusion,
and this naturally determined the course of their
march for the future. This discovery was soon gene-
rally verified and imbued everyone with fresh hope,
leading them to pursue their journey with renewed
vigor.

The path from now on followed an upward incline
scarcely perceptible to the wanderers, who in their
elation almost forgot hunger and fatigue.

Clearer and clearer shone the light ahead and more
and more precipitous became the ground under their
feet. Already they must have been several thousand
feet above the level of the darker portion of the forest,
and fired with hope they forged vigorously on.

How long they traveled thus no one will ever be
able to tell, for not a single timepiece in their possession would keep anything like time. Rust from ex-
posure during the wreck had ruined every watch.
Ever since they had been driven into the forest there
had been neither day nor night, and no token remained to separate one day from the next. Time had
become one vast unbroken expanse like the forest
itself.

When the wanderers finally reached a clearing they

found themselves on the summit of a circular mountain chain forming a tremendous basin at their feet—
an immense amphitheater.

Turf and verdure round about were now of a uniform golden hue and most delicious fruits and melons
hung from bough and vine. Wild peas with pods as
large as a man's arm grew in profusion and nutritious
vegetation on every side was more than abundant.

Two whole days our travelers rested here and on
the third day they started for the broad vale at the
base looking so much like a single field of golden
grain, broken with huge patches of a silvery hue.

Half a days journey down the slope the travelers
began to find the descent very fatiguing.

"Look 'ere," remarked old Captain Bartlett at last,
calling attention to his garments, "if the plagued
things 'aven't growed since morning. They's big
henough to 'old two o' me now, 'n they feels mor'n
twice as 'eavy as they used to."

"An' look 'ere;" remarked another "hi declare as
this carbine is 'eavier 'n hit was yesterday, and hit's
'alf again has long!"

Everyone hereupon began to make comparisons,
and to their astonishment the same freak seemed to
be general of all their garments and appurtenances.

The whole party was dumfounded and did not
know whether to attribute the freak to an illusion or
to some miraculous source. They talked and talked
over the seeming wonder, but the mystery would not
be unraveled, nor would their bloated garments return to their former dimensions. What was stranger
still, the clothes instead of becoming thinner and rela-
tively lighter from stretching had actually become
thicker and heavier.

As a consequence they were obliged to spend the

balance of the day in re-adapting their garments, emerging in a very primitive dress not modeled after the latest fashion plates.

Early the following day carbines and pots became too burdensome and had to be abandoned and then they considered the advisability of returning once more to the summit, but as they looked upward they were amazed at the awful height to which the mountains rose. Mortal eyes had never looked upward to such towering mountain heights and what from above had seemed to be but a low range of hills now appeared so steep and lofty as to form a practically impassable barrier. They had marched into a veritable man trap.

Only one course was left open and that was to march right on until they reached the plain below, and to establish themselves in this enchanted vale.

So they started again on their downward course and after several days arrived safely upon the plains where, to their further surprise, they were met by intelligent natives who received them in a friendly way, and among whom they found a home in which to begin life over amid entirely new surroundings. They were thankful to have escaped with their lives and to have found a refuge at last in the seclusion of this mysterious mountain hollow.

CHAPTER IV.

OUR BALLOON VOYAGE.

I saw with my eyes and I heard with my ears, but beyond that I was a mere dummy. Occurrences transpiring around me were but a pageant of color and sound, nothing more; for my mind was perfectly passive as I lay, helpless as an infant, at the bottom of the car that hung attached to the great Sky Chariot.

I recollect two men were with me in the car, one a stranger and the other Dr. Giniwig. I saw the big thing above but never dreamed it was a balloon. Of time I had no conception.

The cool atmosphere as we rose higher must have become quite chilling for the sensation on my face felt as if pricked by needles. Not an idea went through my head, but I distinctly remember the sensation of pricking although I lay there otherwise like one dead.

A sudden convulsion shook my whole body and I came to.

"Lie still, Ross!" cried Dr. Giniwig, "don't stir now till you see where you are!"

I had raised myself to a sitting posture and now stared with wonder as it dawned upon me that here I was, suspended in mid-air, caged in a frail vessel—in fact traveling in a balloon.

The air was refreshing and delightful. The stars as I looked up were as far away as ever and as I glanced down upon the moonlit earth and then back again to the sky, for the first time dawned upon my mind the immensity of space.

"How do you feel after the shampoo?" the Doctor asked. "Surprised eh, to find yourself up here?"

"Yes, rather agreeably surprised," I answered, though in reality I scarcely knew whether to regard my situation favorably or not, for a sense of terror was coming over me as I thought of our perilous altitude.

A flash of lightning to the southward revealed bunches of clouds massed threateningly in that direction.

"That's a spinner yonder; she'll be on us in five minutes, I dare say," spoke the stranger who had been keeping a sharp lookout and had not yet observed my waking.

Without a word he picked up a sack of ballast and dumped it over the side of the car. The balloon rose slightly in response. A second bag was sent over and then a third and fourth, but our upward course, or as it seemed to us, the earth's downward course, did not appear to satisfy him. He continued emptying ballast, bag after bag, until the last sack was gone and then, as if abandoning hope from this source, he turned to the Doctor.

"This storm means death unless we succeed in striking another current. Our only salvation is the parachute; so good bye!" and without more ceremony he clambered over the side of the car and in a twinkling was out of sight.

Presently the balloon gave a sudden upward lurch almost tossing us out of the car, and then it rose swiftly for several minutes.

That was the last we saw of our friend Charles

Bacelle. His brother George should have joined us
in the ascent, but owing to indisposition failed to
appear and the usual parachute descent did not take
place, Charles remaining to manage the balloon.

The sudden descent of the latter had not been calculated in our programme and here we were left, Dr.
Giniwig and I, several miles from terra firma, with a
storm approaching below, and neither of us knowing
the first thing about the management of a balloon.

The Sky Chariot was now moving due south, directly toward the coming storm, but we were far above
its level.

Bacelle's calculation of the speed of the storm had
been wrong for it was really moving at a slow rate,
and when it passed under us a quarter of an hour
later it was something terrific.

Above our heads the starry guests of night seemed
to make sport of our strange plight and their million
eyes seemed beaming full of laughter.

All was so quiet above!

Such a stillness reigned that a whisper could have
been heard for miles around.

Close to earth there is always a certain amount of
motion, if nothing else the wind brushing through the
trees so that no one who has never been high up in a
balloon can imagine what real silence is like.

In the midst of such a stillness the storm passed
below producing a noise as if the crust of earth were
being broken through in a hundred explosive erup-
tions.

The first rumbling had sent a tremor through my
body, but that noise, terrible as it seemed, was a mere
bagatelle.

Below us black armies of vapor were spitting fire
and roaring in the onslaught; vast layers were con-

tending for space, grinding each other and compress-
ing the intervening atmosphere till the thick mass
would burst. They were composed of vapor, stuff
like steam; but millions of tons were here spread in
fields of almost limitless immensity—a white mist so
thick as to appear black as coal. Nothing could be
more soft and yielding than this mist, yet it lay so
massed that each rupture of its walls sounded like the
most terrific explosion.

For more than an hour the bombardment continued
beneath us, the concussion frequently shaking our
little car in spite of the distance we were apart and
the counter-current in which we were moving.

It was a grand sight watching the storm, and after
it was over we began to observe our balloon was moving at a much faster rate than before, and the speed
seemed to be growing faster and faster. The current
was remarkably even, like a body meeting with no
obstruction, and fast as we were traveling it did not
impress us as in the least dangerous.

Owing to this remarkable rapidity of motion we
decided to keep a sharp lookout and did so for several
hours, but both of us somehow in an unaccountable
way began to grow drowsy and in spite of all our
efforts we could not overcome the sensation.

Meanwhile the sun was just rising on the hilltops,
a queer looking sun of strange violet hue, and as we
looked down the earth seemed broken into alternate
patches of gold and silver—the latter in bright dazzling sheets.

The Doctor looked puzzled.

Presently he began to sniff the air.

Taking a bottle from his pocket he uncorked it
remarking "smell this and tell me what you think."

I took a good whiff.

"Why," said I "it has the same odor I notice in the air."

"My opinion exactly" the Doctor responded, and after pondering awhile he continued:

"Do you know that the earth we see below us is a composition resembling my shampoo?-That's just what it is, and this air is impregnated with the stuff."

*
*
*

Half an hour later a balloon was floating through the sky bearing two apparently lifeless human bodies. The two bodies were neither living nor were they dead. Still the monster of the air sped on with its strange cargo passing o'er a land yet hidden from the world.

CHAPTER V.

"Shake hands, Whiskers!"

"Whiskers yourself!" I retorted in a feeble voice. Then I began to laugh and roar till my throat grew hoarse.

I had recognized the Doctor as soon as he spoke, and to think of clean-faced Dr. Giniwig behaired like a gorilla was enough to make anyone laugh, and for him to be twitting me on my whiskers made it all the more ridiculous.

The Doctor and I were both bewildered and utterly amazed over the remarkable change that had come over us, for seated in a little four by six glass cell we were staring at each other like a pair of Dromios, alternately shaking hands and laughing in the silliest fashion until we became nigh exhausted.

Where were we at, was a question we might well have put to ourselves. It was a conundrum neither of us could answer. The last thing we remembered we were up in a balloon, and just now we had risen as from slumber to find ourselves possessed of more hair than body—beards reaching to our feet and tresses likewise—the Doctor's all white and mine jet black, our finger nails as long as spikes and our only garments a pair of shrouds.

Had a practical joke been played upon us? If so Dame Nature had played an important part in the prank.

"Let's crawl out of this coop, Ross!" the Doctor
suggested, and just then our attention was attracted
by a neatly done-up parcel near the front of the cell.
It was wrapped in a pink cloth of silky texture and as
we unfolded it, lo and behold—two flasks of liquor,
some goblets and a tray of tempting viands.

The liquid in the flasks proved to be a delicious
wine and after we had partaken also of the viands it
seemed to start the old life in our veins once more.

In moving the tray afterwards we found a peculiar
card underneath on which was a communication in
English, reading:

Strangers in Lukka: Though the writer of these lines knows you
not, she takes the liberty to greet and address you as brothers. You
have been left here by the authorities of our city as dead men, but I,
suspecting you to be still living have ventured to place within your
reach these viands, trusting they will aid in sustaining you until you
escape from the vaults. When you are once at large in the city, if you
will enquire for Jurgo, my father, you will find him a trustworthy
friend. Sincerely yours, in the name of humanity,   ARDA.

"Arda! Who's Arda, I wonder!" the Doctor exclaimed.

"She's an angel, whoever she is!" I answered, and
filling the goblets out of the remaining wine, at my
suggestion we drank her health.

After this we clambered out of the narrow cell and
dropped to the floor some five feet below.

Looking around we found ourselves in an immense
chamber, a long gallery stretching as far as the eye
could see, lined on either side with cells similar to that
in which we had been confined, and in each cell to our
horror we beheld a grinning skeleton.

All the material of this strange chamber from floor
to ceiling was of crystal, and the pillars and cells in
dark but rich colors made its bony contents appear
the more hideous by the contrast.

The place received no light but what radiated from clusters of gems of huge dimensions set at intervals in the ceiling.

"Come this way, Ross! Just look here!" exclaimed the Doctor suddenly, and as I came to his side he pointed to an inscription under one of the cells. The lettering was small and pale, but in modern English and read:

Bones of Victor Galbraith, born in Tsor on the 12th day, 1st month, in the year 946 B. C.; died on the 14th day, 12th month, in the year 1005 B. C.

The Doctor shook his old begrizzled head.

"Utterly impossible!" he exclaimed. "Such English was not known in the year 1005 B. C. Why, that was long before even Julius Caesar had landed on Albion's shore. At that time the druids were still offering human sacrifices and spoke a savage tongue."

The adjoining cell was inscribed:

Bones of John Smith, son of Adam, born on the 24th day, 9th month, in the year 832 B. C. Rest, weary soul, in peace, until the trumpet of resurrection beckons thy return.

"Of all the places in Christendom I wonder where we really are!" exclaimed the Doctor completely befuddled. "Such catacombs as these have never been heard of—and these inscriptions are a real paradox!"

I was inclined to think some practical joke had been played upon us, but the more I thought of it the more preposterous seemed that notion. Our situation was a perfect enigma and just as men confronting the riddle of human life find a solution in going onward so we proceeded, trusting in providence.

Wandering further along this mysterious avenue of the dead we came upon a large opening in the center of which rose an imposing statue representing a tall person in a uniform we recognized as belonging to officers of the British navy, and on a slab at the base we read these words:

To the memory of Captain James Bartlett, founder of the British Colony in Lukka, and the gallant leader of the march through the African wilderness and later descent from the Hills of the Heavens, made in the year 1 of the British Colony, the year 1850 by Old World time.

Now we were more puzzled than before.

"So the letters B. C. denote British Colony!" the Doctor began to soliloquize. "That is better than Before Christ, but where in the trail of Father Time is the year 1005 B. C. then? When did this Victor Galbraith really die if the year 1850 corresponds with the year 1 B. C.? At that rate he died in the year 2855, and heaven only knows what year we have by this time. We are liable to be in the year 3,000 if this is correct!"

Both the where and the when of our existence seemed to be an inexplicable mystery and the more I thought the more I began to question the what of our existence.

Was I awake or dreaming? Was I living or had I died, and was this a sample of the hereafter? Was I really sane?

I recalled the blotch with its fearful bulls-eye, and then my head began to swim and only with great difficulty could I remain on my feet.

We started to walk away, but as we turned to the right we caught a glimpse of a great clock set in the pedestal of the statue. It had a large dial indexed for 24 hours and a series of lesser dials indicating not only the minutes and seconds, but also the day, month and year. Over it in raised letters were the words, "British Colony Time." So simple was it we had no difficulty determining it was now the 2d hour of the 24th day of February, in the year 1033 B. C.

"Humph," I exclaimed as I turned the figures in my head, "according to this we are living in the year 2883, and what a pair of old fogies we will be when we get back to Paris! Won't we though, old fossil?"

We moved on and turning to another side of the monument our eyes were confronted with a second clock very like the first but indicating "Old World Time!" This informed us it was the year 1894 and below the figure appeared the word "estimated."

Again the Doctor shook his head. There was certainly an irreconcilable discrepancy between these clocks and the inscriptions, for if it had been the year 1 B. C. in our year 1850, and this was the year 1033 B. C. it could by no manner of calculation be only 1894 now in our Old World time.

We were now more mystified than before (if such a thing can be) and observing there was one side of the monument we had not yet seen I stepped around, and there, to my surprise was a broad yellow slab exhibiting an elaborate inscription in closely-lettered text.

The Doctor, seeing me, came to my side and I read aloud :

The relative chronology of Lukka and the Old World have finally been scientifically determined through the accidental descent of the two now celebrated giants with their colossal balloon, which occurred on the morning of January 6, in the year 1032 B. C. Although the Colonial descendants had heard of such appliances through their ancestors they had not been aware of the existence of such giants in the Old World.

The mystery of their colossal dimensions would never have been solved but that their bodies began at once to shrink from some unknown cause, and as their garments remained unaltered it enabled careful calculations establishing the full stature of the smaller of the two at 192 feet. His reduced stature is but five feet six inches, a shrinkage in the proportion of 1 to 24. His weight shrunken was 145 pounds, whereas in full stature it was computed to exceed a thousand tons, for in each dimension he was 24 times as large as in his present stature, and there being three dimensions his weight figured exactly 13,824 pounds (about seven tons) to each pound of weight after the shrinking.

The standards of weight and measurement employed in these calculations, though acquired from averages taken by the original colonists who remembered their own statures and weights bear evidently the relation of 24 to 1, at least approximately, and this belief is further strengthened by the fact that their time bears similar relations, as their chronometers tallying with each other to the fraction of a second still registered one hour to each 24 hours of our time.

That sound is also strangely disproportioned to Lukkan ears was evidenced by the roar and clang their time-pieces made in ticking, the terrific noise being well remembered by the residents of Tsor, who at the time were thrown into a panic from sheer fright, and the noise proceeded from a distance half an hour's walk beyond the limits of the city.

Why our British Colonists experienced such difficulties with their garments and implements in coming down the Hills is now apparent, for instead of expanding garments it had been shrinking bodies that caused the disparity. This goes far to show that beyond the Hills human beings range from 120 to 150 feet in stature, or else we in Lukka measure but 2½ to 3 inches in height. Either they are giants and we are of normal stature or they are of ordinary height and we are little midgets of the most midgety kind, and outside of Lukka would have to associate with the bees and butterflies.

Another remarkable thing in connection with the dead strangers is the fact that their bodies resist the influence of the flesh-eating plants we strew over our dead, a mystery no one has yet been able to explain.

After this remarkable revelation I turned away, a bitter sadness coming over me as my peculiar predicament impressed the truth upon me. It seemed but yesterday since I had left Paris and I was to have been married there the next day. What would Violet think, or rather what had she thought? Does she ever think of me now? If she does it is only to recall me as one who had perished in that madman-like adventure in a balloon. Could I ever return? Possibly to appear as a midget, and be captured and then exhibited in some cheap museum as another Hop o' My Thumb.

"This seems to you like a puzzle — a 24 puzzle, I suppose," said the Doctor after some reflection, "but it is all very simple. We happen to be in a shampoo country—saturated with the liquid, and we arrived right in the midst of it. According to the story of these colonists this is an unknown country in the heart of Africa, but do you know it may be as large as the United States, being only 1-24 its length in either dimension by Old World measurement?"

"I'm so bewildered, Doc," I replied, "I don't really know what to believe. It seems absurd to me."

"Absurd eh!" my friend exclaimed, "life is full of absurdities. Get accustomed to a new experience and it becomes a matter of fact like lighting a match. Even so simple a thing as lighting a match would have appeared absurd before its possibility had been demonstrated. This atmosphere and shampoo soil is no more mysterious than the loadstone that guides the mariner on the seas—no more mysterious than that fluid that for ages flashed God's wrath from the clouds and was at last brought under man's dominion. Is it more mysterious than the new heavens revealed through the telescope, or the world of life hidden in a drop of water? And the camera and phonograph, are these not new vistas added to the world? My dear fellow, our world is so vast and unexplored that right here on this earth man has yet had but the merest glimpse of its possibilities, and our discovery of a new world is not in the least remarkable!"

Wandering further on we observed the inscriptions were in strange hieroglyphics, indicating we had passed the British Colony section and were now where the natives laid away their dead. There were miles and miles of these long avenues, and they were frequently intersected like the streets of a large city, so

that it seemed as if we would never find our way out
of the grewsome place.   We were almost ready to give
up in despair when I happened to espy what looked
like a great heavy door at the end of one of these long
passageways.   It proved to be a door, but it was im·
possible for us to open it.   It had meanwhile turned
night very suddenly and in the dark we found all our
efforts to effect an egress vain.

There was only one thing to do, and that was to
wait till morning, when, with the aid of light we
would find some way out.   So we stretched out upon
the cold floor, and it could not have been very long
before both of us were wrapt in slumber.

CHAPTER VI.

A STRANGE WORLD.

On waking the next morning we discovered an opening in the wall not ten yards from where we had been sleeping. It was very small, evidently intended only for ventilation. I crawled through first and afterwards, with considerable difficulty, managed to help the Doctor through, he having become wedged in after the fashion of the fox in the fable.

How our eyes did stare as we took our first view of the surrounding country! It was a picture that brought the fact of being in a strange world most forcibly to our minds, for all the colors of Nature seemed either reversed or radically altered. The sky was emerald green and a deep violet sun looked down from over the towering hills so different from the daily image we had been used to see. The ground was one sheet of silver covered with patches of golden turf like huge rugs spread over its surface, and the trees and shrubs were also golden-hued, with trunks and branches black as ebony.

The belt of mountains in the distance fully justified the name they bore, the Heaven High Hills, for within their circle all objects were dwarfed to utter insignificance in comparison. Mingling in hue with the silvery and golden colors of the plain at their base, they grew darker and darker as they rose, giving the summit the appearance of a massive frowning disc suspended in mid-air over this strangest strange lands.

From the top of a knoll near by we beheld in the distance a great city glittering like a huge cluster of jewels. It seemed peculiarly laid out in circles, fold within fold, and in the center a vast tower rose whose gorgeous colors and resplendent beauty were indescribable.

The impression of strangeness brought to my mind thoughts of Violet, now hopelessly separated, at which the Doctor, observing my dejection, remarked, "Don't look so blue, young man. How do you know but this world may be worth a dozen of the old!"

After a pause he continued, "Ah, thinking of the girl, are you? I'm really sorry for you, Ross, but my dear boy, you must forget her now, and remember there are just as good fish in the sea as ever were taken out. Suppose we make for the road yonder and follow it to the city?"

Acting upon the Doctor's suggestion we started on our way to the city in the distance. Here and there, as we jogged along, we passed queer-looking cottages, built of crystal and occasionally we would see some huge idol standing in an inclosure—evidently a place of worship. The only living creatures we met were groups of cattle with ridges rising from their spines like rows of horns. We also passed some peculiar little elephants romping in the fields as playfully as if they had been so many kittens. They were no taller than a western broncho, were as black as coal and had upward-turning tusks of pearl. They had longer limbs and were far more agile than the larger old-world species. We watched their peculiar maneuvers with much interest for they acted with a wonderful degree of intelligence, going through cotillions and cutting capers that bore resemblance to the game of tag played by school children.

After trudging along a good half hour we perceived a rider approaching from the direction of the city. He was mounted on one of these small elephants, called elphies here, and as he came close to us we were not a little surprised to be greeted with the words "Good morning, gentlemen!" in as good English as ever was spoken.

We returned his greeting upon which the stranger exclaimed:

"I presume you feel quite lost, my friends!"

"Like a pair of chicks just out of their shell!" responded the Doctor, acting as spokesman, "but I beg you, sir, not to judge us by our disheveled locks, for I assure you we are peaceably inclined and are neither lunatics nor wild men."

"Your appearance, my friends, is quite pardonable and is readily accounted for;" the stranger explained, "you see you arrived here last year, apparently dead and you were consequently placed in our catacombs. But all this will be easy to remedy and will give you little further annoyance. A closed conveyance is even now on its way and we shall soon drive to the city where a dressing at Barber Zuzo's will put you in presentable shape."

"You have been informed then, in some way, of our restoration to life?" said I, interrogatively.

"I have, indeed;" the stranger responded, dismounting while his elphy scampered to an adjoining field, "the report that you were missing reached us late last night and shortly after sunrise the place of your exit was located."

Recalling the communication we had found with the bundle of viands left in our cell I enquired as to the whereabouts of Jurgo, the person alluded to by the writer of the note.

"I have the honor to claim that name," our friend explained. "I take it, therefore, that you received my daughter's note—a strange fancy that of her's, indeed. All along she has insisted you were still *living* and while many thought you possibly were not dead she adhered to the belief that you *were really living;* and in order to relieve her mind I engaged a watchman of the vaults to see that fresh viands were always by your side and to report promptly your restoration to life."

The Doctor and I were both profuse in expressing our appreciation of their kind and thoughtful attentions.

"Don't mention it, my friends;" Jurgo retorted, "don't say another word about it!" and spreading over the ground a cloth he had borne on his arm, he invited us to be seated while he explained the strange interest he had taken in us.

To begin with, Jurgo informed us he had been a merchant for many years and had always been in comfortable circumstances. Some fifteen years ago his daughter, then a mere child, had been rescued from drowning by a barber called Zuzo who succeeded in saving her at the peril of his own life. Out of this incident a close friendship had developed between the two families and Zuzo proved to be a great student and philosopher, a fact that, owing to his reticence, was known to but a few of his most intimate friends.

It happened that at the time we came down in the balloon Zuzo was the only man in Tsor that dared scale the walls of the car and go down among the prostrate giants to trace the source of the terrific noise that had startled the citizens. On their persons he found chronometers as large as a cartwheel and from these he traced the deafening noise that ceased later in the day, after they had run down. Having discovered the cause of the commotion he began to investigate further the contents of the car and to his surprise found the bottom strewn with precious stones of enormous size and fabulous value. These stones were the fine sands that had escaped from the bags of ballast thrown overboard by Bacelle, and these in this country which is called Lukka appeared like huge rocks and their color was one very much prized here for its rarity and beauty—to the Lukkan eye.

Great a sensation as our advent in Lukka had made it was completely dwarfed by the news of Zuzo's discovery of jewels in the strange vessel that had dropped from the heavens. Here were over a ton of precious stones as fine as any in Lukka—an incalculable fortune, and by the law of the land it all belonged to Zuzo—the children of the stars, as we were designated, being regarded legally as dead, whether really so or not.

"Pardon my curiosity," I remarked if I ask how it is this man of fabulous wealth should be still engaged in a menial occupation — dissipated his fortune possibly?"

"Dissipated it — heaven forbid! Zuzo is not a man of that kind. He was robbed, and in broad daylight at that. He kept the jewels stored in a private safe depository — one he had built expressly for this purpose. One day his head watchman was presented with discharge papers signed as he thought by Zuzo, and the bearer with a new force of men took his place at once without exciting suspicion. The order of discharge of course was a forgery and the new force of guardsmen were a gang of thieves. To this very day they have not been able to trace the robbers nor to recover a single jewel. It is even suspected that the authorities are in collusion with the gang—but no one knows whom to trust and there is very little hope of ever seeing them again. Poor Zuzo feels the loss more perhaps on your account than his own, for he had regarded the jewels as belonging to you in case you returned to life."

While we were listening to Jurgo a strange vehicle resembling a tall coach all aglow like a huge crystal came toward us as if self-propelled but in reality drawn by a pair of elphies in tandem underneath.

The ebony brutes unfastened themselves with their handy trunks and scampered away while a man in a queer dress, evidently a servant, carrying a strange box stepped out and advancing to Jurgo set the box down before him.

The latter, stooping over began to manipulate the "box" and lo, it expanded into a platform answering the part of a table; then at another touch it began to blaze and crackle underneath and by some other hocus pocus he extracted one after another beautiful crystal cups filled with a beverage resembling tea and passing them around invited us to partake.

As if he had been a wizard our new friend drew forth a sumptuous repast in which the Doctor and I participated with much zest, having tasted no food since the previous day.

The repast was soon over and the magic "box" was restored to its normal shape and replaced in the roja, as the tall vehicle is styled. A shrill whistle brought the elphies back to their station under the roja, a slight clanking of chains as they fastened the latter to their harness-belts, while at Jurgo's instance the rest of us entered the strange vehicle and we were soon rolling along at a rapid rate, moving toward the heart of the great city.

CHAPTER VII.

THE UTOPIANS.

The tonsorial art as practiced in Tsor is at least unique if not artistic. Here the customary style is to trim the beard in round patches about the size of a dime, grouped according to the taste or fancy of the wearer.

The upper class train the beard to patterns in imitation of their respective insignia of rank and still others wear hieroglyphics to indicate their names.

Even the descendants of the British Colonists have adopted these customs and Jurgo himself wore a line of dots passing under his chin.

To emblazon a young dandy's face and keep it neatly trimmed called for delicate skill and among the ten thousand barbers of Tsor none were more gifted in the art than Zuzo.

Zuzo was tall, of splendid physique, with classic features and of modest, tranquil demeanor. He had decided views of his own which were not popular with his patrician patrons, but he never obtruded them upon others nor would he conceal them, and in spite of the repulsiveness of his peculiar notions to the aristocratic customer, he was well regarded among them, for his candid fearlessness always commanded respect.

Tsor's aristocracy is very democratic and is not hereditary. It simply distinguishes the bearer of a title for the amount he has contributed toward the

expense of conducting the government and is therefore prized as a great honor.   There are a dozen
grades of the Four Hundred here and the government has no need of assessors, as instead of tax
evasion people overtax themselves voluntarily in order
to enter a higher social circle.

Zuzo and three assistants were busily occupied
trimming the figured beards upon the faces of a like
number of Tsorans while at the farther end of the
long chamber was a crowd of natives engaged in animated discussion.

"Do you believe a Tismoulan league will really be
formed?" asked a young Tsoran of an elderly native.

"They may form a dozen Tismoulan leagues for a
matter of that," chimed the latter, "but when it comes
to withdrawing from the Lukkan Provinces these infant states will first have to provide for the settlement
of their enormous debts, and then—mark my words—.
they will very soon be on their knees begging to be
left where they are!   We shall naturally demand
assurances for the payment of not only the State
debts but all the private debts as well and also for
the security of our investments.   Fudge!   They are
going in deeper every year.   They couldn't pay
fiddlesticks!"

"I have heard," said another, "that their ambassadors are now in the city negotiating for a final
settlement."

"Settlement!" exclaimed the elder Tsoran in a
tone of contempt, "settlement!"

"I hear that they are coming to Tsor one night"
a newcomer remarked "to establish a kingdom and
make slaves of us."

"Hush!   Here come the ambassadors!" exclaimed
one of their number, a noted wag.   All eyes turned

at once toward the other end of the chamber and at once burst into shouts of derision and laughter.

It was indeed a ludicrous sight they beheld for the "ambassadors" were none other than Doctor Giniwig and myself being escorted into a private apartment by our friend Jurgo.

Two hours after running this gauntlet of ridicule no one would have recognized the smooth-faced strangers, dressed in Lukkan costume, as the former "ambassadors," thanks to the skill and kindness of Zuzo who personally ministered to our wants. Of course Jurgo explained the situation in presenting us and Zuzo entertained us with a minute account of our arrival in Lukka and the romance of the jewels; and as he narrated the details of the robbery it was clear he regarded the jewels as a trust he had not properly guarded.

We were soon again in the roja, and Jurgo began to peruse a Tsoran newspaper he had purchased just before entering while the Doctor and I sat eyeing one another, in a study of our new appearance dressed in Lukkan costume.

Presently Jurgo's face assumed an expression of intense interest and twice he brought his hand down upon his knee emphasizing the smile on his face, and then again a frown would reflect some unpleasant communication.

"My dear friends," he finally said "this is the greatest news that has stirred Tsor for many a century and I trust therefore you will pardon my enthusiasm, and if you will permit me I will be happy to translate the lines, reading them to you as we go."

We were naturally eager to hear this remarkable news, and accepting Jurgo's offer he proceeded forthwith.

"To begin with," he said "let me inform you that Tsor is the metropolis of eastern Lukka whereas the city of Tismoul, her rival, is the great center of the western section which is comparatively new and sparsely settled. It is likewise poor in capital and a constant borrower. Bearing these facts in mind you will readily understand this article which I shall now read you line for line as it appears, commencing with its heading," and then he began:

UTOPIA.

THE LUKKAN LEAGUE TORN TO PIECES.

DISMEMBERED BY THE WITHDRAWAL OF TWENTY WESTERN PROVINCES.

HOW SECRET NEGOTIATIONS WERE CONDUCTED WITH OUR MINISTRY.

The New Section Will Be Known As Utopia and Will Be Conducted After New Ideas.

STARTLING THEORIES OF MONEY!!

HOW THE FINAL SETTLEMENT IS TO BE MADE.

It appears that for more than a year a movement has been in progress in our western provinces through the medium of secret political organizations which has culminated in the final dispatch of a commission authorized to negotiate with our general government represented by the high priests under Chief Minister Korma.

Being assured that an honest settlement for all properties would be made and that all outstanding debts would be honorably settled it became incumbent upon Minister Korma to request from the Tismoulans an explanation showing how, in the face of the difficulty they had always heretofore experienced in meeting interest and dividends alone, they would manage to make a settlement for the principal itself, so many times larger than all previous payments.

TISMOULAN DEMANDS.

In reply the Tismoulans explained that all payments would be made in labor or products embodying labor. They stoutly maintain that money is only the measure of their debts, but that labor or its equivalent is the substance of the debt. The source of the debt they argued was at best but labor or products, and money was only a temporary substitute.

The Tismoulans insisted they had been purchasing Tsoran labor with their money which, instead of being applied in return to purchase the products of Tismoulan labor was returned only as loans or investments in Tismoula, the Tismoulans thus sinking deeper in debt and parting with their properties in order to make up for the deficiency in the sale to the Tsorans of Tismoulan labor or its products. Tsorans should have purchased more Tismoulan products in order to make commerce *real* and *honest exchange*. They

contended that if continued Tsor would ultimately
own all the property in the western provinces and
Tismoulans would be worse than slaves, for they
would become as poor as savages while educated to the
wants of civilization.

FINAL TERMS OF SETTLEMENT.

It was a novel proposition and our ministry finally
took it under advisement and after long deliberation
concluded it the part of wisdom to accept payment in
labor or products, and all agreeing that twenty years
was a liberal period to make as the average duration
for products, the Tismoulans engaged to issue interest-
bearing bonds to be good for products only, and to be
payable one-twentieth each year until twenty years
shall have elapsed, the currency issued as annual payments on the bonds to be legal tender and to be void
if not utilized within one year from issue.

Our able ministry had been very reluctant to accept the Tismoulan version of trade, but the latter insisted they might as well agree to pay in slices from
the moon as in Lukkan money over which they had no
control and which was free to abuse exchange making
it utterly impossible to ever pay the debts. Tsoran
capitalists, they said, would have the choice of any
products in their markets at prices regulated by supply
and demand and no longer at prices shrunken by the
absence of the full demand for labor properly due
there.

The new government is already established and
goes under the name of Utopia.

REJOICE, MEN OF TSORA!

For twenty years your markets are to be flooded
with Utopian products brought hither by our creditor

capitalists, and great bargains will gladden your hearts!

While Utopia gains the empty honor of a separate government Tsora, as the remaining provinces are to be styled, will reap the substantial reward of

A HARVEST OF CHEAP GOODS.

Tsor will have great cause for rejoicing, for capitalists will hereafter invest all their funds at home and wealth will fairly roll at our doors.

Let us offer sacrifices to our idols and feast their nostrils with incense! Let us bedeck them with garlands and strew flowers at their feet! Let our gratitude pour forth in thanksgiving! Let all eternity resound with the glory of our victory! Glory to Zmun! Glory to Zrog! May the gods all share with us the joys and blessings to come!"

"In all the hundred centuries of Lukkan history," Jurgo exclaimed, "there has never been a proposition at once so audacious, so foolhardy, and withal so revolutionary. They will deny themselves the profit from buying cheaper in our market and ——"

The conversation was interrupted by the sudden halt of the roja now arrived at its destination, and at our friend's solicitation we alighted following him into the house, an elegant cottage framed entirely of crystal blocks and slabs in variegated colors.

In the center of the lower floor was the reception chamber and here we were presented to our host's daughter, Arda, who acted as hostess, her father being a widower.

Arda was a charming young lady of very simple manners, with the candor of a child and the wit of a philosopher. In reply to thanks we offered for her kind forethought in our behalf she said she couldn't help believing we were alive and anyone but a brute would delight in the opportunity of assisting mortals placed in our predicament.

A dinner was served and table talk, I venture to say, was never more brilliant and interesting, for not only were our hosts fine conversationalists but the variety and novelty of the topics were so refreshing and agreeable that time was absolutely forgotten and the dishes served fared no better. A marked feature of the occasion which I still recall was the wonderful soft light shed by the phosphorescent walls — a peculiarity belonging to the interior of all Lukkan houses whose inner walls shed a soft luster at night —a light that can nowhere be excelled.

Arda often reminded me of my Violet. I remember distinctly the picture of her face when animated by excitement, for in this state I first recognized the resemblance she bore to my affianced. Two faces were perhaps never more unlike than those of Arda and Violet, yet the recollection of Violet's features when elated was a perfect counterpart of Arda's under like condition.

The Doctor to this day has not recognized the slightest resemblance between the two while I on the other hand was several times on the verge of calling our hostess by the name of Violet.

Later in the evening we were joined by Zuzo and his family, consisting of his wife Velva, and daughter Meta, of whom we will have more to say hereafter.

Zuzo, as before mentioned, was quite a student, and being asked his opinion of the Utopian withdrawal his face grew dark while most prophetically picturing the results he anticipated — results totally at variance with those predicted in the newspaper account.

The Utopian wares he said were foreign to the process of exchange. They would bring no money into Tsor through which the workingmen would be enabled to make purchases. The circle of exchange would be broken, for merchants would constantly replace their wares with goods that have not come from the activity of shops, that have not placed in the prospective buyer's hands the money with which to remove the goods from the merchants' shelves. The property still in the hands of the masses would be only too soon exhausted in sustaining life after which the merchant would find the goods on his shelves dead stock while the creditor drove him to the wall. The whole industrial system would be paralyzed and society rent by the almost total absence of opportunity to earn sustenance. Starvation and riot, revolution and despotism—a long nightmare of barbarism were in store.

The priests of Tsor were worshippers of Zmun, the god of gold, and their creed rested upon the prevalent system of commerce. It was not expected they would tolerate aught at variance with their creed. They thought more of their station than of humanity. Creed was to them everything; they could not be expected to stultify themselves in that which they had preached all their lives.

To the Tsorans the Utopian would hereafter be an unclean person to be shunned and avoided lest his iniquitous thoughts contaminated the minds of the good people of Tsor. It was well they were separated —well for the creed of Zmun, and well for its dynasty of priests.

That evening the hours appeared more fleeting than they had ever seemed before, and when I had retired to the room assigned me my mind would do nothing but wander from Violet to Arda and from Arda to Violet.

Did I not still belong to Violet—however veiled in mystery, however barred by space? My conscience was sorely disturbed. It became a huge interrogation mark vibrating between two images.

Then I wished all had been a dream or an illusion like that blotch; but no, it was only too real, and struggling with this stubborn paradox of the heart I lay a long time until at last the veil of unconsciousness buried every qualm.

CHAPTER VIII.

Crystal is the great staple of Tsor. Crystal in this city takes the place of iron and steel, of brick and stone, of lumber and in fact of as many as a dozen old-world staples. Crystal pavements, crystal bridges, crystal ovens, crystal machinery and crystal houses and stores and factories glitter everywhere. The very earth is charged with crystal sand and the air is impregnated with, infinitesimal particles of the stuff.

The manufacture and manipulation of crystal is here the great industry of industries. The glittering substance is charmed into every consistency and framed into every conceivable product. It is made to be capable of being bent, of being sawed, split and pierced like wood, of being drawn out, in fact of being treated in a hundred different ways. It is sometimes as pliant as rubber and again as rigid and elastic as steel. It is converted into threads, into ropes, into cables, into chains, into nails and screws and is also woven into the most delicate and diaphanous cloths.

Lukkan glass possesses a further charm in its wonderful adaptability to assume bright colors in which every shade and hue is shown to perfection. More remarkable than all, however, is its peculiar sensitiveness to the light of the sun, changing its hue with every change of light.

To go through the streets of Tsor is like seeing a

vast panorama of color, for even the vegetation, im-
bibing life from the crystal soil, partakes of the
peculiar color sensitiveness and as a consequence the
gardens and flower-bedecked lawns fall in with the
general color transition pursuing the march of day.

Experts here can tell the hour of day simply by
the shades surrounding objects wear, and ever since
the advent of the British Colonists Tsor has been
dubbed the Chameleon City.

The entire area of the city is laid out in circles
called yims and these are crossed by avenues radiat-
ing from an inner circle surrounding the Kar Yuk or
Royal Temple, the great tower we had seen from the
distance on the morning of our exit from the catacombs.

The original Kar Yuk, built in the remotest
antiquity, was replaced by the present structure about
three centuries ago and has ever since been the admiration of all Lukka. The structure is half-pyramid,
half-tower, covering some five acres at its base whence
a winding pathway leads upwards around its sides
forming a sloping terraced wall upon each of its four
faces.

It is impossible to convey an adequate impression
of the wonderful mingling of colors on the vast surface exposed to view, of the grand symmetry of its
immense proportions, of the manifold delicate intrica-
cies of its design. It rose to the sky, a distance of
more than a thousand feet, like a colossal column of
triumph—an everlasting monument to human genius.

Along the outer sides the walls were replete with
costly ornaments and patterned with historic figures
forming a pictorial review of Lukkan history, commencing with the dim era of tradition. Students
clambered up this winding incline to acquire at first

hand the history of the past and to commune with its characters, now hero gods, here weirdly outlined and moulded upon the massive slabs. Here the idealized characters appeared in gigantic stature cast in the image they once bore and set in the surroundings of their day—studies at once in art and history and objects alike of worship and veneration. It brought to mind the vast flight of years and suggested the immensity of the past. It formed an endless panoramic review stretched over miles of crystal canvas. Five men could march abreast between the outer railing and the eloquent walls. Upon this winding pathway ten thousand persons could be so distributed as to scarcely make a showing, and many a time, on gala days, more than fifty thousand had stood here to view the city.

The Kar Yuk is entirely devoted to the State, its lower floors being filled with shrines at which the populace worshipped favorite idols and sat in awe while their priests conducted imposing ceremonies. On the upper floors the scribes of Lukka registered the titles and transfers of all properties and recorded births and deaths and marriages as well as betrothals. Here also all the aristocratic titles were registered with the particulars as to rank and the price contributed.

Surrounding this temple a large park extended to the circle of palaces, the Kar Yim, or royal street. On this yim were many public buildings among which was the Kar Tuki—the national prison, a sort of combination of prison and poor house. The crystal in the Kar Tuki was a dense black, its walls looking gloomy and forbidding.

This prison was an awful place, but it was a safety valve to Lukka and for this reason was regarded largely as a grand institution.

The Lukkan creed conceives their god of creation, Zrog, as asleep after his great work, having left the world's administration to Zmun. Some day Zrog would wake and then a general resurrection of the dead would take place and universal happiness reign.

Worshipping Zmun, the god of commerce, all sins were measured by a money value. Zmun was the ideal king and commercial integrity was his law. Debt was the first step toward the violation of commercial integrity and was in itself a sin, and inability to pay a debt was a crime.

Crimes were all punished by fines and murder was so heavily fined as to not only impoverish the most wealthy but to carry the debt down to the second generation and involve also the next in kin, brothers and sisters. This terrible punishment, for many reasons, was considered more deterrent than killing the criminal.

All claims, including business failures, are settled in this prison until the last petro (their smallest coin) has been satisfied.

The Kar Tuki was thus also the final refuge of the unemployed. No matter how dull the labor market there was always plenty of work in the prison, for the labor was farmed out to contractors at pitifully low prices and the latter found a certain market for their products by underselling rivals. That prisoners ever succeeded in earning their release was only due to the wretched fare and the utter barrenness of their surroundings.

Begging, as might be expected, is also made a crime and the unemployed are kept on their knees upon platforms fronting the workshops, applying thus for work, and if long out of work they soon drift into the Kar Tuki, where their discontent cannot breed

agitation and trouble. For this reason riots were unknown in Tsor and the Kar Tuki acted as the safety-
valve of Lukka.

Half an hour's walk from the Kar Yuk the famous
Tok Yim rattles and roars. It is a remarkable place
—a tremendous circle of factories the equal of which
is nowhere else to be found. The major portion of all
the manufacturing in Lukka, a country of vast
industries, is done on this yim. No street in London
distributes one-tenth the employment furnished here,
for it comprises a street twelve miles in length lined
with factories and workshops upon either side to a
depth varying from one hundred to three hundred
yards.

Here every morning can be heard the tramp, tramp,
tramp of clattering feet from an army of more than
two hundred thousand strong. What a field of activity! What a bang and whiz and whirl, when these
shops begin their daily grind! What a vast machine is
the whole! Yet this vast whole is but a part of a still
greater whole. On either side of this yim are a series
of circular streets extending to the center and out to
the suburbs of Tsor, forming a line of yims hundreds
of miles in length all lined with dwellings, stores and
warehouses. Here reside consumers, consisting of the
families of workmen, of tradesmen, of capitalists, of
professional men, even to the dark home of the poor
prisoners within the Kar Tuki — every class, high and
low, rich and poor — all combining to keep in motion
the busy wheels that buzz and hum and thunder with
stupendous uproar in this colossal bee-hive of activity.

The circle of the Tok Yim is the heart of Tsor. Into
this mystic circle, this throbbing organ, as in a vast
hopper poured the energies of Tsor, to come out as-
sorted and re-assorted through warehouses and stores

of greater and lesser merchants until they reappeared
in the myriad homes of this mighty city in ten thous-
and forms, representing commodities of every sort—
a variety embracing the useful as well as ornamental,
most necessary articles and absolute luxuries, furniture for the mind and body-serving devices—such a
range and latitude of things whose lexicon reads complete only in that word—infinite! Out of the mystic
energies of arm and brain comes forth this world of
product. Wonderful, wonderful alchemy, this process
—exchange.

All Lukka is one vast machine, a million wheels
co-operating, any one of which alone would be worthless. As consumer or producer, as employer or employed, each was essentially a part of this machine and
each depended on the others for performance of their
part in the operation of the whole. There was no kind
of work sufficiently varied in its product to supply the
multifarious wants essential to any one person living
in this age. All alike were dependent on the activity
and integrity of this process called exchange—on the
harmony of the social machine.

It is indeed a vast social hopper into which the
human energy pours and comes out in shape to feed
the body, the senses and the mind, thereby renewing
the supply of energies—a perpetual evolution.

This vast co-operative process—exchange, is thus
in its remote extreme a physiological and psychological
process, supplying to the organs of the body the food
essential for their preservation and for the continuity
of the grand cycle of life.

Exchange is to the social body what digestion is to
to the human body. Impair digestion and the functions of man are crippled; prevent digestion and you
kill the man. Impair the process of exchange and the

state becomes an invalid ; destroy the process and civilization must come to an end.

CHAPTER IX.

For months after our advent in Tsor no man was more idolized than Dr. Giniwig. The Doctor had performed a number of operations that astounded the surgical fraternity of Tsor and boomed his business till he was literally coining money.

In Paris the Doctor had been only an ordinary surgeon, but here he became a prodigy. The secret of this radical change lay in the antiseptic treatment he applied, a method hitherto unheard of in Lukka. He had now more cases than he could attend to and could stipulate almost any terms he chose.

English was the only foreign language known in Lukka and the educated classes and most of the British Colony descendants were conversant with this language as well as Lukkan.

This prevalence of English opened a ready field for me in delivering lectures on Old World topics, such as history and science as developed since the year 1850. In this I was meeting with flattering success and was already becoming reconciled to my new surroundings; in fact, it was a case of Hobson's choice, for I soon learned to realize how utterly impassable were the Hills of the Heavens and how uninviting were the forests surrounding them.

The Colonists I learned had made numberless attempts to cross the Hills, but invariably failed, it being impossible to convey provisions anywhere near the summit. Balloons had also been tried with like results, the balloon in each instance failing to rise owing to the extreme lightness of the Lukkan atmosphere.

While lecturing I was also acquiring Lukkan, studying the language with a view of delivering addresses also in the native tongue, and the rapid progress I was making was due largely to instructions imparted by Arda, particularly through practice in conversations held in that language.

We were consequently very often together, for when not taking lessons myself I was giving her in return instructions in various Old World branches of knowledge.

Bright and early one morning, while the balmy air was sweet with fragrance from the rich roses for which Tsor is famous and while surrounding objects were beginning to assume their proper colors of day, Arda and I started out to spend the forenoon in a jaunt through a fashionable thoroughfare in a portion of the city I had not yet visited.

We were mounted on a pair of spry little elphies who trotted along evidently enjoying the stroll fully as much as did their riders.

A more sylph-like figure than Arda's, dressed as she was on this occasion in plain attire, I never beheld. I doubt whether her charming grace was due to any feature of her long riding habit. Another of her sex, if attired identically the same, even if gifted with the same natural grace, would have appeared plain. There was something in her expressive eyes and the balanced contour of her face that irresistibly kept the material Arda in the background where the charm that only distance lends could assert itself, clothing her form with the ideal in the beholder's mind

Arda was one of those who would be beautiful and interesting in spite of local surroundings, sub-duing to ideal harmony and contrast the weaker power of material form, under the influence of her higher personality. The beauties of color, form, design, all shrank before the higher beauty of a noble mind whose expression, revealed in her speech and animation, held all things else subordinate.

Our novel steeds fairly shone with glitter from pear-ly-beaded nets, while unique, curiously-shaped saddles were firmly girded to their backs, so that the rider could sit obliquely to the beast and lean back with feet supported in a rest that took the place of stirrups.

Arda never looked fairer in my eyes than on this bright and balmy morning as we started on our way to the Yam Yim. The wakening colors of the day, the blossoming flowers, the bright mansions trimmed with climbing plants and roofed with many a minaret or capped with rounding domes, the tall trees waving in the breeze, the winding, silvery roadways, and the golden heath sprinkled with glittering dew were pleasing to behold while the trills of fluttering song-sters, the distant signal sounds from the Tok Yim, the occasional tramp of foot-steps, the murmur from each tree's million trembling leaves, the roll of wheels, all joined to make day's chorus, filling our ears with a constant hum upon whose current our conversation ran softened and stimulated.

Even our little elphies seemed to catch the music of day's growth, and as if invigorated by its cheer, with a few low grunts they increased their pace, nod-ding their bumpy heads as they trotted along.

Soon we turned into the Yam Yim, so named after the yam or canal that runs in the middle of the yim through its entire length.

Most gorgeous villas and perfect fairy homes are those that line the banks of this quiet stream. The sights here were very novel. On this driveway dogs, goats, dwarf elphies, unicorns and human beings trotted and puffed to the lively tinkling of bells and fierce signal whistlings that voiced the human mandate to the lower brutes. Richly-mounted beasts, chariots, rojas, carriages in various fantastic styles, two-wheeled carts, three, six and ten-wheeled vehicles rattled and ran over this great, showy, bustling highway, and this was only the every-day procession of life along the Yam Yim.

"What a handsome bridal couple!" Arda exclaimed, looking toward the Yam.

Almost hidden behind great masses of foliage intermingled with flowers a bride and groom were seated inside of a floating bower that was slowly gliding over the inky waters of the Yam. A muscular Tsoran at the stern propelled the vessel while at the prow a huge idol stood facing the happy pair.

"They are on the way to the Honeymoon Garden," Arda explained.

"They appear very intelligent;" I said, "too intelligent almost to be accompanied by such a stupid idol."

"Hush!" Arda entreated, with a smile, "our people all worship idols, though not perhaps in the way *you* imagine."

"I am astonished, Arda," I exclaimed, "you worship idols!"

"Certainly, Ross, why shouldn't I?" she replied with a rebellious toss of her head.

"Do you think it very intelligent or right to worship an image—an inanimate substance? Would you then bow your spirit to dust?"

"Do you not worship your god through images?"
Arda asked in return.

"Our God is pure intelligence;" I answered. "He is
absolute goodness and wisdom."

"Then he is an utter stranger to you," returned
the fair idolatress, "for you cannot *think* these things.
Absolute wisdom is unintelligible to the human mind.
To think attributes you must couple them with some
instance, some experience, some person—an image of
some sort, if you please; and so you must borrow a
substantial base on which to found your beautiful
idealization. Your god apart from matter is mere
nothingness—dust like the shapeless matter in which
no ideal is embodied. Our most ignorant idolators,
believing they worship images, rarely but worship
the idealization embodied in the image, and so even
they in some form worship perfection—the God *you
think you worship*, Ross! Am I not right?"

"I confess you are quite right;" I admitted, "it
never before occurred to me idolatry so closely approx-
imated our own beliefs."

"We term this Christian Idolatry;" Arda explained,
"it is the ancient creed adapted to Christianity by our
Colonial ancestors. The natives still adhere to the
old creed, but there is no clash between them for in
religion they are identical, and they even accept our
Bible, which is a brief outline of your Old-World
bible, as an addition to their creed—interpreting its
references to images or idols as referring only to specific idols but not to Lukkan gods."

"I perceive the differences are merely intellectual"
I remarked, "and involve only the question of more
refined methods of defining and expressing beliefs."

"The idol in the boat" said Arda "was the idol of
constancy, preaching a silent and yet eloquent ser-

mon, entreating the novitiates to make every sacrifice toward preserving sacred their marital union. Is that not beautiful?"

"There are other idols we worship besides those you have seen;" Arda continued, "sometimes our idol is a picture or a poem—sometimes a great person, but always some object embodying great truths, great examples—all great models reaching toward perfection in some attribute. These objects assist us in idealizing greatness and worshipping perfection in what we consider a truer way than in wordy worship of a formless god who, having all attributes has really none—at least in the mind of the worshipper."

After Arda's explanation I had more respect for idolatry and began for the first time in my life to realize that I had myself, in some respects, been an idolator. I now subscribed heartily to her belief and when I complimented her she disclaimed credit for the ideas saying they were merely belonging to a creed she had inherited.

With the advance of day the sun's rays threatened to become oppressive, but as we were half way round the circle of the yim we continued onward. Roadway and canal were by this time thronged with pleasure parties on the way to the numerous parks scattered along this yim, and the quaint gaiety of these Tsorans in the midst of the novel surroundings made a lasting impression upon me.

At one time our ears were suddenly greeted with shrill snatches of music as if coming from weird beings high up in the air. Then we heard a splashing of water in the yam and turning beheld a mammoth, richly furnished barge gliding forward our way. Its flower-strewn deck was filled with a bevy of young women and children in gala dress swinging boquets and banners and singing the loveliest of lively airs. In the center on an elevated plane a band of juvenile artists, with strange little instruments which Arda called banjoettes, discoursed sweet strains that mingled with the merry voices from the youthful throng.

The barge was propelled by two herds of elphies marching along one on either side of the yam.

Further on we beheld a vehicle of exceeding length that bore straddled in single file more than a hundred boys and girls and was propelled by a long line of monster goats in tandem with noisy little tinkling bells suspended at their breasts. The strange vehicle seemed to be all wheels and could bend and wriggle like a huge serpent, due to the fact that the wheels were attached to the hinged sections of a long center bar.

Such were a few of the sights we beheld on this yim. To me it was like a day in fairyland. The conversation had been carried on in Lukkan, a charming tongue, and Arda's brilliant and pleasing manner of speech added no little to the romance of the day. I could not help viewing my situation with a feeling of marvel, thinking that if Paradise were anywhere it was right here in this city.

Crossing homeward from the Yam Yim we passed the Tok Yim, which was thronged with kneeling applicants for work, men, women and children being on their knees in front of every shop and factory. It was a sad picture and what made it more impressively sad was a glimpse I caught now and then of the men in the factories who were ordered about by masters weilding a lash over their heads. Arda was no less shocked than myself at the sight of these brutal monsters and explained their course as a form of emphasizing authority. By the Tsoran method of reasoning no one was ever obliged to submit to these indignities. With them there was a saying current that it is better to be in the Kar Tuki than to starve; it is better to apply for work on one's knees than to be in the Kar Tuki; it is far better to feel the lash than to be a kneeling applicant, and it is better still to bring bread to the home than to escape the pangs it costs to procure it.

Speaking of the Tok Yim that evening to the Doctor I happened to mention this saying and received a reply that the ruling classes had always a way of explaining abuse by saying poor folks might be glad they were kicked and not hung, and because their ancestors had been kicked much oftener the present generation had no real cause for complaint.

"Ten to one," said the Doctor, "the people are being robbed in the transaction called employment or else they would be mutually independent and no such humiliating terms could exist."

CHAPTER X.

A gradual dusk was settling over Tsor. It was purely a commercial dusk, a dusk that was felt underneath the roofs of a million so-called homes in Tsor. No interior light could banish this gloomy tinge from home or factory, from store or warehouse. It was a dusk that had settled around the eye of the soul—not a sensual dusk, not a material dusk; and no material light could banish its gloom.

Something was wrong in Tsor. Else why had the number of kneelers in the Tok Yim quadrupled in the first year of Tsoran widowhood? Why was the larder empty and the warehouse crammed? Why rested the factory wheels while famine stalked abroad? Why roared hunger by the side of paralyzed arms? What meant those muffled sounds, the crack, crack, crack of business failures in rapid succession? What meant this spreading commercial conflagration, blazing its destruction with no bells sounding the alarm and no valiant firemen hastening to the rescue? What meant that line of gliding, ghostly figures, the debt-driven stream that is pouring down into the tomb of the living, the Kar Tuki?

WHAT MEANT THESE DISMAL SIGNS?

It meant that Utopian wares were pouring into the warehouses and blockading the path between the factory and the home. They stood a mountainous barrier between human wants and human means. The supplying hands were in chains within tantalizing view of the hungry mouths. This mountain of Utopian wares had brought not a petro into Tsor and it towered over the city a huge mocking spectre of "cheap wares" —a parody on the poverty of the times.

Even the ministry of Tsor was forced to realize this phase of the situation, but they resolved with a stubborn bigotry to adhere to their position. They believed Utopia would soon give out and fail in keeping its payments. How could it be that this section that had hitherto invariably been obliged to borrow should now be able not only to dispense with borrowing but to keep up these exhaustive payments? They had calculated and still believed the Utopians would soon surrender humiliated and make terms redounding to the credit of Tsoran finance and the glory of Zmun.

The temples of Tsor were being well attended; their idols were appealed to in heart-rending prayers; sacrifices were daily offered at their mystic shrines, all to appease the gods, and all to no avail. The priests of Tsor had unbounded faith and with dogged tenacity determined to withstand the siege of wealth to the bitter end.

Dr. Giniwig had always been of an active disposition, and there being no personal attachments holding him here he became very anxious to leave Tsor. We had now been here a whole year and seemed to be faring worse the longer we stayed.

On the other hand I had taken a strong interest in the friends I had found here and I dont know why it was I could not bear to think of a move that would tend to separate me from Arda, to whom I was becoming more attached every day, for hardly a day passed but we took a walk or drive through the yims of the city.

"Put this down as my last week in Tsor, Ross!"
said the Doctor one morning. "You may come along
or not as you please; I will stay no longer in this dead
city. I don't fancy this Kar Tuki frowning on me from
day to day."

"You take too gloomy a view of things, Doctor," I
retorted. "Why not stay right here? These clouds
will break and leave Tsor a gold mine after the
storm!"

"You may have the pleasure of waiting, Ross, till
it rains gold; but as for me I'll pack up for Tismoul."

As before stated, a year had already elapsed since
the partition of Lukka and two years had expired
since our departure from Paris.

It seemed apparently no more than a few months
and whenever my mind reverted to Violet a cloud of
reproach would gather. It seemed to me as if I was
acting false to my affianced. What if after all there
were some delusion in my present situation and I was
forgetting her in my attentions to Arda? If so, I was
really false to both. To Arda I had never mentioned
the name of Violet, for somehow I could not broach
the subject to her. In imagination and intention I
had done so a hundred times but in fact I could not
induce myself to do so once. I could sooner have
held my .hand in burning flames than communicate
this information to her. It seemed to me as if Violet and Arda were but one person. There was but
one ideal that embraced the two. Their personalities
had, in my mind, really merged into one. What was
it, apart from the tender affection, the sincere regard,
the cheeriness of soul, the noble impulses of a true
heart, the quick intelligence, the splendid courage, the
artless grace, the simple candor, the mild but keen
judgment placing the veil of charity around the world

they lived in, that was their real being? Was it the clay of flesh and blood and bone, or was it the barren names that comprised their being? Was their being only in the mortal dust—in which they differed? Was it in the mortal dust that they were two and separate? And had it been but mortal dust I loved as Violet? That could not be!

The Violet I loved was immortal as the stars. I have found her here in Arda. In her ideal lives the ideal of my Violet, the immortal which is one—one everywhere, one throughout all time.

God, the Maker's hand is here in this, revealing to me an immortality I had not dreamed before.

Nor death, nor Lukkan wall can stay the eternal bond of true affection, the affinity of souls.

Should I leave Arda now? Should I deny my heart? What should I do? One answer only was written in my soul: I must leave Violet to God. She would forget, and then another Ross would bring me back to her. My Violet was here!

The same day I met Arda at the cottage of Zuzo in the Zdar yim, and on the way escorting her home we rested in one of the rustic bowers so numerously distributed along the yims in all but the poorer sections of the city. An automatic instrument was discoursing lovely music here while we were enjoying a pleasant chat, in the midst of which Arda artfully seized both my hands and looked into my face, a sweet bewitching smile upon her rosy lips and her eyes beaming with rapturous light.

"Ross, I have a secret to impart to you" she said, in her sweet, charming way, her bewitching gaze holding me like one entranced. "I should have spoken sooner; if you love me, Ross, as I believe you do, accept this triple token in proof of my affection and be my third man——"

She was just in the act of handing me a handsome triple ring when I interrupted her.

"Third man!" I gasped, "what do you mean? I—I, can't comprehend——"

I could say no more, for I was almost choked.

"Why, there's nothing to be alarmed at," returned Arda, calmly, in her melodious voice, "I perceive you do not understand our Tsoran methods. I had always supposed this custom was familiar to you!"

It was plain to me that Arda, though at first calm, was really much agitated and must have been painfully embarrassed at this unpleasant turn, and desiring to set her more at ease, I admitted my ignorance.

"I realize very well that you were not aware of our custom," she resumed, "but in Lukka it is the practice for ladies and not gentlemen to propose."

"I was well aware of this," I responded, "but you asked me, did you not, to become your third man; and you never before told me that you had already been married twice."

"Married twice! How could you think so?"

At any other time Arda would have enjoyed a hearty laugh over such a blunder, but the subject was too sacred to be made light of and Arda was too sensible to jest in serious matters.

"I don't see how I could think otherwise, when you asked me to become your third man. What else is to be implied by a third man?" I asked.

"Oh, you stupid fellow!" Arda playfully remarked, her voice fairly bubbling with laughter, and looking into my eyes she continued "can't you understand that?"

"Well, I'll have to take pity on you and explain,"

she resumed after a pause. "Our custom allows each person as many as six engagements and you are my third."

"But how can you be married to so many gentlemen?" I asked, still bewildered.

"Why, Ross, we never *marry* but one gentleman, and the others become the best men at the wedding. The engagement merely implies their selection as best or preferred company. Marriage is then confined to people who are best to each other, for such engagements must be published and stand unchallenged a year before marriage is permitted in the church of Zmun which is very strict. Our engagements are in no sense, however, promises of marriage, nor does any disagreeable result attach if parties cease to keep company. The mere fact that these engagements can only be made to six persons renders them sufficiently serious to prevent gross trifling, and the fact that the number of the 'best' are so many enables better acquaintance before rash steps are taken."

"I am beginning to see," I said, "you are already engaged to two gentlemen, so that I will be the third. How stupid that I never learned this before!"

"You have had so much to learn in Lukka that it is no wonder; and it has always been a delicate subject which I naturally avoided in our conversations, imagining you would gather it from other sources."

"So these engagements are not a promise of marriage," I resumed after a pause, "but are a permit to marry after a year's unchallenged publicity, provided the parties so desire; and there is nothing binding in it until parties are really married?"

"Indeed," said Arda, "we have perfect liberty to test our inclinations before taking a permanent step, and no two parties are ever brought together so con spicuously as to make separation attract attention to the embarrassment or injury of either party."

"It's an admirable method and strikes me more favorably the more I think of it," I affirmed, "but does it not perhaps supply an interminable field for gossip mongers?"

"On the contrary," was the reply, "so numerous are the possible conjectures as to utterly bewilder this class. It really baffles the ingenuity of their tongues. The public hears nothing more after the engagement until invitations are out for the home dedication on return of the bridal couple from the Honeymoon Garden, which is often in some distant city or town."

I had become so much interested in this marriage custom that I had for the time forgotten Arda's proposal, and now recurring to me, I returned to the original subject and, taking Arda's hand, I made a complete confession assuring her that it was my only wish to be able some day to call her my own.

What was further said I do not recollect. The reader may doubtless surmise, but the precincts of a hallowed love are like our most devout prayers, sacred to silence.

We started for home soon after, arriving just before nightfall, and full of joy presented ourselves to Jurgo, announcing to him our engagement and asking his approval.

To my great astonishment a cloud passed over Jurgo's brow and an expression of bitterness saddened his countenance. It passed away like a flash, however, while an ominous silence followed. It was an eloquent silence voicing a doubt more forcible than wordy utterance.

It really spoke volumes.

For a while he sat in his chair with downcast face,

buried in deep reflection. He had anticipated the possibility of such an outcome but did not look for it so soon and was not prepared clearly and wholly to interpret its significance. Evidently there was some danger lurking behind the curtain of events, of which we had no view.

Arda and I were both frightened at Jurgo's attitude.

Arda spoke first:

"Tell us, father; was there any wrong in what we have done?"

"Forgive me, children, for causing you this anxiety," responded Jurgo, his face lit up with a smile. "I was laboring under a false impression in the belief that Ross' age would be a bar to your union in the church of Zmun, for he appeared to be past the years at which one may be anointed in the Church, but on second thought his Old World years will only be reckoned year for year and this will not prevent his anointment. You understand our creed and can subscribe to our Christian Idolatry, I presume?"

"Oh, yes; I can subscribe to such a faith without the slightest hesitation—and I mean to worship one idol in particular," I responded, with a sly glance at Arda, whose cheeks turned crimson.

Our sky was once more clear and everything seemed bright and rosy now. Jurgo soon after dispatched a note to the household of Zuzo via a small elphy, a family pet, who frequently acted in the capacity of messenger.

That evening Zuzo and his family accompanied with Dr. Giniwig appeared, followed later on by three bearded priests in long yellow robes.

I had met two of the priests before and after an introduction to the third and a general social chat,

Jurgo announced the purport of this gathering and we were requested to take our assigned stations in front of the priests who stood in a row with the high priest in the center. Arda and I faced each other about five paces apart at the extremes of a semi-circle, in the center of which stood Jurgo with Zuzo and Dr. Giniwig on the right and Velva and Meta on the left.

In front of the priests was a small table on which lay the book of records.

Everything was so still one could have actually heard the proverbial pin drop. I felt perfectly at ease, and Arda never looked lovelier.

The high priest who occupied the center finally put to Arda the question whether of her own free will she had invited me to occupy a place in the sacred company from which alone the law of Zmun permitted her to join in wedlock.

Receiving an affirmative answer he put the question to me whether of my free will I had accepted her offer, and as was to be expected received another affirmative reply.

Thereupon he drew from underneath his long robe a quill and proceeded to enter the engagement on record, after which he made the final announcement in a strong, resonant voice:

"Know all members of the Church of Zmun that, having of their free wills consented to enter a bond of engagement under the laws as ordained by the divine Zmun, I hereby pronounce the names of Ross and Arda coupled for the purpose of eventual marriage. If any cause exist why the union by marriage of this couple, Ross and Arda, should not be, the reason must be filed within one year from the day of the entry on these records and must find approval by the acknowledged authorities of the Church of Zmun. Amen."

The high priest's voice was no sooner silenced than another priest stepped forward and spoke:

"Hear! Hear! All men of Lukka, for I that speak to you, Hoki, the Priest of Tears, proclaim this bond invalid."

"What reasons have you?" asked the high priest.

"The groom has not been brought up in the faith of Zmun and cannot share its benediction."

"If he share in the faith of Zmun, he may share its benediction; how is it, you, called Ross?" retorted the high priest.

"I share the faith of Zmun" was my cool response.

The priest Hoki kept his place.

"More have I whereof to speak;" he continued, "the groom has never been anointed in the faith."

"The groom is not yet past the years," was the high priest's rejoinder. "What may be the years of your living, pray?"

"Twenty and eight years have I lived," was my reply.

"Then you may still be anointed," said the high priest.

But the priest Hoki was imperturbable.

"Ask him," he resumed, "whether he is of Lukkan birth."

"That already we know;" was the response from the high priest, "but wherefore desire you knowledge of his birth?"

"Because," said the priest, "in the Book of Zmun it is said each person that is born in Lukka, when he shall have attained the years of judgment, of sixteen years or more and be not yet fifty years out of the cradle, if he accept the faith of Zmun's sacred laws may be anointed, but no mention is made that *anyone else* may receive anointment. In the thirtieth verse of the twelfth division will it be found even so as I have stated. Again hear me! hear, men of Lukka! I, Hoki, the Priest of Tears, proclaim this bond invalid!"

There was an intense silence following this speech. The high priest began rummaging through the leaves of a ponderous volume that had meanwhile been placed before him.

All eyes were eagerly bent on his movements. I felt extremely uneasy. Jurgo's face grew dark as in the afternoon and Arda looked pale.

The high priest had evidently at length found the quotation referred to, for he was eagerly following the lines, leading with his forefinger.

"Though in all the days of Lukka anointment has never been denied to a living person, yet do I find it verily so; for here it is put down even as has been said by Hoki. It is obligatory and I therefore record the bond invalid."

Thereupon the high priest handed his quill to Hoki and that worthy proceeded to enter the protest against the validity of the bond, stating the reason in full.

The high priest had no sooner pronounced the last word than Arda burst into tears. I hastened to her side and endeavored to comfort her

"Do not grieve," said I, "this obsolete form need not deter our marriage. The objection can easily be overcome by a little ingenuity; trust me, it shall be brushed aside. Now, be of good cheer, Arda; see how brave you can be!"

Jurgo was still dark and gloomy when Arda addressed him:

"Do not look sad, father, this will be only temporary. See, Ross is full of hope!"

"It may all be well if you are wise, my children. I know what it is to love; yet if love be true it will see wisely and desist in the face of inevitable calamity."

"What mean you, father?" Arda asked, her face a picture of anxiety.

Jurgo's frown renewed my former fears and I felt as if on the brink of a volcano.

"I mean the Curse of Kodor! Have you forgotten, child, that old but inexorable law that smites as outcast and unclean the person marrying without the Church of Zmun — that gives its blessing to the hand striking the accursed? Have you forgotten the dreadful curse under which the infidel Toora was branded on his face and let loose to be stoned and cut to pieces by the mob?"

"But this curse, father," responded Arda hopefully, "cannot apply to Ross who is not a Lukkan and cannot be held to our creed."

"True, my daughter; but you are born in Lukka and in the Church of Zmun, and this marriage would subject *you* to the curse."

Arda hung her head and wept bitterly.

I also began to realize the hopelessness of our cause and felt keenly the disappointment, but a hundred fold greater was the agony of mind in which I contemplated the parting with Arda which this would inevitably necessitate.

To her it was a Curse of Kodor already; not a distant threat but a present affliction. The stones of the mob came knocking at her heart and the sharp edge of human heartlessness cut deep into the flesh. Poor child! I tried once more to comfort her, but in vain. She broke into great sobs and was inconsolable. The religion of her worship had never before crossed the religion of her heart. It had never before appeared to her in the role of a tyrant. The decree was to her one irrevocable and merciless, a degree of cruelty the more deeply felt coming from the church that should have sheltered her.

Arda was completely exhausted when I left her side, but she did not permit me to go till I had promised not to forsake her.

"For my sake, Arda, do not give way to despair; there is no cloud so dense but light will penetrate," I said, and a smile upon Arda's lips told me my words had not been spoken in vain.

CHAPTER XI.

Zuzo had spent much of his early life within the walls of the Kar Tuki, by the side of his father, Orm, whose business had been wrecked after a prolonged struggle with competition against a power he did not himself understand or properly estimate. All Orm knew was that he had once provoked the hostility of one Omrez, a merchant whose career bordered on criminal transactions. Omrez threatened to ruin him and the persistence with which aggressive rivals afterwards pursued him in business convinced Orm that his enemy was in league with others in the execution of his revenge.

Surmises, however, could not restore his shattered business. He could prove nothing and the fact of his ruin stared him in the face, an argument that would accept no reply short of immediate imprisonment in the Kar Tuki.

His family consisted of but two children, Zuzo, now twelve years of age and Ortro, a child of six. Little Ortro was taken in charge by one of the neighbors, but Zuzo insisted on taking his place by the side of his father to console and comfort him in his declining years and to contribute his mite toward shortening the term of imprisonment, which was expected to run in the neighborhood of ten years.

In the prison Zuzo used his utmost endeavor to cheer his father who found it hard to reconcile him-

self to his downfall, and the confinement gradually
asserted its subtle power, causing his spirit to chafe at
the unnatural barriers restricting its wonted freedom.   Personally he was treated, if anything, better
than others but the incidents of injustice he beheld
rankled in his bosom and burned in his blood all the
more that he was helpless, and powerless to strike
against them.

He knew he could accomplish nothing; but to satisfy the furious passion within he would have unceasingly denounced these outrages had he not dreaded
the extension of his penalty which would have ultimately been meted upon his sons.

Suppressing the voice of his feelings the wrongs
rankled the more and the inward struggle was a constant and severe drain upon his system.   He was only
forty-eight and his face already wore wrinkles and
his eyes had a wandering look as he followed the lead
of young Zuzo to whom he was chained, working
mechanically—his mind far away from the cruel slave
pen that enveloped him.

Nature is very kind and in the cruelest pain she
veils our being in unconsciousness.   Orm was not
weak-minded; on the contrary, his perception was very
keen and intensely sensitive—natural in the highest
degree.   To such a mind the shock from unnatural
surroundings and revolting cruelties came in its
fullest force.   In such a mind the strong natural current of feeling would not yield or bend out of its
course.   The conflict was inevitable and its fury
would not abate.   Nature at length brought relief.
Orm's mind slowly shifted its focus.   Present surroundings slowly but decidedly sank out of his view.
The whole world shrank with his being into a series
of capricious and discordant experiences—judgments

loosely and inharmoniously united, the cradle-life renewed, where dream and action mingle. It was nature's cloak of darkness descending over him to ward off the blows of external severity.

After this Orm worked mechanically, like an automaton, recognizing no one, not even his son. The great drain on his life had been checked and now he lived on year after year, completely oblivious to all impressions from without.

One morning Orm did not rise as usual and when Zuzo tried to wake him he met no response. Orm had crossed beyond the prison's pale.

Zuzo was obliged to work out the balance of the sentence, keeping him here until he had arrived at the age of twenty-one. Then he went out a free man to join the kneelers on the Tok Yim.

This early experience had made a profound impression in his mind, one not any too creditable to the social standard of Tsor. He had met here men of sterling character who cursed the indifference of the ruling class and not without cause. He had learned here to think for himself and to think deeply and he had also acquired habits of industry. It had been an unmercifully hard school, but he had emerged apparently the better for it.

A few years of liberty enabled him to acquire the barber's trade and as the craft plied their work here only in the broad daylight he devoted his evenings to teaching in a little school house adjoining his home.

Such was Zuzo's early career.

One day not long after the events narrated in the preceding chapter he was seated at a triangular desk fitted in one corner of his library. It was a novel but very handy desk, with broad front and a large right-angle frontage of shelves and pigeon-holes for the accommodation of books and memoranda. He was seriously engrossed in summarizing the results of the school season about to close on the approaching election day, the greatest holiday in Tsor.

So deeply was he engrossed that he did not hear the light footstep of Velva, who gently placed her hand upon his shoulder.

"You are in trouble, my good fellow!"

"No, not exactly, my dear;" he responded, "I was just figuring to see what we could do for brother Ortro. Poor fellow! He is so proud and sensitive! He never communicates his difficulties to others; now his obligations have been challenged and before I was even aware of it he has been lodged in the Kar Tuki. Just think! Scarcely three years ago he was enjoying his own home with the most precious darling of a wife, a snug sum stowed away and as brilliant a prospect as any young man ever could desire. Ever since her bones were laid in the catacombs he has lost many an opportunity to work because he would not allow himself to take preference over brother workmen more needy than he was."

"When old Osko was kneeling behind him," said Velva, "Ortro permitted him to take his chance because he couldn't bear to think of Osko's small children crying for bread. So Osko took the chance and there has been no further opportunity for Ortro, as the factory has ever since been reducing its force."

"Poor Ortro!" sighed the schoolmaster, "I have heard some workmen call him a fool, but if all of them were only such fools as he they would be better off. Why, he has been advising them to buy only Tsor-made wares and as long as they had money they persisted in buying Utopian products. But what can be done for Ortro?"

"Get him out of prison by all means;" urged Velva, "I will see Jurgo. With his assistance we may possibly be able to reclaim Ortro at once!"

"We cannot call on Jurgo," Zuzo retorted, "for his business is already in danger of financial collapse. Ortro would rather remain in prison than drag Jurgo after him!"

"But what can we do alone?" asked Velva.

"That's just what I've been calculating. If all my pupils come up tomorrow with their unpaid dues I may be able to do something, but I fear scarcely enough to pay for his release."

"I can add five milos to this; perhaps that will make it sufficient!" suggested Velva, and observing a look of surprise on Zuzo's face she continued, "that's what I had laid away toward a new cloak for the feast of Oz, but it will give me much more pleasure if applied toward helping Ortro."

Zuzo returned to his previous calculations which evidently did not result to his satisfaction, for he arose soon after and began to pace the room nervously.

Then suddenly, as a new idea came to him, he left the room, ascending to a garret where he found a dust-covered chest from which he began to withdraw a lot of odd papers which he laid, one by one, upon the floor until the chest was emptied.

He bit his lip, chagrined at the evident failure of his search, but not wholly disconcerted, he began returning them, this time examining each very closely.

The chest had not been more than half refilled when a yellowish slip caught his eye and he pounced upon it as a cat would upon a mouse.

He had at last found the object of his search and with a smile of triumph he hastily thrust the remaining papers into the chest, closed and fastened it and seating himself upon the chest he unfolded the yellow slip and began to study it.

This document was the identical forged order that had betrayed his head watchman in the depository. The officials of Tsoi had failed to obtain the least clue to the thieves who had stolen the jewels and now an idea had come to him and he was on the way to un-earth the villains himself without their aid.

He was still more elated after a minute survey of the little document at the discovery of four peculiarities, each of which was alone distinctive and a combination of the four in one man's writing would be accepted as equivalent to absolute identification. This would constitute overwhelming evidence and all that now remained to be done was to trace the writer.

His present purpose being accomplished he returned to the library and once more took his place at the desk.

"I wonder where that girl can be! Here it is past the fifteenth bell and no Meta!" exclaimed Velva on his return.

"Don't you think it strange she's not home yet?" Velva resumed in a tone betraying alarm. "She's usually here at the twelfth bell."

"It is rather unusual:" responded Zuzo, "I believe I'll go out to look for her," saying which he put on his cloak and was already approaching the door when it opened and in rushed Meta all out of breath.

She fairly stumbled into her father's arms and after receiving an affectionate greeting was turned over to her mother.

"We were begining to be anxious about you, darl-ing ; papa was just about to step out looking for you."

Meta flung herself into a long rocking couch and called aloud: "Gogo! Gogo! Come rock me!"

A low grunt from an adjoining chamber answered

her call and in another moment Gogo, a little three-foot high elphy, came thumping into the room and at once went down on his knees, trundling away with his prehensile trunk as if to the service born.

Gogo was very vain, and as he kept rocking seemed to say out of those little mischievous eyes, "oh, look at me! just see what I am doing!"

"Why, you haven't told us, girl, what caused you to come so late?" asked Velva.

"Well, ma, we had a meeting, all the girls in the establishment, and we're going to march on election day, and what do you think? They've chosen me to lead the march!"

"Meta!" exclaimed her mother in a tone of mild reproach.

"They're all grown-up girls, ma, and we are going to have a wonderful programme, something new! There'll be no children in it, I assure you. You'll see it, and you too, won't you, papa?"

Her father was just thinking of the new clue he had secured and mechanically answered:

"Yes, yes, my child, certainly——, but pardon me, what did you ask?"

Meta responded by giving an account of the proposed march, adding further details. The girls had designed a programme for the day that promised to be as entertaining as it was original. It was to consist in a long march interspersed with intervals of rest, during which games, drill exercises, a mock election, dramatic sketches, literary and musical renditions and pantomimes would be indulged in. The whole was so arranged that through its judicious distribution of active and sedentary enjoyments no undue strain would result either bodily or mentally.

"A capital idea! I wonder who put that into

your heads," exclaimed Zuzo, after Meta had finished.

"Well, I declare," said Velva, a picturesque look of astonishment on her face, "it's just amazing how girls can invent such a programme. The world must be really turning around now—as they say beyond the Hills."

Meta then proceeded to explain the mock election they were to hold. The girls would be supplied with artificial money called votes which would be used in making purchases from mock merchants and manufacturers, each of whom they considered held an office, and according as they purchased from him and gave him their money or what they called money—votes— they decided who should or should not continue in office. Thus they would wield a great influence and raise men to high office or depose them as they chose.

"In the business world," Zuzo added afterwards, "there are a hundred-fold more offices than in politics, and in the business world the offices are more extravagantly conducted, for the officers are continually in contest with each other and are used to pocket all savings if any are left, so that the public has only an expensive service at best. In the business world all the year was one election day—so much so that no one seemed to realize the fact."

In spite of all attempts Zuzo could not repress a feeling of nervousness that came over him during the week. He was loth to ascribe much importance to the matter and still felt constantly as if shrinking from a duty in withholding his intention from Velva.

Velva herself finally perceived his uneasiness and insisted on his confiding to her the cause. He told her finally, after some persuasion, but did not succeed in drawing from her the least approval.

"Affairs are running smoothly now;" said she "let

well enough alone. Every step is a door leading no one knows whither. You have said so many a time, dear, but you never *apply* your wisdom."

"You know, Velva, I have always taught that we were here to more than 'get along well.' Velva, my love, can I deny the duty I owe the world to expose the cruel hand of crime? Can I go on indifferent to these things and retain that holiest of all garments, self-respect, that sacred virtue without which your own love would perish in your breast? Oh Velva, I must endeavor to recover what remnant is yet left of the wrecked fortune to fulfill the trust I took upon myself for the two foreigners!"

"You are noble, Zuzo, and I am not worthy such a man!" replied Velva, and no more was said.

* * *

At the polling station of the Fourth Precinct, along the Yam Yim a tall, powerful man, his face masked, in plain costume, black from head to foot, presented his voting card which was thereupon examined and corroborated. The voter's pen was then placed in his hand and he was permitted to register his vote along one line in the open registry book while his card was being canceled and filed away.

Having entered his vote the tall masker began turning the pages of the register, searching evidently the entries of previous elections. Page after page was turned over but the searcher scanned them in vain. He had almost reached the last pages when he suddenly leaned forward and became deeply absorbed in one particular line.

This particular line was a revelation to him in several respects, one of which was in informing him through the number of points scored on property issues that the writer held a station only second in rank among the titled gentry of Lukka.

It was still early in the day for this aristocratic district and the masked voters who entered the voting booth one by one, presented their cards, registered their votes and turned away ; and in each instance after the vote had been entered the strange man in black advanced before the register book, glanced over it and again retired.

An hour passed away and the man in black was still at his post.

The election clerks began to whisper among themselves. What did this strange masker mean? Was he perhaps greatly interested in the result and computing the vote in his mind as it progressed? Possibly, yet this action impressed them as suspicious. A few thought he might perhaps be entertaining some sinister purpose, possibly to snatch off the register book.

The great time bells of the city had rung four successive peals and the man in black was still at his post.

The officers of election eyed him closely but maintained silence. There was no specific law against his course so they could not interfere.

The man in black began at length to show signs of impatience, at intervals pacing up and down the hall.

Once more the bells tolled the signal of a spent hour and still the man in black persisted doggedly in his course.

As each masked voter registered, the black masker advanced to glance over the page, only to retire again.

The seventh time the bells tolled and the man in black was still at his post.

A stately nabob in rich scarlet gold-trimmed robes entered attended by two liveried servants, who remained in the background while their master advanced to register. He entered his vote and turned to leave.

The black masker again stepped forward, mechanically looked over the register as before and drew back with a cry of surprise. Instantly recovering self-possession he hurried to the departing voter and in a polite but commanding tone demanded his name.

"My name! Who are you to challenge me? Out of my way!" saying which the stately masker, with a disdainful gesture, turned his back on the challenger and started off.

The man in black followed with quick steps and with an adroit motion of his hand snatched the mask from the face of his adversary.

Unmasked, his face flushed with anger, our aristocratic elector turned upon his plebian challenger, who at once recognized him and in his surprise called him by name:

"Count Urg!"

"Prince Urg, if you please!"

"A prince of thieves then — I apprehend you——"

Prince Urg's servants had witnessed the unmasking and were already advancing to the assistance of their master, and before the speaker could complete his charge they sprang upon him, one of the lackeys seizing him by the throat.

A lively scuffle ensued, the man in black freeing himself only after a severe struggle. Meantime, however, several guardians of the peace had arrived and now all three were placed under arrest.

The man in black, whom the reader has already recognized as our friend Zuzo, had accomplished his purpose. He had discovered the forger and thief.

Unfortunately he was successful very much like the fisherman who pulled in a shark only to make a meal for his catch.

While under arrest upon the charge of creating a
disturbance he was incapacitated from making any
charges against another person and meanwhile a
second and more serious charge was laid at his door,
for he had been guilty of a crime against the State in
tearing the mask from the face of an elector.

In reality he had torn the mask from the face of a
criminal, no offense whatever, but Prince Urg would
now be first to enter the charge and would stand in
the eye of Tsoran law as innocent — Zuzo's charge of
theft and forgery having yet no legal status.   Had
the two charges been brought forward simultaneously
the political crime would have been condoned as a
justifiable step in view of the grounds, even if Zuzo
had failed to establish wholly the identity of the
criminal.

Urg's rise from a count to a prince since the previous election coupled with the identity of the hand-
writing would have been convincing evidence had
Zuzo's charge been legally recognized but as before
stated, the scuffle had defeated this calculation—in
fact, such a possibility had not been considered in
Zuzo's plan.   Had the scuffle not occurred its execution
would have been a brilliant success, but the ifs are
life's stumbling blocks—the hills and bog holes in
the world of events.

Zuzo was completely exhausted from the struggle
and the excitement of his thrilling experience.

Before being taken from the election booth where
a crowd had already assembled, his mask was removed
by the officers and one at each arm, they marched him
out into the yim.

Onward he was led through the crowded thoroughfare, amid the jeers of the thoughtless and indifferent.
Now and then he would meet a sympathetic glance

from some kind passer, for his pale face indicated strongly the suffering underneath and read the word "unfortunate" rather than "criminal."

The yim was more than ever full of liveliness, and the air, fragrant and breezy, was resonant with laugh·ter and mingled strains of music from far and near. The natural beauty of the yim was heightened on this great holiday by a profusion of decorations on every side and the moving figures of man and beast that animated the scene, so that the picture of Zuzo led on between the officers was thereby made doubly sad.

All the loud mirth was lost in the bitterness that dwelt within his heart; the lively music seemed but jarring notes and the sweet, balmy atmosphere crys·talized into lead within his breast.

He traveled on, his mind fled from the life sur·rounding him, in which it seemed to have nothing in common. He took refuge in deep, wandering thoughts in which he lived buried, seeing nor hearing aught. All the loveliness and beauty of the external world was drowned in the awful flood of darkness that enveloped him. All the channels of sense were as if seared and the mind as if it had closed its walls and shut off communion with the material world. The visible man was a walking spectre—a mere automaton.

In the far distance a procession of girls was ad·vancing amid applause from the bystanders. They were singing a patriotic song. Step by step they marched on to the beating of drums. "Halt!" The procession stopped. The girls stood two abreast. Their leader waved apart her hands and the ranks separated into single lines. Further orders were given and the girls went through the movements of a drill with admirable precision.

The two officers were meanwhile approaching with their prisoner.

"About, face!" Now the girls faced the advancing group. All eyes were bent on the prisoner, and when the next order was given the girls failed to respond.

Their commander turned to see what could have caused this breach of discipline. She looked eagerly forward, then with a slight shudder she screamed, falling backward into a swoon.

A scene of tumult followed, the frightened girls rushing wildly hither and thither in answer to their own excitement, and as a consequence considerable time elapsed before water was brought and the girl restored to consciousness.

A crowd of maskers had meanwhile gathered, among them Prince Urg and his attendants who had been released on Urg's recognizance. "Who is the girl?" was asked on every side, and the response came back that it was Meta, the daughter of Zuzo, the barber.

When the girl returned to consciousness she was bewildered by the crowd pressing around her.

"What has happened?" she asked.

"Nothing, Meta dear, only you had fallen into a swoon. Just rest a moment," responded a familiar voice.

"Ah yes, I've been too excited—" she started to say, but suddenly recollecting, she asked if the person led by the officers had not been her father, and then she fell into a second swoon.

Unfortunately the water left over had not been saved, occasioning another long delay. No sooner had Meta fairly come to her senses the second time than a companion was at her side offering to accompany her home.

In the meantime a handsome closed roja appeared on the spot and a gallant stranger, whom the reader will recognize as Prince Urg, placed it at their disposal, assuring them they would be taken safely home.

At first the girls politely refused, but at the urgent appeal of their companions they yielded consent and the two girls were soon after being driven away along one of the fashionable yims of the city.

The two guardians of the peace having Zuzo in charge went right on unconcerned by the swooning of Meta—a matter too trival to deserve their attention; and Zuzo himself, who had witnessed the scene and heard the cry, had been only sensually impressed. After they had gone on several rods his mind was suddenly roused by what had occurred. The full import of the affair came to him all at once.

"My child! It is my child!" he cried endeavoring to rush back.

The officers in return seized him more firmly and forcibly dragged the struggling man along.

While Meta was being driven off in Prince Urg's roja her father was crossing the threshold of the Kar Tuki and the massive doors of the prison were being closed upon him.

CHAPTER XII.

While her father was confined within the walls of
the Kar Tuki Meta was reclining in the midst of
palatial splendor.   All her surroundings were symbols
of luxury and refinement.   Liveried servants bowed
low and awaited her pleasure, and Prince Urg himself
was profuse in his offers to gratify her wishes — being
attentive, even to servility.

Poor Meta! Surrounded by a world of mockery
and sham!   Well was she aware that all this was
only outward seeming, a hollow pretense.   Instinctively she knew that the apparent freedom was an imprisonment; that the stooping and cringing attitude
concealed behind it an unmerciful tyrant; that the
pleasing smiles were a thin mask covering ugly frowns.
The luxuries and refinements were tantalizing; the po-
liteness of the servants was repulsive, and every word
of Prince Urg's was a dagger in her heart.

Falsehood had brought her here.   She had arrived
in an unconscious state, due to a goblet of cold water
served by a liveried servant who advanced to the roja
from a palatial mansion on the Yam Yim at which the
driver stopped, osensibly for the purpose of allowing
his elphies to quench their thirst.   What happened
thereafter she could not recollect.   She awoke in this
palace and was told that while her companion had
been taken home, she had been too ill and the physi-

cian summoned had found her in a high state of fever forbidding her removal.

At first they told her she was sick, but mild drugs administered in her food began to make her really ill and gave some color to their pretension.

She could not understand why her mother had not yet called to see her. She enquired frequently only to receive evasive replies, and at length when a tardy explanation did come it was to the effect that Velva was prostrated by the news of Zuzo's incarceration but was convalescing and would be permitted to call the next day, and the "next day" never came. Each "next day" brought a fresh promise fully as good as the first and usually more plausible. Thus all Meta's remonstrances were alike of no avail, and she was really forcibly detained.

Meanwhile Prince Urg called daily to enquire after her health. He invariably brought her some flowers or dainties which she politely rejected, asking only to be returned to her home. But her prayers availed not. "My dear lady," he would say, "you do not realize your condition. You are altogether too fever-ish to think of going out. Your physician absolutely forbids your leaving the house under any circum- stances." Then he would assure her that nothing in the world would gratify him more than to restore her to her home. He would meet her repulsions with smiles, assuring her that her judgment was at fault, all due to her high fever and that when she was better all the attentions now distasteful would appeal to her in their proper way.

There was such an element of coarse, patronizing pretension concealed underneath the Prince's elegance and grace of manner, and such an underlying air of egotistic superiority behind his servile stooping that it made him inexpressibly hateful to Meta. Handsome as he was in outward appearance she could not bear his sight.

She had no tangible evidence of this man's duplicity of character; she could not reduce in terms of reason the source of her dislike, yet she saw in his person the embodiment of all that was despicable. To her he was a hideous spider who had painted his web in enticing colors and lurked in the rear. Poor fly! She knew perfectly well her presence in his palace boded only evil and that the soft draperies and open doors were a delusion; behind them were impassable barriers. Better far to have been imprisoned within the walls of the Kar Tuki than in this dazzling den.

One day a withered old hag leaning on a stick, entering the room, approached the girl.

She was bent with age, and her dried-up features were one network of wrinkles. Her nose and chin almost met, and the thin lips between were severely compressed.

"Hey-dey!" screeched the wizened witch, shaking her head, "what can have brought hither my little star of beauty?"

Pokety poke, poke, poke, poke, hobbled the hag, advancing still nearer to the young girl, and leaning her head close to Meta's she gazed scrutinously into the girl's face.

"Hee hoo! a sweet dream face! ha, ha! You shall live a queen, child—a queen!" and an animated smile made her small eyes gleam.

"Come! come hither!" she called, beckoning Meta to follow, as she turned toward an adjoining room.

Meta had not yet spoken a word and scarcely knew whether or not to respond. Prompted however by a desire to learn more concerning her surround-

ings, she followed the pokety poke steps of this witch
woman.

The old hag hobbled through several chambers
and passageways and up several flights of stairs,
mumbling to herself all the way.

There was a peculiar nasal twang in her voice as
she went on, growing louder and more distinct as she
became worked up in her excited imagination.

"They try to pen me like a beast! they try to feed
me like a dog! they'd dress me like a beggar—I, who
have been in my days Queen of the Koofim, the mistress of the serpents! I'll be revenged some day. Ha!
ha! ha! I've a tongue, h-e-e-e-e-! I could tell a tale
or two! He'll rue the day I speak! Were he not of
my own flesh, nursed on my flesh he'd die—he'd feel
the serpent's sting—the ingrate! Oh, but I'll be revenged! Ha! ha! I'll be revenged! I'll be revenged!"

Presently the hag stopped before a large room, and
thrice repeated a peculiar whistling stanza.

"Now look!" cried the hag.

Through the almost transparent crystal wall Meta
gazed into the adjoining chamber and shrunk back
with a feeling of horror.

Coming toward the wall on the inner side of the
room were hundreds of crawling serpents. The old
hag called some of them by name and they came,
beating their fanged jaws against the transparent partition, at her feet.

"Their masters, the Koofim, are out upon a royal
expedition; but ere night a wealthy twain of Tsor
will lie, two serpent-bitten beings, stiff in death, and
the dead serpent—lying by the twain, will tell the tale
of death—but not tell all! not all! not all! In the
great shock and clamor of surprise when they are discovered, the dead serpents by their side will conceal

the crime, and the pillage wrought will remain in darkest secrecy, while here the Koofim will share their gathered wealth—gold, precious metals, gems and jewels, rarities, such things as are a feast to look on! Ha! ha! The cunning Koofim are the kings of Tsor."

The young girl shuddered hearing this speech, and the sight of the mass of writhing serpents rolling against the glass partition, under her eyes, caused her whole frame to quiver.

"Fear not, bright one," the hag screeched, in an assuring tone of encouragement, "you have naught to fear. You shall be Queen of the Koofim, and in the eyes of Tsor you shall be the grand Princess Urg."

Meta was speechless with astonishment at the hag's words.

"Ah, you shall rule in this house, my dearie! You shall be Queen; but mark, when your beauty fades and you become wrinkled and bent, they'll try to hide you from the world, and place you in a pen, as they do me. Yes, yes, it is better so than stagger out into a frowning world, to be shoved aside and shunned— to go forth into the darker side of the open world, worse pen than this—worse, far worse than this!"

The hideous creature seemed human through all her callousness.

Meta began to regain self-possession, and realizing the desperate character of this place, determined to take advantage of the hag's garrulousness and learn what facts she could with a view of effecting an ultimate escape.

"Who are the Koofim that you speak of, pray?" she enquired coaxingly.

"You have never heard of the Koofim, child? My son has not yet mentioned them? He-e-e-e-! Ten centuries have they ruled in Tsor. And you have never heard of them? He-e-e-e-e-! They are the master serpents though! The cunning of the fox have they; the tiger's ferocity; the lion's courage and the serpent's stealth and sting! They wield the serpent as the mechanic does his tools. The serpent is the crowning and final implement of the order that rules Tsor in the dark. The Koofim are the real kings of Tsor! At every vital organ of the State a Koof is stationed to ply our work and hold secure our place. In its very cradle we chain the law and train it to our ends; among the courts and guardians of the peace our spies and agents act. From us the Lukkan lords of wealth purchase the law as they buy merchandise; but they are in our power. Let but a word escape their mortal lips, and serpent sting will seal those lips for us. Ha! ha! ha! ha! He-e-e! Our Koofim rule the lords! The men of Tsor stand single, each lost in a million scattered aims; but we Koofim are as one, with yet a thousand bodies plunging through the dark and death to those that cross our plundering path.

"We live by plunder and our plunder has a thousand shapes and forms! We make and unmake values, do works of bribery, execute revenges; we carry forgery to the very documents of State; steal purses, rob houses, betray men and women—do all things that may yield revenue.

"Oh, it is a grand order! Our Koofim, child, are known by no badge, no mark, no secret word—they've nothing but the serpent's instinct to know each other by. It is a glorious order, child; its word is the true law behind Tsor's mask of law."

"My man, Count Omrez, was in his day Grand Master of the order, and now my son, Prince Urg, is Master! He is now King of the Koofim, King! And you, my duckling, are to be the Queen. Ha! Ha! You shall be queen! He-e-e-e-!"

When Meta heard this strange recital she felt as if the world were sinking beneath her feet. What hope could she look for in this literal den of serpents? Where could she anchor hope while Tsor, that great city, was powerless in the folds of this monster serpent — the order of the Koofim?

Should she endeavor to escape? The Koofim would pursue her to the ends of Lukka; they would hesitate at nothing. Father, mother, friends, were guardians no more; against the vengeance of the Koofim they would all be powerless.

The whole world was turning into sickening chaos in her mind — home, safety, order and humanity all seemed as if swept away in one terrific flood; her world was lost to her and in its place there reigned one dark, primal vast, without a landmark; a dismal, cold and grisly, horrible cave of utter darkness.

A thousand times more pitiable and hopeless seemed now her fate than ere the hag had spoken.

Poor, poor girl! from the warmth of that sunny home in the Zdar Yim to be plunged into this wretched haunt of evil.

The girl could hardly stand on her feet. In sheer desperation she would have made an attempt to escape from this dreadful place, but she was altogether too weak to think of such a thing, and it was only with difficulty that she dragged herself back to her apartment.

The old hag, who was the mother of Prince Urg, had sought, by informing Meta of the brilliant future in store for her (as she regarded it), to ingratiate herself with the future Queen of the Koofim—though well aware it was an interference in the affairs of her son which he would resent with terrible punishment if discovered. Therefore, before leaving, she secured from Meta a promise not to betray the information imparted to her.

From his roja Prince Urg had witnessed the march and drill of the girls led by Meta. Her wonderful harmonious physique and the classic distinctness of her features, the simplicity of her movements and the calm, quiet dignity and the decision with which she delivered her commands attracted his attention.

"What a queen that would make to command my Koofim! And reign as princess in the palace to a dot! A fine woman!"

He had scarcely thus inwardly expressed himself than Meta swooned.

The prince was sufficiently interested to mingle with the crowd, where he learned her identity. Zuzo still held the forged order. An idea flashed in his mind; he would secure the girl as a hostage until he recovered the paper. It was an altogether unnecessary step, and its purpose was ridiculous. As King of the Koofim he had other and better means to nullify the document. In reality he was being driven by an impulse, and the real meat in the action was an infatuation and not anything rational as he imagined. His reasons were merely mental pretexts, not daring to face the fact of infatuation which impelled them. He therefore took immediate advantage of the opportunity, with what result the reader already knows, leaving it for later hours to speculate just to what extent he would make use of it.

As the days passed Prince Urg became more and more infatuated with his captive. She would make a grand Princess Urg, and it was only a matter of time and custom to these characters when she would prove herself a mistress of the Koofim fit to be their queen. She had just the qualifications that would hold them at a distance, yet command their respect. Once she was bound by the tie of the order, a first crime—as a pledge of secrecy, and they would yield her absolute confidence and fairly worship her.

He delighted in having brought Meta here as a hunter would delight in adding a fine horse to his stud, one that would lead in the chase and gratify ambition or vanity, as the case might be. Urg was a true idolator, a materialist, an animal who saw only the animal and could worship only what he saw.

As Prince Urg nothing was objectionable to him in the union contemplated, inasmuch as the aristocracy of Tsor was one of cash and not of blood, and the prize of beauty, grace and youth outweighed all else for the present—for after all he was swayed only by impulse. He looked not far into the future. Why should he? As King of the Koofim he could discard the girl whenever he chose.

It requires two to make a bargain, however, even in Tsor—even in the den of the Koofim, and Urg realized one obstacle in the fact that Meta thoroughly despised him. It was not likely under the circumstances that she would entertain a thought of union with His Highness unless he could bring to bear a powerful motive. Back of all else he knew he had brute force to rely on, but he preferred if possible to avoid appearing in so harsh a role. He would much rather appear as a friend, and to bring this about he set himself at work with a determination worthy a better cause.

CHAPTER XIII.

SAVED FROM SHAME.

At a long table in an upper hall of the den the King of the Koofim sat one morning surrounded by a motley crowd of rough-looking men who had just finished their repast and were on the point of dispersing. No two of these men dressed alike or in the least manner bore resemblance to each other; their individuality was strongly marked and their appearance was very picturesque, owing much to their dare-devil, defiant freedom from restraint, for these men belonged to the Order of the Koofim.

The room was decorated with stuffed serpents coiled and hung in long lines of loops, from each of which loops peered a glaring serpent head. The ceiling was literally covered with coils and in the center hung a monster python whom they called mother of the serpents.

The assemblage was tumultuous with loud talk, ribaldry and coarse jests, when a stout Koof leaped on the table and in an instant had all the dishes round about spinning in the air while a shower of the un-eaten remnants was being scattered over the heads of the spectators. A whole bowl of some liquid was thus poured over one of the outlaws, who sprang to his feet amid the jeers and laughter of his companions, who thereupon gave vent to such cries as:

"Give your snakes a bath, Urkan!" "A bath is good for snakes!" "Now, let's see a snake performance next!"

Urkan, the man addressed, was a snake charmer and a professional assassin through the serpent's tooth. He always carried a number of serpents on his person concealed under his garments, and this sudden bath enraged him, as it gave a shock to the serpents, who at such times are liable to strike with their deadly fangs. As he was not immediately bitten the danger was over, but not so his rage, and forthwith picking a ladle from the table he flung it with full force at the head of the conjurer. It struck the latter square in the face, inflicting a bloody gash on his cheek. The bleeding man sprang to the floor and was at Urkan's throat in an instant.

A single word from their king parted the men, but not till the conjurer, Kislig by name, had sworn vengeance. He would be satisfied with nothing less than Urkan's life. "The viper's tooth be your death!" swore Kislig between his clinched teeth, and his eyes glared like two living flames.

Kislig was a stranger to serpents. He wielded no power over the reptiles; on the contrary he felt a perfect horror for them. But there was a show of delight, a sort of anticipation of actually expecting to carry out the threat, preposterous as it seemed, that made Urkan regard the vow with alarm.

He appealed therefore to his chief for protection. Kislig must renounce the threatening vow or suffer imprisonment or death, according to the traditional custom of the order.

The King of the Koofim laughed outright at the appeal. It was only an oath ; not a vow. Kislig could not execute the deed even if he really meant it seriously. He durst not come near a viper—much less cause one to strike Urkan, who had such a wonderful influence over serpents.

"You have dipped in the goblet too much," said his chief jestingly, and therewith the subject was dismissed. Then, as if to heal the snake charmer's wounded egoism, he handed him ten gold milos, saying:

"There, my boy; look lively now!"

"Ten milos!" exclaimed Urkan in a tone of contempt, "why, the jewels I brought you yesterday are worth a thousand milos if they are worth one. By all the adders and asps! Didn't I lie in that cellar two days and a night before the inmates were out of the house! Four times they were close to me and once I had to plant a viper in their path so as to gain time and find a new hiding place. But when the coast was clear didn't I carry the house off though over the roof! Just think of it! two necklaces, the finest you ever set your eyes on; three pins and a dozen jeweled rings, and table-ware in silver and gold till my back ached with the burden. And you offer me ten milos! Bah! May the mother of serpents swallow you alive! May your carcass sink to the bottom of the boiling earth!"

"How much do you want?" the chief curtly demanded, virtually admitting the justice of Urkan's supreme disgust.

"Oh, a hundred milos will do."

"A hundred milos! You are mad. It would be gone in one night and you'd have all eyes on you, besides. No, no, my duck, ten milos will last you much longer than a hundred! They ought to last at least a week. There, take these, and I'll hold ten more to give you next week."

By this time the outlaws were all dispersed and Urg withdrew to another chamber where he immediately rang for a servant and ordered writing materials to be brought in. Arriving, the servant was ordered to wait for further orders, while His Highness penned a few lines and then addressed the servant:

"There; take this note to Lebo, the printer of Tok Djun, and have him insert this paragraph in a single copy of the Djun. Mark; I want it only in a single copy and no more. Lebo will be glad to do so, at least if a milo is pressed into his hand. No one else shall know of it. Here, that's for Lebo; and here is one for you, and when the paper is here there will be another milo for you. The paper must be here to-night—to-night without fail. You understand?"

"I shall do as Your Highness bids," said the attendant and with an obsequious bow he retired.

Prince Urg inherited title, wealth and profession from his father Omrez, who had raised himself from obscurity to a position of eminence and respect in the highest circles in Tsor. Few in those circles could disclaim a share in the same profession; trampling down all human obligations whenever the glare of public scrutiny did not reach their deeds. Prince Urg's was only a more scientifically organized method and a much deeper shade of the same ghoulish practice of fattening upon his fellowmen—a species of financial cannibalism.

At an early hour that evening Prince Urg made his appearance before Meta much agitated.

"Scandalous! scandalous! Perfectly shocking! It is simply outrageous, the way tales are circulated! Oh, it is most shameful and vile!" The Prince went on in this manner, pacing the floor, apparently worked up to a high frenzy.

Meta arose from a couch on which she had been lying, and gazed at him, mute and bewildered. Why should he be airing his troubles in her presence? She had never betrayed any sign of faith in the man or the least interest in his affairs.

Prince Urg continued pacing the room; he looked disconsolate and sad. A pale melancholy had settled upon his face and his chiseled features seemed coldly beautiful. It was a sadness, however, that was incapable of kindling sympathy. His thin features could assume the shape but not reflect the expression that speaks from heart to heart.

"Oh heavens, I haven't the courage to speak of it!" he murmured.

Then, as if done with the greatest reluctance, he placed in her hand a copy of an evening journal, directing her to read an article he pointed to, after which he abruptly left the room.

Meta cast her eye over the lines which read as follows:

PROSTRATED THROUGH SHAME!

It is now clearly established that the lady, Meta, who had been missing ever since election day, has been traced to the house of a certain Urg, from which place all further trace of her has been lost. Her father has been given a sentence that will confine him to the Kar Tuki at least two years, and now the mother of the girl lies prostrated with sickness caused by grief and shame.

A flush of crimson mounted her cheeks as she read these lines. Her eyes filled with tears and she fell upon her knees and prayed to the Lukkan God of Fortitude for strength to bear her through this trying ordeal.

Presently Prince Urg returned and Meta, still on her knees, begged piteously for permission to go home.

The tears in that innocent, childish face would have moved a heart of stone.

"I must see my mother," she cried in a burst of

passion, reading refusal in his silence. "Let me go, I pray! My poor mother!"

"You may go," returned the Prince, in a kind tone that brought a quick impulse of joy to Meta's heart; after a lengthy pause, however, he resumed, "but not as Meta. Clouded with shame you shall not leave this roof. Yes, yes you may go — but only as Princess Urg — my wife!"

His last words were uttered in a tone of appeal.

Meta gazed wildly into his face, her eyes turning with scorn.

"Your wife! your wife!"

Then she burst into a fit of hysterical laughter, alternated with weeping and a profusion of tears.

"Your wife!" and pointing to the newspaper now lying on the floor she resumed, "as if this slur will not be shame enough! But your wife! that were a blot upon my conscience! No, that, that can never be!"

"What has all this sentiment to do with it, I pray!" sneered His Lordship, his brutal self coming to the surface as his anger rose, in disgust at Meta's speech.

"It has this to do with it," Meta replied, in calm, decisive tone, "that I prefer to wear the name of shame before all eyes rather than by my conscience, even in a whisper, to be reproached. It means that I would not be your wife though to the world you were fifty times a prince; though fifty threatened shames darkened the path before me. It means I could not be your wife. It means I could not love you—I look on you with loathing; I despise you; I shrink from you as from a scorpion. I fear you — but there relations end."

Meta the girl had in these few words become a woman. The ordinary self had surrendered the reins of being to that heroic counterpart of self, ever guarding by its side, ever urging upward to higher planes.

The ideal Meta had come to the rescue and had revealed a power and strength of personality the ordinary Meta had never felt before. It was the revelation of a new self, bringing with it a reinforcement of strength equal to the emergency of the hour.

Prince Urg was thunderstruck. He looked for certain opposition, in fact a stubborn one, but not for such an outspoken, fearless and implacable determination.

His role as a self-sacrificing hero, shielding her honor with his own name, was a back number. It was a flat failure, but did not deter him from his fixed purpose.

He addressed her once more, this time in the tone of an injured person:

"My honor may suffer, your mother may be driven to the grave overwhelmed with shame — that it is no concern to you? And your father? He my perchance perish in that unwholesome prison — that is naught to you! There is a conscience somewhere in the moon you'd have no blot on! How sensible you are!"

As he progressed in this speech his manner became more and more sneering and he betrayed a coarse exaltation over the display of his apparent wit, adding further cause for the contempt with which he was regarded in Meta's eyes.

"You do not know my father; nor my mother, nor conscience. I therefore pardon what you have thus far done—all you have sought to do. But I beseech you in the name of heaven, let me go in peace! I know my mother waits and suffers by my absence. Oh I beg you, give me leave to go!"

"I have listened to your sentiment long enough," retorted Urg harshly, "and now, as your own sense of shame does not prompt you, a prince's honor will compel you."

"Compel me! Great heavens, what do you mean? For your honor? Oh shame! Why was it that you brought me to this place? Why have you coined pretenses to hold me here? Why was I not taken to my home long, long before this slurring publication? Why has there been no word uttered against the author of this slur? Because *you* have done this thing! *You* have blackened my name. *You* like a loathsome reptile, have dragged my name into your slimy pool seeking to drag me after. You would compel me to be your wife! A man would never stoop to such a deed!"

"With this Meta started for one of the doors moved by a blind impulse to get away from his detested presence and also with a vague aim to seek escape through the darkness. The Prince, however, stepped quickly in her way, addressing her in a half-flattering, half-patronizing tone:

"Not so quick, my little artful—my sweet daughter of eloquence! You have done superbly well and will grace your title most royally. See, here is your diploma—all certified to and witnessed by priests and registrars—all legal forms complete and perfect; and all the public records, even to the entry of engagement a year ago, are unimpeachable. This is a perfect marriage license, lawfully recorded, and we are already man and wife. Calm yourself therefore, my dear; accept the inevitable."

He fairly chuckled with delight, a look of triumph lighting up his face as he crossed the room.

Meta turned deadly pale. For a few moments she was paralyzed by the diabolical audacity of the man. Wicked as she regarded him, she did not expect to see him act such a fiendish piece of outlawry. The poor girl was perfectly helpless. She could only appeal to his mercy. With tear-bedimmed eyes she sank to her knees and once more addressed her persecutor:

"If there are any dear ones that you love—a mother, sister, brother or a friend, even a dog, or any object toward which your heart is moved, O let the least spark of that yet lingering love speak now in my behalf! O do not let the dread name of destroyer haunt your memory like a curse and weigh upon your spirit! If not for your own self, then yet for me, I plead for mercy! Save me! if you are human, save me! In the holy name of love, stand now aside; stand aside and let me go my way! She calls me; my mother calls. My mother!"

"Spare your words. Forget these lingering fancies of your past. You are now my wife! Do you hear? You are the Princess Urg. So come! come! Come with me!"

The last words were spoken as a peremptory order, and as the ruffian advanced to seize her hand Meta instinctively shrunk back.

"No! no! no! It cannot be! it must not be!" she burst out sobbing, while Urg, who had seized her hand, was already dragging her away.

"Stop—one moment!"

These words coming from Meta in a thrilling tone of command had a startling effect—they were perfectly electrifying.

Prince Urg instantly came to a halt and Meta faced the ruffian, a strange fire gleaming in her eye, as she leaned forward saying, in a low subdued tone, "I will be your wife," and then with a dextrous move she snatched a dagger from his girdle. The Prince fell back frightened, under the impression that he was to become a victim, but before he could reach her again she had completed her sentence with the words "as

dust and ashes!" at the same time plunging the weapon into her bosom, and a moment later she fell forward in a pool of her own blood.

CHAPTER XIV.

Tsor was still tottering on the verge of ruin. Not a day but betrayed new evidences of impending revolution. Into the mouth of the Kar Tuki still poured the daily stream of downcast wretches, victims of social disorder.

In the stores and warehouses, these public but privately-controlled highways of exchange, cheap Utopian wares lay piled up waiting for buyers to come — buyers who did not exist. It is true, Tsor was full of men and women; full of hungry mouths, but the wage-paid men and women, the true demand for labor, were absent. The Utopian wares had not put a single petro in the hands of a Tsoran wage-earner, and therefore buyers did not exist.

Society was seized with a fright. Every petro in Tsor was clutched as if life depended on its possession. The wheels of enterprise were clogged. No new buildings, no new roadways, no new factories, no new equipments, no new household furniture, no new garments, nothing more seemed wanted.

Idleness breeding idleness; vice breeding vice; in the home savage squalor; in the streets savage riot, were the logical and inevitable consequence.

Exchange, one of the most vital processes in the life of civilization, was being arrested. The market — that great distributing organ in the industrial body of Tsor — was paralyzed. As long as the Utopian wares kept pouring in, the market of Tsor could never be restored to its former activity. The seed of mistrust had been sown in these foreign wares and a crop of famine was ripening. Foreign, indeed, were these wares—foreign to the process of exchange.

Priests preached economy; prayers ascended in sacrificial smoke, and burnt incense was given their idol gods to sniff. Moral instincts and moral laws were appealed to. Faith, hope and patience were each exhorted, and the great reward of a glorious future life were pictured as the price of virtue and economy. But while the ghost of starvation leaned over the cradle and while the specter of death stalked in the streets peering out through the sunken eyes of pale-faced men and women, while the dead cinders from Utopia were pouring into Tsor's dying heart, all these words were an aggravating mockery.

The power of law could check the rising savage in a single individual breast, but should the sparks, now separate, unite into one bursting flame, what tinder would Tsor be!

The priests of Zmun continued deaf to all verbal appeal; deaf to the appeal of facts that spoke in dismal eloquence on every side.

They had their creed, their religion to vindicate. What were mere worldly woes to the eternal judgment? Faith, pure, blind, unyielding faith, would bear them o'er the threatened tide of horrors. Then, what a triumph would be theirs! Then would faith be exalted—high above all sordid earthly thought! This was a supreme test of faith, and the righteous would surely win and the vain be humiliated. Woe unto them that dared to interfere or sought to destroy the grand harmony designed with infallible wisdom by the almighty Zmun!

The Doctor had for several weeks been declaring he would no longer remain in Tsor, urging me to accompany him to Tismoul, and loth to part from Arda, I still cherished the hope that some deviation in marriage customs might by this time have been effected, now that the Utopian government had been in existence over a year, it being naturally disposed toward progressive reform.

Attendance at my lectures meanwhile had gradually dwindled until at last I had only empty benches to count on so that finally I yielded to the Doctor's importunities and one fine morning, bright and early, we started on a journey to Tismoul.

It is two day's travel by fast elpbies to the city of Tismoul and the entire route is over a lovely country where vegetation is tropically luxuriant and sweet songsters seem to imbue every tree with music.

We spent one night on the journey at a town called Lepsa which was curiously laid out in squares every one of which comprised a village in itself and more than a dozen of these squares again formed a larger square in the center of which were located the public buildings of the town. No fences obtruded their obnoxious presence here and the whole place was beautifully parked.

Everything in Utopia, we learned was to be laid out on this order and the city of Tismoul had from the beginning been thus planned. For the short stay we found everything so remarkably convenient and practical, so pleasing and cheerful and the people so agreeable that it formed a decided contrast with our late impressions in gloomy, grumpy Tsor.

On the evening of the second day we arrived at Tismoul which we found as had been represented another Lepsa on grander and more magnificent scale, the dwellings in each block being grouped in varied figures such as circles, squares, octagons and other geometric designs, whose outlines were often broken to vary the impression they would make.

We were fortunately supplied with letters of introduction to a number of former residents of Tsor and entering the city we enquired of every person we met until finally an officer directed us to the residence of one of the parties, a certain Tasha, by whom we were cordially received.

Tasha was a very prominent person in Tismoul, being in charge of the Utopian Bureau of Manufactures, and among the first acquaintances made here was the Utopian Minister of Finance, Aggra, a fine old gentleman, who knew more by far of our Old World affairs than either the Doctor or I. It fairly made our eyes bulge the way he talked about the American Industrial Republic, whose material wealth in 1930 he assured us with the utmost gravity had grown eight times as large per capita as it had been in the year 1890.

"You don't mean to say they have passed the year 1930!" I ejaculated.

"By the nearest calculation we are able to make" His Excellency replied "it is now the year 1946 in the Old World. You are astonished? I will prove it to you. In the first place we have discovered the fact by direct communication with your former world through a special process discovered some three years ago and gradually perfected until now it is the easiest thing in the world to steal ideas from over the Hills by our power of thought transference."

"Stealing ideas is easily comprehended," the Doctor remarked, "but stealing them from such a distance and getting ahead of time, too, that really paralyzes me!"

"It is no more wonderful," retorted His Excellency, "than your electricity — simply a latent power in the mind that, once discovered and the necessary training applied, became as simple as the falling of a stone and not a bit more wonderful. In this new art we have now attained such a command of the mind that we steal ideas from other planets no matter how remote, for distance plays no part whatever in matters of pure mind. We have a copious literature from the moon, but its thoughts appear as if in a different key or from a different strata of mental vision, rendering it thus far utterly impossible to obtain the slightest clue to its meaning."

"But that does not account for the lapse of almost half a century," I remarked. "From calculations made in Tsor the Old World time recorded but one year to our twenty-four, and this lapse just reverses the proportion."

"We do not attempt to account for it," Minister Aggra replied. "We have simply discovered the fact. Our theory of the fact may be wrong entirely, but even that would not deny the fact itself.

"The accepted theory accounting for this disparity of time," he resumed, "is based upon a comparison with the motion of the planets. To all appearances our earth is stationary. For ages no one believed it moved. Today we believe it revolves with a fearful velocity in spite of its apparent rest. It might double its speed or reduce it by half and would yet to all appearances remain just as at present. Sensual observation is no criterion. The harmony of a wide range of observation is the true test. Change celestial phenomena and calculations must be readapted toward achieving the broadest harmony. Theories must accommodate themselves to facts.

"As to solar time we already know that our Lukkan atmosphere is a deranging element, else time would run day for day alike. Impressions of time are also unreliable, else the long days of childhood would not be measured by the same twenty-four hours as the adult's day. There are nations living slow and nations living fast under the same solar sun. There are also fast and slow periods in each nation's life. Remove from consideration all solar measurements and it is then easy to conceive cycles flying swiftly onward and again others that creep along, scarcely moving.

"Now, then, for our theory: Until two years ago we had been dragging our existence, as in childhood, in a creeping cycle, and since then we have passed into a condition the reverse, in which Old World time lapses twenty-four years to our one. This is regarded the most plausible theory and is universally accepted by our scientists. But as I said, even if this theory is wrong the fact still remains."

The Utopian revolution we now learned was the direct outcome of ideas procured through this marvelous process of thought transference, and, as we were informed, it had already doubled the material wealth of Utopia besides freeing the multitude from the bondage of capital and bettering their present welfare while they were acquiring a gradual collective ownership of the entire capital of the country.

Utopia had simply modeled after the American Industrial Republic and the revolution had been to the withdrawing provinces a veritable Aladin's lamp.

Looking backward now they perceived how close to the precipice of ruin they had already got, under the impression that forms of law and forms of government could give what its accepted institutions denied. Society had become too complicated and unwieldy through its division of rank between rich and poor and justice had become a witch's cauldron into which were poured bits of honesty, stupidity, intelligence, knavery, bribery, precedent and chance, all so mingled that no man from common intelligence and sense of right could foresee what the law would decree. Corporations openly performed such acts as brought law into contempt and the older judiciary, developed in a period before the intrenchment of corporations, were being supplanted by a class brought to the front through the influence of the ring of corporate vultures that hung around our legislative bodies. It is now universally acknowledged that the State could not long have survived before it would have been sent back and forth vacillating between the rocks of anarchy, monarchy and oligarchy, sinking at last into barbarism.

The Doctor and I listened with rapt attention as Minister Aggra and our host Tasha recited the wonders achieved in Utopia as a result of American ideas, and observing our anxiety to learn more concerning the later history of America our host brought us a small volume containing an outline of American history from the year 1896 to 1930 which will be reproduced as our next chapter.

CHAPTER XV.

AMERICAN HISTORY, 1896–1930.

The year 1896 will ever be memorable in the United States of America for the rise of the Free Labor party, and for its platform, which has since become known as the Second Declaration of Independence.

The document charged that the moral obligation of government was not being fulfilled because it sheltered one class of men privileged to destroy the property of workingmen, and through this privilege subjected the latter also to endless blackmail.

Modern production, the platform further charged, was a co-operative process involving the combination of many kinds of labor, through exchange, to produce the variety of articles necessary to sustain life, and BEING A CO–OPERATIVE SYSTEM *under which the isolated individual is helpless to produce,* IT COULD NOT RIGHT-FULLY IGNORE THE MONEYLESS MAN, *subjecting his property of labor to confiscation in idleness and holding it thus also subject to extortion* or partial destruction as the only alternative by which it may ever be saved from *total* destruction in idleness.

The issue between capital and labor is whether labor shall be consumed in idleness while capital is being continuously preserved to control the avenues of employment and through this control to perpetually prey on the working classes, or whether capital shall now consume in excess and enable the working classes to secure the full product of their labor, preserving thereby their own property and thereby acquiring also sufficient wealth to enable them to control for themselves the means of employment.

Property is a surplus of wealth reserved for the purpose of adding to personal comfort and rendering personal energies more effective. Capital is excessive property so applied as to yield a revenue without performing any labor—exacting the revenue from others who are deficient in ownership of property and who, if possessed of a full share of property would not surrender any portion of the product of their labor.

Capital has no fixed form. What is capital to-day, may become property to-morrow and *vice versa*, according to its use. That portion of a man's wealth alone is capital that yields a revenue over and above the full product of his labor. Capital is not exactly wealth loaned, for many lend on one side and borrow on the other, the wageworker thus paying interest in the surrender of a fraction of the product of his labor and sometimes recovering a portion out of the profits accruing from lending or investing his savings.

Capital is formed through a process in which one person gradually acquires two homes to another's none. It substitutes the loan of the second home to the homeless man in place of purchasing the equivalent in labor from him. The first home is legitimate property, but the *second home* is CAPITAL and measures the amount of the homeless man's labor previously destroyed in idleness—labor that should have been purchased by the capitalist to pay a moral debt in completing the act of exchange—a debt capital still owes.

In its very origin CAPITAL IS A SURPLUS PRODUCT. *representing an excess of labor sold by the capitalist, as*

*compared with the poverty of the working classes which
represents a deficiency in the sale or preservation of their
property in labor.* Capitalists, by not reciprocating in
the purchase of the workingman's labor, acquired sole
possession of that surplus that is the medium of employment, limiting the amount of labor that can be
preserved and dictating whose labor shall and whose
labor shall not be preserved, acting in defiance of all
principles of equity, rendering the property of labor
thereby insecure, restricting consumption and its
reciprocal production, and repudiating all recognition
of the element of exchange and equity in the
co-operative process of modern production. Thus

CAPITAL IS A DESTROYER OF PROPERTY,

In its origin repudiative and in its action profiting
from the legalized authority to continue the immoral
repudiation involving the unrestricted destruction of
the labor property of others.

COLLECTIVELY CAPITALISTS SUBSTITUTED LOAN IN PLACE
OF RETURNING EMPLOYMENT DUE TO COMPLETE AND PERFECT
THE ACT OF EXCHANGE AND MAKE THE INDUSTRIAL PROCESS
HONEST AND THE TERMS OF EXCHANGE ON AN HONORABLE
BASIS. The responsibility of capital is collective, but
controlled and held individually its duties are evaded.

Apparently the consumer has invariably had employment prior to consuming, but this can be said only
upon the assumption that his standard of ownership
is to be permitted only on a level with that of the savage, or lower still, that of the debtor or the slave.
Civilization has a large surplus as her collective
standard of ownership and each member of civilized
society should therefore permanently retain ownership of a reasonable share of property without disturbing his title to the reciprocal obligations of ex-

change, regardless of the fact that some employment may have preceded his consuming. *Employment is the reciprocal obligation morally following consumption just as returning is the reciprocal obligation to borrowing.* Money is a medium but not an end in the transaction of exchange.

LABOR IS PROPERTY.

The platform affirmed that the workingman's labor or energy, whether discharged in work or not, still entitles it to be classed as property, declaring that *the pain and hardship involved in doing work are no greater than the anxiety of parents over a breadless family and over the uncertain morrow* in the absence of the opportunity to work. Such idleness it declared was not a vacation. *The man standing ready to work when employment is due him* IS ON DUTY, and wages are MOR-ALLY due him just as if he were working—the fulfill-ment of the act of exchange being an obligation as sa-cred to society as the enforcement of any laws under civil government. All precedent of contracts recog-nized the principle involved and decided in favor of the workingman! *Nor is this energy called labor ever obtained except at a cost of food, shelter and raiment* and IT IS THEREFORE IN EVERY LEGITIMATE SENSE PROPERTY.

To the oft-repeated defense of capital that it is the product of and interest the reward for abstinence from enjoyment of surplus wealth it replied that *the capi-talist had meantime enjoyed the pleasure of possession* and *the security involved in the surplus wealth.* Cap-ital had also caused the multitude to suffer from insecurity and the feeling of dependence and abso-lute destitution, and the poor had also been denied the pleasures of possession—an abstinence, if abstinence alone were a sufficient title to wealth, that would jus-tify them in claiming an equal share in the ownership of all capital. *The capitalist had also demoralized the workingman by enforced idleness*, thereby leading him into dissolute habits (among them indolence and loss of skill and special aptitudes dependent on the continuous use of trained faculties), to which losses is also to be added the confiscation meantime of the workingman's labor.

Had the original lenders said to their brother workers, "We will do your work while you take a vacation, and as fast as you dissipate the value of your homes we will purchase them and thereafter loan them to you for the rent," the workingman would have had no moral right to accept the offer. The property needs and requirements of civilization increase with each generation and no man has the right to dissipate these or forego the opportunities leading to their production or their preservation and force his offspring to begin anew on a level with the savage or slave. Children inherit the wants and they must inherit the means of civilization, and any sale bartering away these rights for the present pleasure or ease of the parents is an unholy and indefensible act, virtually being paramount to the sale of the children to the children of the capitalist.

Society had been gradually rising more to production by the process known as division of labor, brought about largely through commerce. It had increased in wealth and productive capacity in a marvelous degree but all along *it had increased the minuteness of its division of labor, multiplying occupations, man and man becoming more separated as the process developed, and thereby it had intensified the difficulty of making ends meet.* The freeman became less and less self-employing and more and more dependent on the efficiency of the process of exchange, which was growing more and more imperfect as its field widened. The absence of integrity in this process played havoc everywhere. It drove mothers, daughters and small children under the yoke of the factory and drove men out of work or to standards of wages insufficient for family support without the aid of little ones and those who should have remained under the parental roof. Poverty under the roof of the self-employing pioneer in the wilderness made a cheerful home compared with those homes, apparently free, under the shadow of a labor market that sent the wolf to the door to compel acceptance of humiliating terms.

It is true wages measured by quantity of product have increased steadily, but wages measured by the ratio of the products produced to the product received have constantly decreased increasing the mental burden of "making ends meet" and decreasing also the chances of acquiring an ultimate competence. Real wages in an economic sense have declined.

In the discussions evolved during the campaign of '96 eminent economists insisted there had never been a violation of the act of exchange. Every sale of commodities, they said was for gold or for its representative in some form, equivalent to a commodity, so that all purchase and sale was an exchange of commodities for commodities, or labor for labor. Thus it was also claimed that exports and imports invariably balanced.

The fallacy of these claims was exposed by showing that *gold in such transactions does not* ACT *as a commodity*, NEVER *being consumed*, coming back very often to the lender only to be utilized in interest-bearing investments or re-loaned, while the commodities the borrower purchased were being invariably consumed. *The mere fact that it required labor to produce the gold does not elevate it above the sphere of a counter*, gold being merely a sort of security attached to the counter for use where the issuing government's credit is not good; this is the only part gold ever played in connection with money, and this use of the metal is one of the chief factors enhancing its commercial value, for destroy this use and its utility for ornaments would be greatly depreciated. Nations that can demonetize silver will some day find safer methods of foreign interchange and are liable to suddenly leave gold a much debased metal.

The platform of the Free Labor party admitted that SOCIETY AS A WHOLE *had countenanced the growth of capital* and AS A WHOLE *was responsible for the result.* The party pledged itself therefore to protect all capital as property and to protect all labor also as property. Labor, it declared, has the prior right to be preserved through employment, even though the excess, capital, measuring the debt of employment still due the multitude as unfulfilled exchange, be totally annihilated in being consumed. Such a transaction would only transfer ownership to the multitude, *as it would be an excess employment to them* OVER AND ABOVE *that created in answer to their own consuming.* It would be ANNIHILATED *as capital* and CREATED *as property.* In its origin CAPITAL had been *created* and PROPERTY ANNIHILATED.

Society in the past as much as said to all: "Obtain all the wealth you can under the law and you shall be protected in its possession and in its enjoyment. Neither society nor the capitalist recognized the true significance of either capital or interest or how society could be shaped to avoid the alternative of these evils or others appearing equally as bad or worse. The part capital and interest played was beyond doubt the equivalent of theft, but theft sanctioned by law, and not in defiance of law.

IT WAS UNINTENTIONAL THEFT,

And while not a crime in the sense of a voluntary act, knowingly and willfully performed, with choice of less vicious methods of conducting commerce, *it was still* IN EFFECT *identical with other theft*, *and* ON A FAR MORE STUPENDOUS SCALE.

The title to ownership of capital is merely one to ITS VALUE — what the capitalist may hold for USE or for CONSUMING BUT MAY NOT WITHHOLD TO USE FOR INTEREST OR USURY. The duration of time in which it is to be consumed is justly measured by the average duration of products in general, liberally estimated to be twenty years at the utmost, and *the employment to result from this consuming is a debt of employment still due the disinherited.* PRACTICALLY IT IS BEING LOANED *and the borrower should therefore have the privilege and opportunity to repay — and to repay in labor, the true unit of ultimate exchange. In reality the employe is a borrower of factory, tools, machinery, stock, and all the essentials involved in the process in which he is engaged at work, and he pays for the loan by allowing the employer all the profit he can make over and above the stipulated wages.*

Workingmen as borrowers of collective capital are entitled to all the advantages of use *to the extent of having the benefit of* ALL *the employment to be derived therefrom, and not only a limited employment.* In the absence of the full demand for employment wages are curtailed and the volume of savings so reduced as to debar them from securing their own properties.

To buy out capital with ordinary money is utterly impossible, for the disinherited could not acquire the necessary money without *surplus* employment, and this they could not get, unless the CAPITALISTS *voluntarily consumed their surplus, which is not to be expected of them, as they* PREFER *to charge for its use, the cost of wear and tear, thus perpetuating it, and also charging for its loan a profit of some sort, whether interest, rent or ordinary business gain.* Capital is thus practically intrenched and cannot be dislodged. Simultaneous saving on the part of the multitude would be met with a CORRESPONDING SAVING ON THE PART OF CAPITALISTS and a contraction of production that *would make the saving result only in increased idleness* and would produce no accumulation of property for workingmen. Simultaneous saving is the process following financial panics, being destructive and in no sense creative.

THE PURCHASE OF CAPITAL.

The method in which capital was to be protected as property was by its purchase with bonds payable in annual installments bearing interest at 4 per cent., each annual installment to be made in money legal tender for one year only at market prices determined by the ratio of supply and demand — the government assuming control of all industries. *This transfer was not to take place until a satisfactory organization of the industries in question had been effected,* and THE ULTIMATE LIMITATION WHEN FINAL PAYMENT WAS TO BE MADE WAS NOT TO EXCEED TWENTY YEARS FROM THE TIME OF PUBLIC DECISION AT THE POLLS.

The possibility of being able to pay such an enormous indebtedness lay in the fact that the prices of labor would rise PROPORTIONATELY HIGH through the increased demand for labor to enable the absorption of capital, however large the sum. In reality the workingman would not feel it, for the saving of wastes and the extra portion of the now increased wages, besides the profits of labor before wasted in idleness, would more than meet the payments, leaving him fare better than ever. *Hitherto the* LABOR MARKET *had been overstocked through deficient consuming; now the* CAPITAL MARKET *would be overstocked through the excessive accumulations of past years, and would represent an excessive demand for labor,* and *whereas before* LABOR WENT UNDERPAID, *now it would go* OVERPAID. The paradox of the ease with which capital accumulated in large volumes absorbed from the masses would now be reversed, and the masses would now just as miraculously accumulate and absorb it back, where it belonged.

Were the sum to be paid a hundred times as large, or to be paid within a hundredth part of the time, its payment would be just as easy, *for the possibility of being able to pay the sum depended entirely upon* LIMITING THE TIME *in which the purchase is to be completed.* If left for an indefinite period the previous condition of dependence and poverty would prevail, for labor would then be at the mercy of capital as before. In fact, THE SHORTER THE PERIOD *within which the final payment is to be consummated* THE LESS WILL LABOR HAVE TO PAY— *the price of labor rising proportionally high.*

PROTECTION TO AMERICAN INDUSTRIES.

Protection was unqualifiedly endorsed, all efforts to withdraw it being rebuked as retrogressive and as an unconstitutional assault destroying the property of those directly engaged in the industries, ultimately injuring all industries.

What is true among individuals is also true among nations. A nation may beggar itself and its people may perish with hunger while commerce in its conflict of accumulation ignores all reciprocal obligations, substituting loans and investments in interest-bearing properties in place of return purchase of the products of the impoverished nation's labor. The countries of the world all suffer from the abuse of capital and their low prices are a barometer telling the extent of the abuse, everywhere greater than in our own comparatively new country, where it has not yet had time to work the extreme effects.

So-called trade with these low-priced countries is a delusion; it is not trade, but purchase—a continuous exhaust by which our property passes into foreign hands, and we afterwards become borrowers of it, instead of remaining its owners. This process is practically and economically *borrowing*, and IN NO SENSE. TRADE. Besides impoverishing us it would confine us to fewer channels of industry, converting us largely into laborers, and the burden of idleness and loss of skill would be an enormous destruction of property as a substitute for the so-called profits of buying cheap goods from abroad.

In its application during and after the civil war protection produced a golden era in our country, causing a vast material wealth to be created out of our energies. We were obliged to stock up rapidly with new factories, new machinery, new railroads and millions of new homes with their furnishings. The labor of brain and hand had never been better rewarded than when engaged in the creation of this vast wealth; but once created, the process of absorption into fewer hands and the greater restriction of demand for labor and increase of non-productive pursuits involved in the competitive system tended to separate our people into classes, widening the gap between rich and poor from year to year, as in older countries.

Quite recently we have madly leaped from the frying pan of lowering wages into the fire of conflict with the still more abused foreign labor and discovered that "free trade" was only free buying. The buyer saved a few cents, but as the "trade" is chimerical some one was left idle in return, betrayed by the buyer. Thus free betrayal was found to be a more correct name for the act.

The theory of free trade is perfect as far as it goes, but it only touches the surface of trade, confining its attention to products (that represent labor exchanged — in being combined in the product), but it ignores entirely the labor destroyed in idleness — the unex- changed, and thus the most vital part of economics — to ensure exchange and protect against waste, fraud and destruction is left out, resembling a love story with- out lovers or a perfect house resting upon quicksands.

TARIFF REFORM.

Among other things the platform declared "TARIFF REFORM" UNCONSTITUTIONAL; for according to its own advocates it was to admit foreign goods, essentially supplanting the American product and essentially also destroying the property of American labor.

In discriminating against specific products it dis- criminated also against specific classes of labor. If there were grounds for discriminating against partic- ular monopolies or trusts these grounds must be estab- lished, and if proven, it is clear that other methods of punishment are open than that of subjecting innocent workingmen to the loss of their labor property through idleness. The law has a right to its pound of flesh, but to no drop of blood; it must avoid acting like the bear who killed his master in attempting to kill the fly. The constitution guarantees the citizen all the protection possible under government, and the with-

drawal of any portion of this protection is contrary to
its spirit and intent.   This is not a government for one
city or for a body of foreign importers, but a government for the whole people — a government bound to
protect their property — their labor, against the cupid-
ity of commercial pirates just as it would against any
other common thieves.

If tariff reform is right free trade is right, for if it
is right to steal one dollar it is right to steal ten dollars.
If lawlessness in trade is right then all lawlessness is
right and the simple law of beasts should be the law
for man.   If restrictions in the interest of law and
order are to be encouraged then they should also be
encouraged in finance and industry, for to banish the
hope of bringing law into finance and industry were
as bad as to banish all law entirely.   The tariff legislation of 1894 has been a step towards anarchy and
that step cannot be too quickly retraced.

RAW PRODUCTS.

All products, including labor, are raw products.
Coal is raw product to the cooked meal, the cooked
meal is raw product to labor and labor is again raw
product to coal.   Buttons are raw product to garments,
garments are raw product to labor and labor is raw product to buttons.   There is no break in the chain of
production, each item being a link at once raw product and finished product ; *but none are exclusively raw
products.*   There are mechanically crude products,
usualy cheap, but these, as raw products, are subject to
no different conditions than the same quantity in value of other products, and can cheapen production in
no higher degree.   The plea for free trade in raw materials like the plea for tariff reform is only a plea for
a degree of free trade and must stand as beneficial or

injurious by the criterion of free trade. It may be
urged that there is an element of land rent in its price,
but all products aside from labor involve an element
of unjust monopoly and are all governed by the same
standard — that of interest, *and land is no greater
monopoly than capital*, FOR WHOEVER HAS CAPITAL CAN
HAVE LAND.

Protection had been a virtual declaration of industrial independence *between nation and nation*, and now
the new Protection declared industrial independence
BETWEEN MAN AND MAN.

The Free Labor Party pledged itself to stand by
AMERICAN PROPERTY AGAINST THE WORLD and to stand
by AMERICAN LABOR AGAINST ALL CAPITAL.

IMMIGRATION.

Regarding immigration, the claim was made that
the immigrant, once in our country, purchased the
product of *American* labor. For every thousand foreign workmen there were probably $200,000 worth of
American-made products annually consumed, besides
causing demand for construction of additional machinery, apparatus, buildings, etc., involved in the annual manufacture of these products. They also required additional residence buildings—all operating
to reciprocate for the employment the foreign workmen receive.

Where it operates injuriously is when they flock
into manufacturing districts, displacing large numbers
of workmen and demoralizing local wages. The demand for labor they cause is diffused and is so scattered that its benefits are not locally felt. The rem
edy for the evil is therefore clearly in better distribu
tion of immigrants, who will work less harm if dis

tributed throughout the west and south, or if their
numbers in manufacturing districts were restricted.

The evil lies evidently in bad distribution and not
in the immigrant himself—at least not in the Cau-
casian immigrant, and the comparison so often made
between the imported workman and the imported
goods is not detrimental to immigration properly controlled—the one exchanging labor with us and the
other failing to purchase our labor in return. The
difference is as great as between two customers entering a store, one an honest purchaser and the other a
shoplifter.

A MEDIUM OF EXCHANGE.

Fearing the contemplated changes would frighten
foreign investors into a return of American securities,
or a withholding of interest and dividends from re-
investment, causing thus a heavy draft upon our gold,
which might thereby precipitate a panic, the platform
recommended the prompt issue of a bond currency, to
be distributed pro rata among the states, counties and
municipalities according to population, this currency
to take the place of future local bond issues, to bear
interest at the rate of 4 per cent., and to be legal tender, with 1 per cent. for each expired quarter elapsed
since its issue.

This bond currency was to ultimately supplant local bonds, without acting as a burden to the country, which was now paying higher rates on such
bonds. At the same time it was to become a great reserve currency, strengthening our financial world by
enabling it to carry larger safety reserves than they
could profitably do with any other form of currency.
This bond currency was designed also to go into circulation by being expended in local improvements and
would so increase the volume of employment as to

stimulate that confidence on every side so necessary to revive the depressed industries.   Where one dollar was expended it would stimulate an increase of production equaling ten times the value expended, all being wealth that would otherwise not have been created. It was to be the signal stroke that was to start all the wheels in Uncle Sam's factory going at once.   Concerted action was needed and no one could give so effective a signal as Uncle Sam—the government itself—*and this is one of the purposes for which government exists.*

The world's gold was declared altogether too scarce in proportion to the amount of produce to be exchanged or sold.   As a result, a vast system of fiat of the worst kind had come into use, and the number of banks from which it was being issued equalled the number of citizens of the republic.   *Every man who purchased on credit was such a bank, issuing his promise to pay, whether in writing, on a note or in a ledger.*   The corner grocer held the family's fiat and the wholesaler held the grocer's fiat, and so on to the banker and capitalist.   If you refused to accept these fiat bills you could do little business.   Business adapted itself to it in a fashion by charging risks or insurance, in raising the margin of gross profits.   Commercial and collection agencies were organized to report the standing of these personal-fiat banks and to enforce redemption by both legal and persuasive methods.   It was recognized as a very expensive medium, costing consumers from 10 to 50 per cent. for exchange by the time the manufacturer's, wholesaler's and retailer's risk and collection charges were summed.   This was really free banking on an enormous scale.

More currency was unquestionably needed, but ordinary fiat currency had been tried with the result

that it would become a disturber of values. No one
desired to carry reserves that yielded no revenue compared with other investments, for reserves are an investment and so fiat currency for this reason would
soon be at a discount, causing rise of other values and
still further contrasting its inability to yield a revenue. Particularly speculative properties, such as lands
and stocks that are not to be consumed, would boom,
and later precipitate a panic in the reaction when
everyone sought to liquidate, the expansion of values
having followed the expansion of currency and currency proving once more insufficient in volume.

The interest-bearing currency on the contrary, it
was urged, would enable the combination of a large
volume of currency together with steadiness of values
and would also largely eliminate credit in favor of
more economic cash transactions; and to supplement
the bond currency, it was urged greater restrictions be
placed upon credit.

A CONSTANT MENACE.

The platform warned the country against the danger
threatened by foreign ownership of American stocks,
bonds, mortgages and other properties. *Any sudden
withdrawal of these investments, or failure to reinvest the
interest or dividends accruing could so abstract gold from
our country as to at any time impair our financial stabil-
ity and precipitate a destructive panic.* This ownership
the platform condemned as a nuisance and menace as if
it were dynamite at our doors. American dignity and
American security could not tolerate the continuation
of this danger. *It was not necessary to discriminate
against these investments, but* IT WAS NECESSARY TO RENDER
THEM HARMLESS.

It is an act of egregious folly to suppose any maintenance of "parity" or propping of public credit abroad can in the least condone the destruction of private credit at home and INCREASE OF ALIEN OWNERSHIP OF OUR PROPERTIES — A VIRTUAL BORROWING on our part, going deeper and deeper into the toils. Any maintenance of credit or parity at such a price is merely postponing and aggravating the evil. It is making tribute grow and rendering impossible the payment of the debt itself.

On this basis we are already borrowers to the extent of probably from eight to ten billions and the shortage in balance of trade from the dividends and interests on this sum, the volume spent annually abroad by Americans and shortage from other sources like these not reckoned in the ordinary balance of trade account, is increasing this debt at the rate of more than half a billion annually. In the face of these facts the acceptance of the gold basis is a virtual declaration of bankruptcy with no escape except by perpetual tribute bondage.

It is an economic blunder to issue an obligation to ultimate settlement in anything but labor. The gold borrowed left our shores again to purchase products or labor, and WHAT WE REALLY BORROWED WAS THEREFORE LABOR, and WHAT WE OWE IS THEREFORE LABOR.

THE CIRCULATING MEDIUM.

The platform declared it an impossibility to conduct an industrial society without money. *Without money a country's property would be almost worthless. Infuse money into a moneyless country and you may possibly add more to its wealth than* TEN TIMES THE VOLUME OF THE MONEY INTRODUCED, *simply because of the greater efficiency imparted to its paralyzed energies that before were being destroyed.* Infuse law into a lawless country and you add value and wealth to that country. Improve the morals of a community and you increase the effectiveness of its forces and the quality of its social atmosphere.

An infusion of bond currency, even a fiat on printed paper, WOULD ADD REAL WEALTH *until the full activity of energies are fostered,* BEYOND THIS BECOMING A MERE DILUTION OF THE COUNTRY'S NOMINAL WEALTH but not altering its real worth.

An ordinary fiat currency in large volume sinks in value, because, as previously stated, *when held as a reserve it fails to meet the standard of other investments— namely,* YIELDING A REVENUE.

Money is the only form of wealth convertible at any instant into any form of commodity desired, and in a crisis when no one can rely upon the receipts of the morrow everyone needs a larger hoard than usual and is loth to part with it. For this reason a larger volume of money is required to tide over such periods, as individuals, consulting only their immediate individual safety, at such times restrict their consumption, shun new enterprises and through these causes largely produce stagnation. For this reason a LARGE volume of currency held in reserve by individuals and business concerns would enable the commercial world to hold out longer under a threatened change or crisis without breaking down. The volume of consumption would not decline so rapidly and coming slower and feebler to be met with a greater reserve fund would never be able to produce a crisis. SECURITY IS A FUNCTION OF MONEY CO-ORDINATE IN IMPORTANCE WITH EXCHANGE.

A national law was also urged for the protection of the family and the repression of credit and speculation, to allow the combined creditors but half the proceeds from the forced sale of real property, stocks or other securities.

There is only one redemption for money, and that is redemption in labor—the *ultimate unit in exchange. Money should be simply legal tender and be guaranteed protection before the law like all other forms of property — neither more nor less.*

Property is not redeemable in gold, and why should money be? The entire gold supply is probably 1 per cent. of the total property value. Suppose all desired simultaneously to be secure by converting their property into gold? They might as well wish themselves transferred to Jupiter. Of money likewise the world's currency is much larger in volume than its gold and universal redemption would be impossible. Redeemable currencies are good only as long as there is no simultaneous call made for redemption, and while the holders of gold can be bribed by discounts or tribute to continue its loan. *A real redemption accompanying the gradual payment of all practical debts in gold could not possibly be accomplished.* The whole theory of redeemability in gold, or even gold and silver, is purely visionary—an utter impossibility and is only a subterfuge by which perpetual tribute may be exacted.

The plentifulness and security of the gold basis, or any non-interest-bearing money basis, may be compared to a large theatre built with a single narrow door—safe in the absence of any alarm, but criminally negligent none the less for its effect in inviting alarm, and the disastrous consequences liable when a case of alarm occurs. The gold basis seems safe as long as we sink deeper in debt, but attempt to reduce the debt and its fallacy is at once exposed by a depleted currency and panic.

Checks, notes and credits are backed only by one

or a few individuals, and prove utterly incompetent to take the place of money in the hour of danger. They are like the narrow door, merely tolerated through carelessness and indifference, and like fair-weather friends, they vanish in the face of peril.

MAINTAINING PARITY.

It is presumptive to assume our unit of value or our dollar shall be equivalent to any given quantity of gold. The latter is a commodity absolutely essential only for foreign trade, and being without international or other regulation, it is the duty of our government to prevent it from debasing our currency or deranging our commerce. To do this further gold obligations should be avoided and to provide for those already made gold should be purchased at its lowest price. By closing all sources of drainage whereby we could be called on for balances of gold the dearness or cheapness of that metal would ultimately no longer concern us.

The interest and dividend payments sent abroad and the money expended abroad should be calculated in our balance of trade and further investments prohibited, to the end that the excess of balance against us be taken out in products or else held in our currency to be *ultimately* taken out in products.

In many directions prohibition of imports should take the place of tariffs and the free list should be substituted with high tariffs to discourage consumption of products that drain our gold supply and compel us for want of gold to make up shortages by selling our products, particularly those depending on foreign markets, at a loss, or paying a premium on gold, whether directly, or indirectly in general depreciation of prices and contracted production

Our hotels and home resorts, as well as the farmers supplying them should be protected against foreign competition, through which Americans are enticed abroad who would otherwise spend their money at home. Such travelers should be taxed according to the time spent abroad and according to the quarters they occupy aboard ship. These people have acquired the means of travel on the American standard of wages and profits and should be made to pay the difference and in addition a further tax for disturbing our balance of trade, for which we are taxed with discounts, interests and indirect losses of various kinds.

Measures were also recommended toward rehabilitating our shipping in order that we control our own share in the carrying trade of the world.

The industrial and financial derangements of 1893 and 1894, the latter beginning with the passage of the tariff reform bill, were so universally felt and acknowledged that the platform had little to say in comment upon them. It condemned the administration in being instrumental in their enaction and also for the attitude assumed in discharging employes and reducing expenditures in the midst of the industrial fight — thereby adding fuel to the fire of panic, an act to be compared only with that of a general who at the first gun of the enemy turns in alarm and leads his troops into ignominious rout. *Fifty millions at such a time added to the government expenditures in improving roadways would not only have saved the equivalent from being wasted in idleness, but have so stimulated the paralyzed industries as to have prevented the destruction of ten times the amount in idleness.*

Commerce is a conflict of accumulation — a strife to substitute exchange with loan. Low prices are the barometer of restricted markets — markets that possess far more eagerness to sell than willingness to buy — markets overstocked, forestalled with capital and forestalled also to a large extent with products for current consuming — markets where the standard of consumption is low — markets burdened with the greatest amount of non-productive labor, the fruit of extreme competition.

Surrounded by a large world with immense commerce but all on a lower plane in every respect than our own, the administration had opened channels connecting us with the world and let out our trade — our very life and blood — expecting it would return up hill; but instead of returning it piled into capital abroad, while our entire industrial system was being toppled into ruin. The strikes, riots, bloodshed and starvation following this abandonment of partial government in industry to the complete trade anarchy of open commerce with the world were only manifestations of the revolution created by plunging a people into a primitive standard of livelihood.

CAMPAIGN OF '96 AND ITS FRUITS.

Such was the substance of the platform of the Free Labor Party in 1896 and such the course of reasoning adopted in urging its endorsement at the polls.

As might have been expected it brought on a vigorous campaign — a campaign of education that after a bitter struggle ended in triumph and heralded a new era in the history of governments.

Among the first acts of the new administration was the appointment of a commission to prepare and report in detail plans for arranging the final purchase of capital and for its conduct and conservation thereafter.

After great labor this report was completed in the year 1898 and was revised, approved and adopted in the year 1900, and on Labor Day of that year the eyes of the whole world were upon us as our new Ship of State was being launched.

It was a colossal undertaking but our experience with large undertakings, particularly the Columbian Fair, especially fitted us to lead among the nations in modeling the first grand industrial government.

The history of the country from 1900 to 1916 is a tale of such a. metamorphosis as would require volumes to minutely record. It was a prosperous era, and contrary to the predictions of pessimists it was an era of personal liberty in a higher degree than had ever hitherto been attainable, for now liberty was more than ever reinforced by the power of collectivism and collectivism was more than ever stripped of license and of stimulus to abuses.

Property and private earnings became now more sacred than ever and rank by personal merit acted as a better stimulant to develop latent capacities. A more liberal choice of occupation and greater certainty of opportunity developed self-respect and manhood and love of work, and now no longer were foreigners a menace to our workingmen.

Under the new order government was administered largely through channels of industry, each industry becoming a representative government in itself. In affairs of health the physician had the greatest voice and in the making of garments the tailor's voice was potent. Each of these industrial bodies was again represented in a general body or industrial senate which acted as a check on the special industrial bodies. Most general legislation was devised by professional students of government and had to be approved by the senate before it became law. *In this system everybody did not vote on everything and on a long string of candidates besides all at one time, but the fountain of all regulations came from those most competent to understand them.* Legislating mainly through industrial channels voters knew most of the candidates personally and a bad man had less chance for election than where few knew him personally and the political clamor was so loud no one knew what really to believe—resulting often in utter indifference as to results.

There was no longer a limit to opportunity for production, for nature knows no such limit, and no more competition remained to divert labor to non-productive pursuits so that as a result *wealth began to accumulate at a wonderful rate, the annual surplus of accumulation reaching a sum five times as large as formerly,* for now production under an eight hour day was double the former total (accumulation had formerly only been less than ten per cent. of the volume of production) still leaving an increase of fifty per cent. over former standards for immediate consumption. All the surplus accumulation went into more comfortable and commodious homes, better equipped and better surrounded and also better distributed. Larger and better equipped stores and factories resulted and the distribution of cities, towns and villages as well as farmers' homes was altered to yield greater social and economic results.

THE EFFECTS ABROAD.

During all this time Europe was undergoing an agitation hitherto unknown. England, the home of capital, was paralyzed by the revelation of her real attitude to the world, and her future commercial importance was circumscribed. The world she had conquered could not be much longer held under her sway. For the individual Briton the future was a glorious one, but the nation's rank as ruler in the world of commerce had vanished.

Russia, contrary to expectation, adopted the new order, but retained the aristocratic government under a 100 year license, at the end of which time it was to become an industrial republic. Forty years was set as the period for her reconstruction, as greater preparation and education were necessary to bring her people up to the necessary standard.

The monarchies of Europe adopted the monarchical method of inaugurating the reform taking from twenty to thirty years for its consummation. The reform was at first met with a storm of abuse, but that soon subsided as rulers and thinkers recognized the practical economics and moral force of the issue.

Following in our footsteps, the South American governments and Mexico adopted the industrial form of government and in the year 1920 a movement was begun to incorporate the American states, embracing the entire continent in one government on the industrial plan, the act going into effect in the year 1930, when the last payments in the transfer of capital were settled.

It is now confidently predicted by the most competent authorities that within one century the entire orient will have adopted the new form of organization and the dream of Tennyson of an ultimate federation of the world will become an accomplished fact.

CHAPTER XVI.

Utopia was more modern than Tsora and her streets and roadways were models of cleanliness and beauty, being smoothly paved with glass blocks in varied shades and colors combined in most fantastic patterns. This paving, like everything else, conformed to the general design of the whole, producing a symmetrical and charming harmony of effects.

The average square was at least double the length of ordinary city blocks and hence the length of roadway to be provided for was but one-half as much in proportion to the ground covered.

There being no back yards and no fences its pretty walks crossed squares so conveniently that all parts of the city were readily accessible to each other. Then there was a nice uniformity about their system of building in groups or squares, the structures aging all at the same time, so that the entire group can be simultaneously reconstructed with great economy, avoiding also the continuous tearing up and obstructing of streets so often a nuisance in Old World cities.

As previously stated most of these homes are without that common manufacturing establishment known as kitchen and laundry, meals being procured at the family restaurants conveniently located in the central group of buildings in each square. Excellent meals are served in these peculiar restaurants; for, as I learned, the cooking conforms readily to the patrons, some of whom retain a special cook for the exclusive use of a single family only, while others combine in sets of two or more—particularly small families, to divide the expense, natural selection tending to bring tastes and cooking into harmony.

The dining rooms, large and small, are the exclusive family property during fixed hours reserved, and each family have their respective and exclusive table service or may use one in common, according to their choice and means. All the advantages of privacy are thus more economically and effectually secured while reserving the elasticity under which, if desired, the advantages of further co-operation can be obtained. With an absolutely individualistic base, communistic methods can be entered or merged into just as little or as much as the individual sees fit.

One feature of the central group of buildings in each square that I almost forgot to mention is the kindergarten where children receive their first elementary instructions. Among these buildings are also to be found a library, reading room and public hall for social gatherings, lectures and other entertainments.

In the entire breadth of Utopia no isolated dwellings or farmhouses exist, as the square is the base of the smallest village and town, and its cities are only aggregates of squares. The farmers here go to their fields every morning in a species of motor-carriage propelled by a stored power, not electricity, for that force is not manifest in the atmosphere of Lukka, but a force the Doctor has hinted to me as being the negative or reverse of electricity—though whatever he meant by that I am not prepared to say. These carriages take the place of elphies in Utopia and the same peculiar stored power does away with a vast amount of manual labor on the farms.

The Doctor and I had read and reread that story of the rise of the American Industrial Republic and had discussed all its phases, and to say we were astounded over its revelations is a mild way of expressing our surprise. We could not believe it, and yet we could see no way to avoid accepting it. Some matters, however, were stil dubious to us and the next time we met Minister Aggra I asked him how it was a man should not be entitled to interest for the accommodation of a loan, being only the price paid to the lender for the advantage it gave the borrower. It seemed to me very much like the righteous reward for a service.

"What perhaps puzzles, you my dear friend" replied the venerable financier, "is the fact that when a business man borrows a sum and agrees to pay a reward for the loan, he invariably expects to make a profit somewhat larger in order to justify the step. This is what you mean?"

"That's exactly what I mean," I responded, "and I don't see anything unjust in that. The lender would be a fool to give the loan without interest and permit the borrower to have all the profit."

"My dear sir," was the response, "your business man IS PAYING NO INTEREST AS I UNDERSTAND INTEREST. He is merely acting as a go-between, collecting the interest from the public out of the prices he gets for his goods *for which the public pay*. THE PUBLIC PAYS THE INTEREST IN THIS CASE."

"Your borrower," he resumed, "merely sees where he thinks he can make a handsome revenue out of the people should he get control of the capital requisite to carry on a given transaction *but he expects the people*, OUT OF THE PRICES HE CHARGES, *to pay the interest*, and he is merely a speculative go-between, *neither a capitalist nor a borrower in a true sense. To the people he appears to be a capitalist and to the capitalist he appears as the borrower."*

"Is interest then really a species of blackmail and not the price of utility?" I asked, finally.

Minister Aggra replied:

"While it is true that the ground underneath our feet and the air above our heads are absolutely essential to our being, still it would be a presumption akin to gross idolatry to assume that these inanimate things performed a service or belonged in the category of human exertions such as are to be exchanged between man and man in modern production. To be able to shut off a man's access to air would give great power over the man but it would be no evidence of personal service to the man. Under such circumstances to permit a man to breathe would appear to be a service to him, and the man would no doubt pay well for it, whether a real service or not, *but it would not be* A PRODUCTIVE SERVICE. It would be a service of the same type as that of the highwayman who kindly condescends to offer me my life on surrender of my purse. I may have created wealth represented by my purse, but my creation of wealth does not make the robbery a creation of wealth. *Although he* ACCUMULATED wealth as *a reward for giving me my life, when he had me in his power,* IT WAS MY ARMS AND BRAINS and not his pistol that *created* the wealth in question. *Human labor* and *not capital* creates wealth.

"Viewing capital in different forms we constantly witnessed in it a source of violence and waste," resumed the speaker, "being a very crude and primitive institution. In the shape of lands it distributed population with reckless extravagance. It constantly readjusted prices so that the least advantage a piece of land had in its location became an indifferent matter to the person seeking land, for the buyer was obliged to either compensate these advantages in a higher price for the land itself or in a higher rental price ; if he wished to escape high and extortionate prices he was compelled to locate where the difference was wasted in freights and other disadvantages inherent in the extreme isolation of the locality to which he was driven.　To get land free he was obliged to go where he wasted his labor for years before markets and other advantages were brought near enough to him to permit his labor to net a reasonable reward.　Thus in the general distribution of population an appalling waste is apparent, both in the scattered residences within cities and towns and in the scattering of farms and of cities, towns and villages. In the spasmodic and capricious development of towns and cities the street mileage to be controlled baffled the means of local authorities, because the expense of their care was divided between too small a number of people and these of very unequal means.　Thus between suffering from lack of care and extravagant cost in the little care bestowed on the streets, the poor distribution of the population is a heavy drain on the community.　The same general fact applies to the entire country whose scattered population had previously been eaten up by freights and harrassed by inefficient roads at heavy cost of maintenance.　Then again in sections it led to huddling human beings like beasts, to the moral and physical ruin of thousands.　The capitalistic or speculative ownership of property beyond any doubt is directly responsible for these results, which I trust no friend of capital will claim was a service to humanity.

"In business enterprises likewise the savage, reckless standard of extravagant waste prevailed.　Immense fortunes were first sunk before a business influenced sufficient trade to follow steadily in reliable channels to its doors. Tremendous business conflicts occurred over the establishment of trade, and enormous wastes ensued. Business was a perpetual warfare to hold positions gained. The established business was a castle under continuous siege from greater and lesser foes. The opportunities of labor were uncertain and so also the opportunities of trade, and trade was left to be fought for in the open, free-for-all field, where the scramble became greater the older the country grew, more concentrated on one side and more split up on the other, and then those who had secured an established trade pocketed all its advantages, so that the public payed invariably at the standard of cost under the friction of severest conflict where trade was most split and most burdened with non-productive labor.

"Capital, under a system of production, conducted through division of labor without a correlative distribution of employment was a manifestation of anarchy —a power to hold men up and forbid them to go to work (synonymous with permitting them to live) unless they submitted to the tributes levied.

"It had never been and was not now denied that PROPERTY *is an aid to production,* but *along with the accumulation of capital it had been observed insecurity of employment likewise began and human efforts became more and more restricted.* Looking backward it was noticed that public prosperity had been greater and *property* had increased at a more rapid rate as long as wealth had been more evenly distributed and consisted more of property and less of capital, as may be observed in new settlements in contrast with older communities.

"The mainspring of civilization is property and

capital is an abuse of property; it antagonizes the social order and restricts progress, being an element of anarchy in the system.

"We have advanced so far now," continued His Excellency, "that every school boy, every school girl, every mother who has the care of home and the home education of children in charge receives an income — an independent income."

"Are you not going too far?" I exclaimed, utterly amazed at the statement.

"Not at all," he argued; "you admit that you always pay the architect and the engineer although they only plan, but do not erect structures; then you must also admit that the first study of the school boy is a portion of the work executed in later life. The fireman at the engine is not paid for all the work turned out by the machine, but he is paid for the work he does as fireman. The inventor must be regarded as well as he who turns the crank of the machine. Study is work to children as well as to men and it is a necessary work for the good of the future State; it is a part of the co-operative process of production; and children working should be recognized by the State that they may be better regarded at home where too often their position subjects them to abuse and disrespect as non-producers.

"Every child has special protection here in the guardianship of its school teacher, who investigates and reports home abuse. The parents are a check on school abuses while the school teacher is a check on home abuses.

"You will also admit," His Excellency continued, "that mothers serve humanity, and their welfare cannot be guaged entirely by the peculiar skill or ability of the husband. *Men are rewarded here according to ability and skill, industry or merit,* BUT NOT UNTIL THE OTHER MEMBERS OF THE HOUSEHOLD HAVE BEEN REWARDED ON AN EQUITABLE BASIS. This is by no means communistic, but rather individualistic, protecting the property of children and mothers against being falsely and inequitably absorbed into wages. *It sends into the household a surer and more continuous stream of income* and gives greater impetus to development by giving each member of the family a distinct individuality and standing in the household and in the community.

"Aside from this," suggested the Doctor, "the State would command more respect by the early object lesson involved in this fulfillment of its responsibilities, making it loved like a father rather than merely feared for its power. In our country the older one gets and the more and more one sees of the agents of State—the politicians, the less respect and the more fear one acquires for the State, which becomes a vague and unreliable element in calculating our movements."

Beyond Utopia's boundaries home in Lukka is a barbarous institution; it is a mere thing of chance and man is more helpless than the savage. Today all is bright; tomorrow all is dark. A man rises worth millions, but ere sunset he may be penniless.

If chance be against him, he cannot as a human being, of his own right, claim the shelter of a roof, nor the privilege of working to create wealth in answer to his needs.

Lacking the cloak of hardihood—man's first roof, he is more homeless than the savage. Nature's open hand that in the wilderness feeds the wild wanderer, is to him forever closed. Of his own right the higher man has naught but chance to shield him from the quick hunger that gnaws its way to death.

Outside of Utopia, I repeat, home is a barbar-

ous institution. It is not so within this glorious
realm; here home is sacred—here home *is guarded as
part of the living man.* Here man is regarded as something more than a moving bundle of flesh and bones.
Like the fish without its fins, like the bird without its
wings, like the turtle without its shell, so is man
divorced from the true home—an absolute and essential part of his very being.

Outside of Utopia the home is like a pool waiting
for fortune's rain; the hands that bring it bread waiting on chance for privilege to work. It is not so in
Utopia, for here the workshop is regarded as part of the
home—its second roof to resist the pouring rain of
want. *The factory with its implements is here an extension of the human hand, as much a part of the true
workingman as the hand itself.* THE FACTORY IS A SUP-
PLEMENT TO THE HOME—AN INSEPARABLE PART OF IT, AND
THE HOME IS AN INSEPARABLE PART OF THE MAN.

Home is here in its broadest sense. It is something
more than four walls covered with a roof. It is an
institution sacred to the family and its needs. It is
provided with doors of opportunity and is ventilated
with the air of individual independence. Upon its
hearth the warmth of an infallible income glows, and
the shadow of want is a dim memory of the past.

Sacred to man and of his very being, home is not a
thing to buy and sell and loan. Home is the property
of the entire family—old and young. It belongs not
to one member ; it belongs not to one hour — to be converted in a moment to transient stuff and frittered into
nothing. The family is a continuous stream, and
home must be as permanent in its shelter, as fixed and
immovable, as is its crying need — its title inalienable
and unassailable.

The family is not one person nor the plaything of a

day; it is a continuous institution, and the home, inseparable from it, is perpetuated here and guarded against the chance of bargain, sale or loan. No member of a family can at one time represent the present and the future nor arrogate to himself the disposition of this sacred property. No man is permitted here to discount his own future nor to hazard leaving a homeless posterity. The property of the helpless, of minors, of infants, of the unborn, yea of the man himself, are all guarded against the despotism or the folly of any one person.

All property is therefore rendered self-renewing— the home, the workshop and all public institutions, highways and domain.

Production being a co-operative process, the co-operative gain of the worker is not at once placed in his hand. Only his own strictly private and personal gain goes directly to him. He is not made a custodian of the future, inasmuch as experience has demonstrated that conducted singly this trusteeship is liable to gross abuse and on the whole is utterly impossible to properly conduct.

Thus a special portion of the product of his labor is directly applied to the perpetuation of houses, factories and publicly-held private properties whereby these reappear as fast as needed, and any failure to be ready when the wear of the old structures demands new ones in their place becomes a public warning of misappropriation. Such a failure, however, is almost impossible to occur as the opportunity for misapplying or concealing wealth in any large sums does not exist, nor is the temptation present as in Tsor.

The weekly accumulations are at once applied, as in a building association, the rising new structures becoming a tangible evidence of the proper appropriation of funds and are a constant check, aside from many others, against abuse.

Only personal wealth can be owned and bought and sold, but family wealth and factory wealth are held under special titles befitting their functions and their greatest use, consistent with security.

It is now estimated that the savings by the substitution of emulation in place of competition ; the elimination of a large force of practically non-productive workers ; the determining of methods and systems by absolute and unvitiated calculations; the larger concentration of trade, beside the increased production resulting from greater confidence on the part of consumers, have brought the net product of labor to more than double its previous measurement, while the savings in interest and wear and tear have done as much again.

True, the Utopians must now also pay for wear and tear, but now it gives them ownership whereas before they lacked this right and they were subject to frequent annoying and expensive removals.

All in all this change has converted Utopia into an El Dorado which is manifesting a wonderful growth in material wealth in spite of its paying the enormous debt to Tsoran capitalists and the much larger one to the ex-capitalists at home.

CHAPTER XVII.

IN THE KAR TUKI.

The Kar Tuki at Tsor was not a resort for pleasure. Its dismal avenues; its death-dealing dampness; its foul and stifling air; its gloomy silence; its iron-clad rigor; its brutal discipline ; its meagre and unwholesome diet; its niggardliness, and its inhuman recklessness made it an abode of horrors. Prison and poorhouse at once, it mingled the unfortunate with the most hardened wretches. Saints and demons were chained side by side and the same forms of cruelty meted out to both.

Poverty was a crime. That which made men poor was an emblem of sanctity in Tsor. The wealthy were idolized for their past "abstinence;" the poor were trampled under the heels of State. If poverty is a crime, what name in all the languages of speech harbors enough venom to be applied to excessive wealth, that crime of all crimes—the crime creating crimes?

Poverty was a crime; inability to pay debts was a crime; but men were denied opportunity and with it were denied the ability to pay debts, being thus literally driven into borrowing and into poverty. The Kar Tuki could not arrest the tide pouring into its black depths. It could not stop what the whole engine of State was driving into its doors. The State was greater than the Kar Tuki. This great gallery of gloom; this colossal theatre of misery, was each day attracting new inmates by the score. However full were its dark cells there was always room for more.

The burden of Tsor's idleness was, however, borne outside of the Kar Tuki. Within its walls the worry was not how to secure work but how to endure it with its endless hours and its hard driving.

Never in the history of Tsor had this prison held so many inmates. It now contained a whole city within itself. The four lower sub-cellars, two of which hitherto had been occupied for storage were now entirely taken up with prisoners, and materials were delivered and again withdrawn daily as fast as the work was completed. Cells that had previously been occupied as sleeping apartments were used as workrooms and its victims ate on their benches and slept on the hard floor.

The sick—there were no sick. No one was permitted to be sick. The prisoners were kept in harness and must either remain in rank or be flogged into rank, between the two alternatives of work or death. The same mistrust of feigned poverty that crystalized in the shape of the Kar Tuki reappeared within its walls in the shape of this discipline against sickness.

The prisoners were fettered in pairs with strong, steel-glass chains attached to their ankles. The partitions between the cells were of heavy, glass-brick masonry, each floor being divided into six large compartments, within each of which were confined several hundred prisoners, and these divisions were separated from a circular outer hallway by a solid wall of heavy steel-glass. This hallway was guarded by a score of armed sentinels on each floor who alternated in marching through the hallway in full view of the prisoners and were relieved by a fresh squad every eight hours.

The cell in which Zuzo was confined covered probably an acre, though in the dark, under its low roof, it looked much larger. In the center of the room was a large furnace surrounded by hundreds of small, glass ovens in tiers one above the other. In these ovens a mixture of fine sands in combination with a species of purple pitch were burned over and over until the requisite clearness was reached, coming out in lumps of pliant, putty-like glass, ready to be trans-ferred to the moulders by whom it was further treated until it finally emerged in a thousand and one shapes as household utensils, working implements, orna-mental articles, in short an innumerable variety of desirable appliances.

One peculiarity of all the Lukkan glass is the fact that heat alone will not melt or cause it to dissolve. Only through a chemical process, when heated and combined with this peculiar purple pitch will it resolve to liquid form, one of its constituents being withdrawn by its strong affinity with the pitch.

The entire furnace with all its ovens were of the clearest and most refined steel-glass and as long as the pitchy liquid was carefully kept from direct con-tact with any portion of these ovens they were per-fectly safe against the effects of heat.

Even cooking and baking in Lukka is done from steel-glass ranges which afford great advantages to the operator, who has full view of the material in prepara-tion, and thus controls it with perfect security.

The prisoners were ranged in this cell by the side of long tables, each of which was supplied with a stock of raw material, and each pair of workers had a set of trays, measures and such vessels as were needed in the work.

Owing to the heat of this room all the men were stripped above the waist, their limbs bare below the knees, giving them a picturesque appearance as they moved in the glare of the furnace light with their long, unkempt hair, their rough beards and their haggard, careworn faces, expressing oft a defiance as if daring the fates to their worst.

Early every morning the work of the day was assigned to each group of twenty, and late in the night it was taken away; and woe to the group that failéd to perform its allotted work. Each member would be led separately into the hallway in full view of all the prisoners and there flogged, going around the entire floor so as to be an example to all. This daily transfer of the material for the day's work constituted the only method by which prisoners distinguished night and day.

Neither Velva nor Meta had appeared at Zuzo's hearing before the court. Did they know where he was? This question was uppermost in Zuzo's mind. What would be their thoughts? As he reflected upon their situation, even though they knew where he was, he realized the terrible anxiety in which they must suffer, and in the contemplation of their agony the whole current of his feeling was absorbed. The fetid stench, the gloomy darkness, the burden of oppression that frowned in everything around him — the outward doom to which he had been sentenced, were felt not even as much as a feather's weight upon his shoulder. His only thought was for the anxious, beating hearts in that ruptured home from which he now was banished.

His own exile was not regarded, but the ravished home roamed in his mind like a destroying spark inflaming all it touched.

As was to have been expected Prince Urg's charge had precedence in court, though the august judge had it in his power to disregard priority of occurrence which would have placed both parties on an equal footing. Zuzo, however, now resting under a charge, the court had the option of refusing to recognize the charge against Urg, and so decided, declaring it detrimental to public interest that a person rest-ing under a charge should be clothed with full civil rights. The court had not been directly bribed or even approached for this opinion but the shadow of the Koofim behind the Prince determined its decision, and while Urg went scott free, Zuzo was sentenced to a fine equivalent to about five years imprisonment, reduced to two after his properties had been seized by the State and half-confiscated by its auctioneer.

When he was at length aroused one morning after the trial and was almost kicked to his feet, he rose, feeling great relief in the prospect of being set to work. The supervisor called aloud asking "H 9" to come forward; "H 9," whose partner in captivity had worked out his own release, was seen advancing from the further end of the room. As this person neared Zuzo their eyes suddenly met. A cold, stolid, indiffer-ent look checked Zuzo, who would have uttered a cry of surprise, but managed to suppress it without being observed by the supervisors.

"H 9" was made to stand close to the side of Zuzo while their ankles were being manacled, and with the chain clanking at every step they marched off to table H at the further end of the cell.

The prisoners at table H looked with astonishment to see the two men embrace.

Ortro spoke first:

"Zuzo, my brother!" he exclaimed, his eyes flooded and his voice choking with emotion.

"It is very shocking, I know," responded the elder brother, "but dry your tears and let us forget where we are. Tell me, how you have been all this time."

"Until now I have felt light and merry in spite of this dismal world but seeing you here is too much for me! I could easier be merry while the lash was cutting my soles! How come you hither, pray?"

"I will tell you later," Zuzo replied, "but in the meantime if you will instruct me in the work you have in progress, it will enable me to do my portion, for you know there's no escape from the Tuki's harsh discipline."

For a while not a word was spoken save the directions concerning the work in hand and soon after both were busily engaged with the sticky putty and glittering moulds.

"This place has often brought to my mind the philosophy you taught me years ago," Ortro resumed, breaking a long silence, when almost through with the alloted work for the day, "and whenever I have been much discouraged it has come in like a good friend to soothe and quiet me. I have found your philosophy a good coachman to my feelings when I have a hard road to travel. It is a splendid spur and now and then is a check against the rebellion of the moods. Our moods are such untamed steeds and shy so dreadfully at each new turn in fate!"

"Ah," returned Zuzo, "Old Adversity is a splendid teacher, whether we like his school or not. To him we are all runaways and must be taught by force. He brings us face to face with the airy monsters we build up in our fear, and then they melt away. But what a bluff fate is! Fill our cup of suffering once and as you know all the rest is overflow, causing no change in feeling. The pangs of life are strewn along the course from cradle days until the eternal sleep; they are often touching the extremes of our capacity this side of unconsciousness, ever soothing the own sting with callous covering or smothered life, retrenching as it were, even to the last relief in death."

"Why, as I perceive, our fears and pangs are but forms of resistance," added Ortro; "they seem like a force impelling us on—they are life resisting death—in fact resisting all depressing agencies."

"I am now more than ever convinced my philosophy is correct, and that in feeling measured there is a strange adjustment that evens up our lives, look on them as we will!" Zuzo half soliloquized. "The outward experience and the inward moods constantly modify each other's tendencies forming impressions in feeling differing from what would be expected from either source alone. Prolonged depression becomes a normal plane at length from which feeling begins anew to take her measure and this is true likewise of exaltation. I believe that purely in feeling measured we are all swayed alike between the extremes in every phase, and by this measure fates all read alike."

"I do think that our fears more often than our afflictions strike us down," responded the younger brother, "and now, our day's work finished, we may before retiring thank Zmun we have passed a day unwhipped!"

Before preparing to retire Zuzo handed over to his brother the forged order still in his possession, fearing it would sooner or later be stolen from him at the instigation of Urg. Ortro was soon after asleep and as Zuzo stretched his body upon the hard floor the picture of his home came before him and the terrible realization of his plight caused him to heave a deep sigh.

CHAPTER XVIII.

At the time the Tismoulan states withdrew Zuzo had taken a deep interest in the affair, and their protest against a settlement in anything but labor impressed him very strongly as embodying an important truth, and the germ now in Zuzo's mind began to develop. Zuzo was a deep thinker and once on the trail would pursue an idea until he brought it into harmonious relation with experience.

His early imprisonment had been in his favor, for there he was able to contemplate the world and reflect over its phenomena unbiased by the preconceived notions of instructors; and if he came out with less knowledge he was more self-reliant in thought and more capable of original study, and in beginning anew to extend his judgments of the world he was not warped by superstitions and prejudices, the assumptions posing as facts in the science and theology of the times.

The development of ideas is a slow process, but as the tree rises from a seed so ideas slowly develop from a germ and gradually, branch after branch and leaf after leaf, sprout forth until the whole truth stands up as evidence of progress.

By the same process Zuzo was gradually gaining a clearer insight into the problem of the poor. During this time he had not the faintest conception of what the Utopians had been doing, but he was at first inclined to think that a sort of free banking would enable more freedom in the exchange of services and products, but the idea was not altogether satisfactory and his studies were brought to a temporary arrest by the suddenly developed plan to recover his lost fortune which terminated unfortunately in his incarceration.

Conversing with Ortro one day a new idea flashed in his mind. It was the missing link and now everything became clearer, and within two days there was not a doubtful point left in the whole range of the problem. Both brothers became highly elated over the ideas and one morning a few days after, when Ortro arose he was surprised to find his brother stretched upon the floor scribbling away upon a long scroll, a task he had begun just before Ortro's retiring. He had been up all night and, as he said, he had fastened his thoughts to the scroll whence they should never escape, whatever happened to himself.

Then he began to read — at first very slow, but as many of the prisoners, pair after pair, stopped to listen he seemed to gather inspiration from his auditors and became more and more spirited in his delivery. By the time he had finished quite a crowd had assembled and he was obliged to commence over from the beginning. It was a strange appeal and is given below in the exact form in which it had been indited upon the scroll:

Men of Tsor,
What right have the rich
To preserve their idol of wealth,
The cold, inanimate stuff,
While the living—
The God that flows in your veins—
That energy, labor,
The skill of hand
And cunning of brain,
Must perish unused,
Plunging you
Into debt and despair,

Into this dark Kar Tuk!
Or into the suicide's grave!

Is not your labor wealth?
Why should it be denied
The right to survive,
Being your life
And the life
Of your dear ones all?

Was it meant
That the peace of the State
Is for the rich man alone—
That he should undisturbed
Rattle his hoard,
While you
In placid silence
Behold the daily murder
Of body and soul
Of those nearest your heart?
Is it peace
When men are driven
To shame and to crime
And down the pathway of sin,
E'en to the doorway of death?

Lo, the power of State
In neglect
Her palsy proclaims
And her trust
Like a glass is shattered
And her great bond burst
When the first corpse
Lies cold on the floor,
From God's household driven
In being banished from work.

Not one of the rich
Alone can shoulder the debt
That together they owe the poor.
They are blind to the debt,
In the craze of their cursed greed!
Oh, shame on the State
That worships the idol of pelf
Before the true god, life!

Oh, shame on the greed
That clutches its wealth
To traffic on need!

Are you aware, men of Tsor,
Employment due and denied
Is labor destroyed?
Are you aware
That the legalized power to destroy
The wealth that is bread and life
Is a power to starve and kill—
And waiving the power to kill,
Is a right to rob
In the name of the law?
Employment is loan disguised
In which the worker
Borrows shop and tools from the rich
And as price of the loan
Surrenders all he earns
Above the wages agreed?
The price of that loan is theft—
For employment is due
And should neither be sold
Nor denied.

Your wealth—your labor,
Is mortal as breath;
Unless applied on the instant,
Converted at once into product,
It dies in its birth—
It is burned as in flames.
But capital,
Your master's wealth,
Returns repaid and enhanced
By interest's tax
Getting eleven for ten
When nature returns but nine—
A fool's trade
In which
A bankrupt forever are you
And your children
Forever are slaves.

From the same cradle
Came his wealth as yours;

But by partial and wicked law
The one is but mortal—
Oft denied and destroyed
At its birth—
And the other
Is clad with a power
To live forever and ever
And to grow—
Its root being planted
Deep in your flesh
And the flesh of your flesh.
Its eternal vigor and life
Is the eternal bondage
Of you and yours.

On the highways of Tsor
The wealth that is—capital
Stands barring your hands
From the toil
That should create
That *surplus wealth*
Wherewith to *return*
To the lender his own—
The capital loaned—
The capital YOU *should have*
To be free
And free to remain.
Yours is the right to return,
To repay the loan of the past;
Yours is the primal right   -
And the right for all time
To hold in possession
The instrument, capital,
The roof o'er the head
And the means
Wherewith the hands
Are free to create
And supply the home
With its needs.

Whence the master's wealth
If not through labor preserved
In excess, till the master could loan
While your labor meanwhile perished

And you were driven to debt?
How can the debt be paid
While the masters' wealth prevails
Being favored under the law
And yours is forever destroyed?
To be free in your homes,
To wield a free arm,
To be free to repay
All borrowed and binding wealth,
Your wealth must prevail
As *first* and *foremost of all*
To be preserved.
You must have work
Though capital all be consumed.
As long as excess exists
Must the lender buy
This wealth of yours—
Preferred for all time
By the right of your needs—
A right transcending excess.

Tsor's capital all is yours
To hold and to use
By the prior title of need;
Its present masters are stewards
Whose rights are to value alone
Delivered in labor
Within one generation,
At prices the market shall tell.

Awake! Men of Tsor!
Rise to your duty!
Stand up in your battle of life!
Assume the heritage
That is yours for all time!
Take possession of Tsor!
Your solemn duty fulfill!
Stop the flame of misgovernment
From devouring in idleness
Your's and your children's
God-given wealth!
Take possession of Tsor,
And let a flood of labor
Drown the wealth of the past

In a whirlwind of shame!
Purchase your freedom
With the wealth—the labor
Now in tribute and idleness burned,
And hold forever
The wealth of the freeman—
The family home
And the highways of work—
The factory, warehouse and store.

From this highway—capital,
Drive the false stewards,
Who, apart as they stand,
Can never fulfill
The mission of stewardship—
To employ as employment is due —
Who will only unite
To plunder the more.
They themselves are at war
And cannot stay
The hand of mistrust and abuse
And the downfall of law,
Since gold is plied
At the font
Where law is born,
At the court
Where law is dealt,
And no place
And no life is sacred;
And the voice
Of a charity sweet
Seeks to drown
The death groans
And the howls
Of those
Dying devoured
In the flames
That snatch
Our bread from the mouth—
In destroying
The wealth in the arms.

Strike, men of Tsor,
If in your breasts

The hearts of freemen dwell!
Duty—God's voice—commands,
Bidding you strike
Against this foul oppression
Of the years.
Let it not live
To cloud in shame
The record of your day!
Let it not live
To spread its infamy!
Let it not live
To plant its galling yoke
Upon your necks
From father unto son!
Let it not live
To read its mandates
Through your courts and laws,
Your State's broad roof
Converting to a prison ;
Changing the arm of law
Into an assassin's knife!
Let not the earth of insecurity
Be quaking 'neath your feet ;
Anarchy's wild torch
Be flaming o'er your heads!
O, break loose
The bonds of this enchantment vile!
Be free!   Be free
As God designed you be!

O, men of Tsor,
If men at all you are,
If human vision
Dwell within your brain,
If human hearts
Within your bosoms beat,
Strike now for liberty—
For eternal liberty!
Strike for yourselves:
For your wives and children strike!
Strike for the unborn world
Whose stewardship is yours,
Whose fate is in your hands!

O, men of Tsor,
Go forth into the marts;
Proclaim the word!
The debt of worth assume
And take your own—
Possession that is yours,
The liberty to work
Repaying what you owe—
The liberty to work
Untaxed by tribute—
The liberty to work
Free, and unfettered
By cords of human bondage !

O, men of Tsor,
It is for you to speak,
It is for you to think,
For you to judge;
It is for you to act!
Upon the threshold
Of a thousand
Generations coming,
You stand now
To judge and act.
I charge you but these words,
Be men!

As the reading progressed a number of prisoners
gathered around Zuzo attracted by the earnestness
and fervor of his eloquence. Their numbers gradually increased and an intense interest was aroused,
the scroll being read and re-read and explained in
detail. Zuzo spoke in a low tone, intensely earnest,
making it very clear to more than a dozen men who in
turn assisted in expounding to others, continuing until the entire division was absorbed in this one theme.

The reading itself did not consume much time, but
for the balance of the day nothing else was thought of,
much to the detriment of the prison work, and ending
in a brutal flogging exhibition that night.

"If we were only free," said Zuzo "we might then

reach the Tsoran workmen along the Tok Yim and persuade them to strike for liberty. But here, what can we do!"

"What if we were all at large? Do you think Tsor ripe for such a change; and how would you proceed?" asked Ortro, anxious as to the practical side of the problem.

"I cannot say exactly," was the reply, "until I have given the subject more thought; but for the present I am satisfied we will be able to accomplish our freedom as commanded."

"Commanded!" exclaimed Ortro.

"Commanded;" repeated the elder brother, "my conscience tells me we have no right to waver or defer this duty. We have no right to shirk this task, leaving it for posterity. We have no right for any present consideration or comfort to barter away the liberties of our children. Whatever the past has done was done unknowingly, but we can make no such plea; we are in duty bound to face this call now and fight its battle to the very end. For my own part I glory in the fact that I live to share the noble work before us. My conscience leads me on, and conscience is God's voice, the true command from heaven."

"God then commands me also," said Ortro, "and all my future days I here dedicate to this cause of liberty."

The two brothers were much moved as they rose to their feet and embraced, while they pledged their future to the great cause of Tsoran liberty.

That night, after the finished work of the day had been withdrawn, the benches were pushed aside and the men, clustered in groups, stretched themselves at full length on the floor. Contrary to the usual custom, they remained awake and in low tones dis·

cussed the strange appeal for liberty. It shed such a
new, striking light into their world as to dazzle the
intellect. It seemed too good to be true—to be even
possible. It seemed like a dream—like a fairy tale.
It puzzled some; others could understand well but
could not bring themselves to realize its possibility—
it appeared so unbelievable.

The two brothers were busy moving from group to
group taking part in discussions to elucidate the doctrine of which Zuzo and Ortro both had a clear, firm
grasp.

Zuzo informed them that primarily in the exchange
of services some had sold their energy or labor in
excess of their needs becoming lenders to those who,
by this very excess, had been unable to sell their own
services, which had been destroyed in involuntary
idleness forcing them of necessity to become borrowers.
The capitalists were today the lenders who in justice
and to make exchange complete and a true process (a
moral necessity as much so as paying other debts)
were bound to purchase the services of the borrowers
until the relation of borrower and lender ceased.

The borrower—owing to the fact that production
is a co-operative process, cannot employ himself as
would a savage, who picked the wild fruit from the
tree; he must wait on the lender for the privilege of
selling his service. The lender, however, only grants
this privilege for a consideration and lives from the
proceeds of this consideration, retaining his excess of
wealth for this very purpose. Meanwhile the total
service the combined capitalists will buy of the working classes is no more than what the workmen require
for their transient needs, plus interest and wear and
tear of capital. Out of the interest capitalists live and
swell their capital, but they buy no more. They con-

trol the machinery or avenues of production and virtually deny the opportunity to more than a limited production.

The borrowers cannot return the borrowed if they wish to — at least as law in Tsor now stands, for the lenders demand, not service, which the capital at best represents, but money. Money the borrowers can never pay, because capitalists limit the amount of labor the borrowers can convert into money, and by virtue of this power hold a perpetual title, the borrowers being perpetual slaves. *No abstinence whatever can save these borrowers, whose saving in the aggregate would at once be met with increased idleness in place of increased wealth.* A few individuals might have work while yet extremely abstinent and thus acquire a small competence, but they would be essentially exceptions to the rule.

Tsoran law cannot afford to protect creditors who refuse to accept payment for loans when offered in the very coin in which the loans were made. Tsoran law cannot permit public functions — the control of the great highways of exchange (capital in other words) by private individuals to the jeopardy of the rights of the many.

Tsoran law must rise to justice or Tsoran life must sink to anarchy.

The issue was so clear that finally not a dissenting voice remained in the entire division, and when they turned over to sleep that night a halo of hope shed its luster upon their dreams.

During the following week all sorts of schemes were concocted, and already a movement was on foot through which to acquaint the prisoners in the other divisions with this new doctrine.

Two sets of the prisoners requested to be removed

to other quarters, complaining of having had a quarrel with some of the prisoners and also between themselves. The request was naturally refused, but on the petitioners offering compensation in the shape of an extra allowance of labor for the privilege they were promptly removed to two other divisions. Soon after further dissensions were reported in the divisions to which these prisoners had been-taken, and fresh removals resulted. Thus by degrees the doctrine was being spread through all the cells in the Kar Tuki.

The spread of this doctrine was followed by a plot to escape in a body and afterwards take possession of Tsor. Ordinarily no plan for escape would have enlisted such unanimity, as the ancient religious doctrines and prejudices and the force of custom would have prevented the majority from giving their assent—the institution of the Kar Tuki having heretofore been regarded as ideally just. Then ordinarily an escape would have led to their inevitable re-capture and return with heavier penalties on their heads. It was only recently that their numbers had been augmented to make them a telling force in Tsor.

While this constant agitation and this plot was in progress many a bench of prisoners were caught short in the allotted work of the day and were marched out in pairs around the circular hallway to be flogged all the way as an example to the rest, but the cruel exhibition only served to nerve these desperate men to their purpose and strengthened the bond that united them.

One evening, after the men had been served with their customary stale bread and tepid water and while they were still engaged in crushing the hard crusts between their molars, the night guards, as usual on relieving the day force, made a circuit of the hallway peering into each cell as they passed.

In the third division in which the two brothers were confined all did not seem quite right, for from the dark at the further end of the room loud words and scuffling could be distinctly heard. There Zuzo and Ortro were engaged in apparent conflict with another shackled couple. The rest of the prisoners were still at their benches grinding away at their solid chunks of bread with apparent indifference to the quarrel.

The guards, observing the commotion, stopped, unlocked the door and half their number entered the cell. At the approach of the guards the combatants separated, taking opposite directions and the guards, following, were broken into two divisions. At this stage the pursuers were suddenly stunned and confused by a volley of sticks and empty vessels. This was followed almost simultaneously by a rush upon their rear and flanks, and before the astonished guards could realize the situation their arms were pinioned and their weapons taken from them. Five spears and five swords were thus secured.

While this had transpired the door had been barricaded by a detachment of prisoners so that the ten armed guards on the outside were unable to effect an entrance.

The prisoners had now a force of ten armed men besides over two hundred supplied with sticks, vessels, chunks of glass-putty, and a few clubs made from table legs.

The outer guard, perceiving the odds now against them started for the upper floor to secure assistance, but were confronted on the way by another armed body of prisoners who were coming down. They turned back, only to be met with a shower of missiles from the now advancing prisoners of the third division. "Down with your arms or die!" was the cry coming from front and rear, and out of their wits with confusion and fright they surrendered at once without any attempt at resistance.

They were immediately disarmed and placed under confinement in the cell of the third division, by that time already vacant.

The attack had been conducted simultaneously on each floor of the prison in order to prevent the guards from reinforcing each other and also to make success more certain should any single move fail. In the struggle but one prisoner was seriously injured, and the Kar Tuki was now in full possession of the prisoners.

CHAPTER XIX.

The wound Meta had inflicted upon herself proved very serious, though not necessarily fatal. She had been removed to a secluded chamber on the upper floor, where her wound was dressed by a surgeon who visited daily and gave orders to the old hag who waited on her. Excessive loss of blood had left her very weak and rendered her chances for recovery slight.

The wound had caused intense physical pain, but the mental anguish she had suffered in a large degree nullified its violent effect, leaving a severe general feeling of dull heavy pain as the sole conscious being. Self-consciousness gradually became more faint and the exhausting pain grew less day by day as it fed upon the system. There would have been good chances of recovery yet but for the gross carelessness and ignorance of the surgeon who one day washed the wound without looking at the water the old hag brought. It had been standing for a whole day and bore within it the seeds of death, infinitesimal blood-poisoning germs.

As a consequence symptoms of fever soon after set in and the patient then began to speak out of her mind. She would imagine herself at home with her parents and would be reviewing her plans for the Election Day celebration. Then again she would discuss the day's programme with her father, saying very odd things. Sometimes she would toss her arms restlessly in the belief that she was struggling with Prince Urg and she would cry "never, never!"

One time she called her father and asked whether they were taking him to the Kar Tuki. Then she said she would hasten to his relief. "We had a hundred thousand milos on election day. I'll gather it from the girls and then I'll vote your release, papa. We'll be wealthy, papa, won't we?"

Thus she spoke capriciously at intervals, seldom in her right mind and whenever she was self-possessed she would enquire for her mother, wondering why Velva did not come—evidently forgetting the actual circumstances leading to her present condition. She would ask what became of her father. Was he free or still in the Kar Tuki? She lingered thus many days growing weaker and weaker, more and more emaciated, as the terrible blood-poisoning spread in her system.

One day the Prince called the surgeon aside and asked what chances she had for recovery.

"None whatever;" replied the surgeon, abruptly, "she may survive a day, two or three days at the utmost. But in all probability she will not survive through the night."

"She made a confession to you?" asked Urg.

"She did."

"She admitted that she inflicted the wound with her own hand?"

"She did, saying it was done in a fit of despair, wandering between the residences of the yim. She talked incoherently and I never ascertained her name."

"And this occurred?"

"Just a week ago, I delayed reporting, expecting from day to day to ascertain her name."

"Good! Be seated now and I will detain you but a few moments."

Urg thereupon left the room.   In a few moments he returned followed by two servants and a number of Koofim.

The surgeon was requested to repeat before the ''servants'' what he had before stated to Urg, after which the ''servants'' were dismissed.

Then Prince Urg most graciously thanked the professional gentleman, placing a number of gold pieces in the latter's hand who then made his departure.

This surgeon had been retained for special reasons, his peculiar merit consisting in a wonderful moral elasticity.   This peculiar merit had been previously tried on numerous occasions and found to be reliable, for the purpose intended.   He was a man not exactly ''true and tried'' but honorably false and tried.

The step Prince Urg had just taken was merely a fortification he had raised for possible danger in case the girl should be ultimately identified and her death in any manner laid at his door.   As King of the Koofim he did not anticipate any real danger, but his shield in the strength of the order was only a shield, *if used*, and this was merely a precautionary form of its use.

One source of possible annoyance however did cause him some uneasiness.   In a small town an unknown corpse would be seen by everyone, but in Tsor it would attract no notice whatever except from families in which some member had been reported missing.   Members of such families would be notified and would be absolutely sure to come to the morgue. Velva, the mother of the girl, had reported Meta as missing and Urg had also learned that the girl had been already traced to the home of the Koofim which went under the name of the Red Villa.   The body of the dead girl might have been hidden in the vaults underneath this den, but Urg expected a search of the building to follow, now that Meta had been traced there, and it would be safer to boldly report the matter, as the surgeon had agreed to corroborate the version of self-inflicted death, and deliver the body to the authorities. If Velva were only quieted it would end all danger of further investigation. He could easily arrange that search for the girl would be abandoned, and long before the father was at liberty the body would be past identification.

Velva must be got out of the way. This seemed the easiest way out of the dilemma. She was the only menace to his security and it was foolish and needless for him to run any risk. It was less risk to remove Velva than Meta. For that was he King of the Koofim.

The shallow-minded force the solution of their difficulties. All outlawry and despotism is of this character—a horrible manifestation of impatience, often in the form of calmness. The King of the Koofim was no exception to this category. He dispatched a messenger after the snake charmer Urkan, who came soon after, and the two were closeted together a long while.

In their counsel they came to an agreement on all but one matter and that was the question of price.

"Three hundred milos," exclaimed Urg, "you are mad! A hundred is enough where there's no booty for the Order."

"Rot the Order," ejaculated the outlaw, "I want booty! I tell you I want cash!"

"You're daft, old man. Do you think my vaults are filled with gold?"

"Gold or no gold, I never kill one of my pets unless there's booty in it, do I, my little darling?" retorted

Urkan, stroking a small viper that had crept out from under his blouse and was crawling over his shoulder.

"If you want sure work, the woman's as good as out of your way already and the whole world knows why and is satisfied. Send for another charmer if you wish; but if you want my work I take not a single petro less than three hundred milos."

"You're a robber—a cursed usurer to take such a price," protested his chief. "Were I to wait a day longer I could get a dozen Koofim who would do it for a hundred. I tell you you'll do this at my price or you'll miss many a thousand in booty before the season's over. Mark what I tell you."

Urkan, reminded by this of his chief's power in keeping him out of important exploits after booty finally came down to two hundred milos, though not till he had hurled a number of imprecations on his chief's head.

Urg yielded at last, though with poor grace; for his face grew black with anger and for a full minute he looked a continuous scowl at Urkan. Taking a number of gold pieces from a drawer in the wall he tossed them contemptuously to his companion in crime. "The balance when all is done; I have never broken my word."

"No, not with me!" retorted the outlaw fiercely, and he looked intently into Urg's eyes, conveying in that look a threat of terrible vengeance should his chief seek to evade full payment.

Such is the honor among thieves.

*   *   *

Toward midnight that evening a man might have been seen entering a chamber in the upper part of the den. It was the chamber of serpents into which Meta had peered. In this chamber were a thousand living venomous serpents, most of them coiled in slumber. Some, startled by the intrusion, now vented their resentment in fierce hisses The man marched boldly through the colony of coiled and tangled serpents lying in his path, in the dim light reflected from the phosphorescent walls of this inner chamber. Before a large dark coil lighted with bright yellow stripings he stopped, and proceeded with weird gesticulating of the hands and a wild song in broken irregular cadence, to bring his snakeship under control. Following the motion of his hands it slowly began to unwind its coils revealing underneath a brood consisting of half a score of little vipers striped like their dam. On went the mother viper following the charmer's hand until she was removed across the room and once more coiled in slumber. The man then returned, quickly stowed the young serpents under his garments and retreated from the room before the mother viper was freed from the spell he had cast upon her.

About this time a dead silence reigned on the Zdar Yim. Cloudy and dark overhead no star looked down into the deep gloom that had settled over Tsor. Not even a footstep disturbed the lonely stillness. The residents of the Zdar Yim were all in the embrace of a fresh slumber. What a contrast a panorama of their present active dream-life would make with the chaos in which the yim lay enveloped at this hour. Every soul on this yim was now resting—enjoying a vacation, traveling in strange lands, wandering far, far away; for this was nature's season devoted to recreation. Not a soul is at home and the yim is completely deserted. In the sunny spring-time of morn the souls will all come back. Did I say all? All but one. One is doomed never to return.

Later on a slight sound begins moving through the

yim.   To the man gliding through the dark each step is dangerously loud.   But there were no ears in this yim and where there are no ears there is no sound.

Close to the Zdar school house is a small hut. Here the man disappeared and his footsteps no longer disturbed night's stillness.   For three full minutes thereafter no sound was audible ; then, through the chambers of this house a man on hands and knees started creeping stealthily from room to room until he came to one from which the noise of breathing was perceptible.   He stopped, pushed aside the intervening drapery and in the dim phosphorescent light advanced to the couch on which the sleeper reclined.

From one of his pockets he drew a small platter and a large vial the liquid contents of which he poured upon the platter, which he then placed on the pillow above the sleeper's head.

This done he drew from his bosom a small bit of a serpent and gently laid it across the body of the unconscious woman.   Stooping on one knee by the side of the couch he watched the movements of the reptile. It had lain there scarcely a moment when it raised its head and with a slow waving to and fro drew itself up advancing in a straight line toward the platter whose liquid it had scented.

The man next drew a long sharp needle from his sleeve.   As the head of the serpent neared the woman's face she moved her arm as if to brush away a fly, when he plunged the needle into the serpent and the latter, angered by the pain, thrust its fangs blindly at the first object in the way, striking them deep into the woman's wrist.

Expecting the woman to wake at once Urkan instantly got down on the floor and rolled under the couch.

The woman did not instantly awake, but lay motion-less for several minutes. Later on a convulsive tremor shook her frame, breaking her slumber. Her body was bathed in cold sweat and she felt deathly sick. Her eyes began to distend; assuming a fixed stare. She tried to cry for help, but her lower jaw seemed as if nailed in place. A terrible agony came over the woman. She had no idea what ailed her. In an in-terval of calm she seemed to suddenly realize her desperate condition, and acting on the impulse of the moment she sprang to her feet reeling toward the door.

In an instant Urkan was up, and before she reached the outer chamber he stood in her path, pushing her from the doorway without as much as uttering a syllable.

The feeble victim fell over scarcely realizing what had occurred. She lay a long time upon the floor while the murderer stood in the doorway still and immovable as a statue. Her face became livid, froth covered her mouth and her limbs grew rigid and icy cold. Her arm had meanwhile swollen to a shapeless mass. Now and then a calm spell would intervene and she would lie motionless on her back staring vacantly at the ceiling. At times convulsions would shake her, or her face would suddenly take a distorted shape through the capricious, ungovernable action of the muscles—no longer under control of the nerves. Then a spasm would contract the spine so that the whole body would bow itself like an arch, the head and heels thrown back. All the active functions of the system were thrown into a vortex of disorder. Within, the muscles, the nerves and the blood were all dis-cordant, issuing wild and inharmonious notes upon that fine instrument, the human body.

Urkan stood at his post determined she should under no circumstances escape to communicate with neighbors. His connection with the deed must die with her closing breath. He stood there watching indifferently the contortions of the writhing body until, at length, the violent changes ceased and only occasional muscular twitchings occurred. The latter he knew would continue long after death; and satisfied that the end had come he stealthily left the house after returning to his pocket the platter and killing the little serpent which was left lying upon the floor near the body of its victim. The dead viper was to corroborate the cause of death and be a final answer to all inquiry.

*   *   *

The same night Prince Ürg was sitting at the bedside of Meta, who had sunk into unconsciousness out of sheer exhaustion. Her pallid face was a mere outline of the bones from which the flesh had all been absorbed. There was something in those sunken eyes, in the expression of that wasted countenance, that had in it an air of triumph—a look that mocked the pallor and the grim, bony outlines of the face—a calm of one who had crossed beyond the narrow life of self while living, of one who had cast herself upon that eternal stream, humanity, through whose pulse the girl had learned to live until her hearing and her seeing, her feeling and her breathing, were all through that one channel whose life is eternal—humanity as one. The self-life, the brutal being, lay there at length, dead and dead forever.

The broader life goes on—that of humanity; and all that makes life dear lives in that stream—in its love and brotherhood, those dear attractions that through all time hold true hearts fondly to each

other; in whose affections mother and child, brother
and sister, friend and friend embrace—not the perishable self, the dress and name—outward identities,
but the higher phase of self, the self-eternal. That
self is boundless; the other is a gross being of a day,
unworthy re-creation.

The Meta of outward identity lay dead. Humanity had not ceased. She had dared the death of clay,
conscious of this. She had refused to pollute that
sacred stream with a life of shame. Living in humanity, she had drawn a higher inspiration from that
stream; drinking of its waters she had grown to loftier
being and she had left that eternal stream the purer
for her living.

The higher self that lives beyond the singleness
of each may well brave the death of clay—living its
after-life today, spanning the ages far beyond today
in its true fatherhood, embracing all mankind in its
true brotherhood. Its life is this life and that next,
the life beyond the narrowness of self, life in humanity—one being and eternal.

Prince Urg sat gazing a long while upon that face
and its calm defiance seemed to work strongly upon
his mind. By degrees it slowly broke through his
icy self-conceit moving him to pity. For a moment he
felt a touch of contempt for himself, something entirely new in his experience. It was the first dawn of
an inward self-consciousness—a precious jewel though
purchased at a price of infinite extravagance.

He himself closed her eyelids, and as he looked
down upon the image of her whom he had wronged
the thought came to him, how strong we are to destroy, how feeble to create. He sat by the side of the
corpse a long while, in dreamy reverie. His entire
past came back to him like a vision. It was a blank

desert without a single good deed stored to feed his memory. He could point to no good he had done at a sacrifice; none but what was incidental to his own self-worship.

A sudden resolution took possession of him and he started away. He called a servant; he enquired for Urkan desiring to see him at once. The servant entered and again left the room; he explored the place high and low in search of Urkan but no such man was to be found. He enquired of all the inmates, but in vain, and at last he reported that Urkan had not been seen for two hours.

The Prince heard the report with a sigh, and his head fell upon his breast. It was too late. The deed had been done and was beyond recall.

CHAPTER XX.

A DREADFUL SUMMONS.

The prisoners in the Kar Tuki were not yet free, although a portion of their number had obtained control over the interior of the prison. Their first move now was to force open the doors of the remaining cells, thereby liberating a body of almost ten thousand strong, and as all these prisoners were still manacled in pairs the next step necessary was to disengage themselves.

In accordance with this need therefore they proceeded to batter in the door of the chief supervisor's room where, after a brief search, they were rewarded with the discovery of a set of keys. These were promptly put to use and rapidly one couple after the next danced with delight at the newly-acquired freedom of limb, overjoyed at this first symbol of the approaching era of liberty.

The liberated prisoners scattered through every portion of the building and ransacked rooms indiscriminately, soon bringing to light a whole library of prison records, including the latest in which their own names and sentences were inscribed. These records were at once brought down to the lowest floor where large bonfires were started and their identity as prisoners was being washed away in flames.

Delighted with their success the prisoners on this floor joined hands in a circle and danced around the flaming piles which shed a wierd light upon their haggard faces They sang and shouted, fairly intoxicated with joy, making the ancient walls ring with repeated echoes. The strange tumultuous scene was in odd contrast with the quiet monotony that had for centuries ruled in this sub-basement.

Above, in the Kar Yim upon which the Kar Tuki fronted, all was quiet. A dozen sentinels were stationed on the yim to give warning of any approaching danger, and all persons who passed to enter the precincts of the prison were made captives and placed with the imprisoned guardsmen.

Each of the thirty-six divisions had its own leader and these now joined in council to select a commander-in-chief. As the most ardent advocate of the movement and one who displayed a capacity worthy the trust, Zuzo was chosen to act in their behalf, and with very little ceremony or talk he accepted the charge and at once began the work of selecting a body of men to act with him in private council and to formulate a general plan of action.

As a result each leader was assigned the responsibility for several adjoining wards in the city, in which they were to apprehend the heads of the civil, police and military authority. These leaders, in turn, each selected a number of men who were to move in squads under the guidance of special deputies, each of whom was assigned the particular officials he was to apprehend. Even the heads of the general government were proscribed and a large special squad was delegated to make the seizure.

The entire work was to be done under cover of darkness, and the aim was to have all the heads of despotic Tsor safe within the walls of the Kar Tuki ere sunrise. Then they were to announce the industrial liberty of a true self-government and proceed with the work of giving it a more permanent and lasting form.

As a prelude to this move a body of men left the prison shortly before midnight and succeeded in capturing a large store of supplies, including weapons of warfare such as swords, spears, maces and shields.

Over eight hundred persons were on the list of the proscribed, and inasmuch as officials in Tsor were provided by the city with free headquarters, each deputy knew exactly the destination to be reached.

A half hour had scarcely elapsed before a little army of Tsoran ex-prisoners, broken into petty squads led by deputies, were wending their way through the yims of Tsor. The solitary guardians of the peace whom they met on their march were seized and gagged to their utter amazement, for such a thing was hitherto an unheard of event in this most ancient democracy. Thus a great revolution was on the way while Tsor was peacefully sleeping.

The last squad had already departed from the Kar Tuki and the remaining prisoners were divided into uniform sections and allowed to sleep during the balance of the night, while a sufficient number remained on guard.

Once more all was quiet at the Kar Tuki, and Zuzo had only to wait for morn in order to follow up the developments of this momentous day. His aim was to march on the Tok Yim and address the working people whom he would find there in large numbers and obtaining their sanction he would assume the reins of government for Tsor for the time being. The State was to assume authority over all property and take the responsibility for it, including particularly that form of property, the cradle of all wealth — labor. There was to be no impediment to exchange of this wealth. *Compulsory exchange was to supplant* THE FREEDOM NOT TO EXCHANGE *hitherto posing under the name of free ex-*

change. To do this the highways were to be controlled absolutely by the State and conserved forever subordinate to one purpose, namely production, involving exchange as a part of the process. These functions must be more fully performed and must be performed honestly.

That which is in its nature co-operative was to be controlled co-operatively—never more to be trusted in private hands where it had hitherto been subject to infinite abuse. The home that was in its nature private was to be conserved for privacy and was to be maintained sacred to privacy. No lender's title would hereafter be sheltered by the law.

An age of unbounded wealth and unexampled security was about to dawn. No rich man was to enter this little "kingdom of heaven;" no poor man would be found there; and merit and demerit alone would mark distinctions. A sickly patchwork of socialism, communism, individualism, democracy and despotism was to be replaced by a human government.

There were many hours yet intervening before dawn and Zuzo could not restrain his anxiety and impatience to communicate with Velva and Meta. He therefore commissioned Ortro to take charge of the prison in his absence, while he hastened away in the dark.

What a surprise it would be for Velva! How glad would his sweet little Meta be to embrace him! In his mind he pictured to himself the joy and happiness that were soon to be realized at the family reunion. He feasted in imaginary scenes of delight; in ideal words of welcome and surprise. Faster and faster he moved along the circling yim.

Nearer and nearer he came to the little home. As he approached close to it a strange anxiety came upon him. He now recalled the last vision of Meta as she fell in a swoon while at the head of the company of girls and a vague dread, an oppressive uncertainty filled his mind. The very gloom of the darkness seemed to have joined forces with the preying mood that was rising within. A peculiar tremor tingled in every nerve as he hurried on. Now he passed the school house ; the next house was his own. All within was still.

He shook one of the doors. No response came. He rapped loud ; he waited, but again no response. He rapped still louder, in fact he fairly thundered at the door. Still there was no response. He tried another entrance, but with only a like result. Strange thoughts passed in his mind. Could they have abandoned the home? Impossible! He was much perplexed ; sorely perplexed. His anxiety was greatly intensified.

Presently he heard heavy footsteps and saw a dark object approach. It came nearer. Then he recognized Gogo, the family elphy. Gogo knew his master and coming to his side began to grunt and press his head against his master's limbs. Zuzo patted him with his hands and then a thought came to him of utilizing the brute. He induced the animal to advance a few steps and remain standing close to the house, where, climbing on his back, he was able to reach an opening used for ventilation and from his elevated perch he climbed through this aperture into the house.

· Passing through the first chamber to reach the central ante-room he saw his own figure through a large mirror and he started back with fright at his image, which he had never seen look so wild and emaciated. His own state of mind no doubt contributed much to the wierdness of the apparition that rose thus suddenly before him.

Stepping into the ante-chamber, however, a more

terrible vision greeted his eyes. Stretched on the floor lay his wife Velva — a fearful spectacle.

He stooped over the body on the floor, perusing it with a half-doubting look as if to question whether the distorted form could be the identical Velva he had left. He felt of her body which was rigid and cold as ice. A twitching of the muscles of the face gave him sudden hope.

"She lives! Velva, my own Velva! Speak!" he cried, seeking to arouse her—but all in vain. Tears welled from his eyes and the agony in his heart began to grow, but it seemed as if it could find no vent and would choke him. He stood transfixed with terror. He could not realize the awfulness of the calamity that had befallen him. His wife, his Velva, she whom he loved dearer than his life, was no more.

In the midst of his grief he was startled with a groan from the further end of the room. He looked in the direction whence it came, and sure enough, there lay a large man stretched out as if dead. It was Urkan, the assassin.

The reader will be surprised to see Urkan here once more after having witnessed his withdrawal, and it will therefore be necessary before proceeding further to explain his re-appearance.

Five minutes had not yet elapsed after Urkan had left the serpent chamber when the form of Kislig, the conjurer, whose face still bore a scar from the recent set-to, might have been seen climbing the stairway leading to the chamber of serpents. By this time the mother viper was already emancipated from the influence of the charm and was rushing to and fro in search of the missing brood. Kislig went directly to the door of the chamber, opened it wide and peered in, but hearing the hisses of the furious parent who was already on its way toward the door, he took to his heels and was soon safely barred within an adjoining chamber.

The young vipers Urkan carried about his person emitted a slight odor, perhaps imperceptible to human nostrils, but to the mother viper it formed a trail of odor marking the track of Urkan as distinctly as if a line had been drawn in the path of his footsteps. Kislig was aware of this peculiar faculty of these vipers and had relied upon this to put his threat into execution.

The old viper moved with unerring precision along the path taken by Urkan, the outlaw. She was a monster serpent, and when she at length arrived before the door through which Urkan had entered the building in the Zdar Yim she drew herself into a coil and waited, not guided by reason but by the animus of her fury.

Urkan on leaving had no sooner stepped over the threshold than he stumbled over the coiled serpent which had already raised its head to strike. As he sprawled upon the ground the viper twined round his body so that by the time he had regained his feet it had one coil already fastened around his neck and was choking him to death. His eyes bulged out, his face grew black and in another instant it seemed as if all would be over with him.

With rare presence of mind he at once threw his body against the wall of the building rubbing the serpent against the hard and sharp edges of the glass bricks. The effect was instantaneous, the muscular coils relaxing at once, and taking advantage of the moment, he seized the snake with both hands and with a quick and herculean effort pulled her off, dexterously hurling her to the ground and an instant later he was again inside of the building with the door safely fastened.

In the excitement Urkan did not realize that he had been bitten twice during the scuffle, once in the left arm near the elbow and once under the chin close to the neck. Realizing the likelihood of such a possibility he immediately proceeded to divest himself of all garments above the waist; and by this time, his excitement lessened and the circulation of blood once more restored into the usual channels, he began to feel sharp local pain, indicating the spots attacked.

His usually dark face turned pale as a sheet on realizing the truth. Undaunted, however, he quickly produced a vial which he had used effectually on former occasions, whenever promptly applied. Considerable time had, unfortunately, elapsed in this instance, and it was doubtful whether the remedy would now more than slightly alleviate the pain. He unscrewed the cover and was in the act of applying it to the wound on his neck when a sudden convulsion dashed it from his hand scattering the contents upon the floor. A dizziness came over him and soon left him stretched upon the floor, a prey to successive convulsions and spasms.

His eye catching the form of Velva during one of the quiet intervals, he was so horrified that he dragged himself as far away from it as possible. He could not bear that apparition whose distortion seemed now to mock him.

Lying there he recalled the events of the day and his mind reverted to Urg's scowling look at the time he finally agreed to pay him the compromise price for the hazardous work. Then another thought flashed on his mind.

"He has done it! He! 'Twas he loosed the she devil on me! A thousand fiends roast him!"

Dying, the wretch had only curses on his lips. No remorse; no thought of repentance shed a ray in this dark closing hour.

As if in a dream Urkan happened to observe the figure of a man bending over the corpse across the room. He surmised at once who the man was. He was still filled with bitter animosity to his chief and now a pathway to revenge was opened to him. He uttered a groan to attract the man's attention.

"Who are you?" asked Zuzo in the instant.

"I'm a dead man," feebly came the response.

"Can I assist you in any way?" Zuzo anxiously inquired.

Urkan lay there a horrible sight. His neck was swollen so that the skin over his face was stretched almost out of semblance to human form and his left arm hung distorted like a huge bag of flesh.

"You can ease my soul; I wish to make a confession. I killed this woman."

"You!"

Zuzo was too much agitated to say more. He had all he could do to restrain himself from laying hands on the miscreant.

The dying man continued:

"I was hired to do it."

"Hired, by whom; speak, man!" Zuzo exclaimed, growing more excited as the fellow showed signs of sinking.

"By Prince Urg — as you knew him."

"Prince Urg!" Zuzo exclaimed, his whole frame quivering. "What made him do this? You powers above, can men have hearts so black!"

"Her daughter lies at his mansion, the Red Villa, the Den we call it; and ——"

Here the speaker was seized with another spell of convulsions. His eyes almost rose out of their sockets above the bloat of that disorted face. His exposed body glistened with great beads of sweat and streaks of froth ran down from his mouth.

Urkan had spoken his last.

A brief course of symptoms like those in which his victim had been borne away now made themselves manifest, and soon after he lay rigid in death's embrace.

Zuzo remained a long time by the side of the dead Velva, venting his grief in bitter recollections. The name of the instigator of her death brought thoughts of his father's sufferings, his own early imprisonment and his last incarceration. Omrez, the man who had ruined Zuzo's father, had been the parent of Urg. Through the whole history of Zuzo's life the name of Urg was interwoven — a thread of continuous crime — of wrongs unpardonable. And now Meta was in his mansion! What could this mean? Could the dastard not even spare her innocence?

The thought of Meta at once aroused him. His resolution was instantaneous. Not another word passed from his lips, but leaving the dead bodies where they lay he went forth and with great strides hastened toward the Red Villa, in the suburbs.

Urg could demand no mercy at his hands. From this moment his mind had become inflamed and only thoughts of vengeance inspired his heart. Urg was to him a venomous spider that must be crushed at sight — a wild beast at large that defied the power of law and should not be suffered to live. He must be struck down on the spot once and forever.

A tremendous passion had been kindled in his

bosom. Under its powerful influence all his philosophy was swept away. It came like a roaring torrent of flame sweeping through his mind thrusting aside all recollections of the great responsibility he had just assumed to lead in the impending revolution.

The absolute self-world in its most terrible form had closed its walls around him and impressed its chaos upon his purposes, drowning all relation to the world of all. In the darkness of his present mind the world had narrowed itself to but two persons, and those were one too many.

His eyes were lit with a fierce flame and his upturned face bore an expression of defiance, conveying such an intensity of passion as exists only when a single object holds sway in the mind to the utter exclusion of all else.

* * *

One hour after the departure of the servant who reported on Urkan Prince Urg was still seated beside the dead girl. Disappointed in his vague intention to turn a new leaf, he sat there overcome with drowsiness, nodding in a semi-wakeful state. In this dreamy condition he was startled by a terrific knocking at the door.

A tremor went through him from head to foot. He would gladly have doubted his senses, but the sound was still in his ear and he felt in his soul as if a dreadful judgment were upon him. He attempted to call a servant, but was unable to utter a syllable.

A second knocking louder than before shook the great front doors as if they were being pummeled with a battering ram. He sat motionless for a moment and then, summoning resolution, rose to his feet and started for the door below when he heard a loud crash followed immediately by heavy footsteps on the stairway. In another instant Zuzo came striding in, his eyes flaming, like a demon of wrath.

Prince Urg sank back paralyzed with fear. He had not the strength in the instant to move from the spot.

"Where is your master, Prince Urg?" he demanded, looking the fear-stricken noble straight in the face.

The latter was dumb with fright and his silence betrayed him at once.

Zuzo recognized the man and with a demoniac look of exultation he advanced toward Urg as a cat would approach a mouse that had been cornered. Deliberately he planted his iron fingers upon Urg's throat and proceeded to choke him. The sputtering and struggling of Urg was totally unheeded by his frenzied assailant in whose hands the Prince was like a mere infant. The parent demon was being throttled by the demon of his own creation.

While clutching the victim's throat he repeated through his clenched teeth the single word "vengeance!"

That one word spoke a whole volume. It told the intense exultant passion in which the man was lost in the demon.

He gazed a long time upon the livid face of Urg, never relaxing his grip. He thus retained his grasp long after resistance had ceased and life had departed; in the violence of his passion he did not even realize the weight he was supporting, and when at length he loosened his grasp and the limp body fell in a heap at his feet, he exclaimed in his madness: "Fool that I am! Why did I speed him so and not torture him! Live, live again! Live, reptile! Do not serpents come back to life? Come back, I say, come back! You have not paid the debt of vengeance yet! Come back I say, come back!"

A feeling of disappointment came over him as he viewed the limp body at his feet and it seemed to stir within him an insatiable hunger for revenge. From violent exclamations he broke at length into a spell of terrific hysterical laughter alternated with cries for more vengeance.

After a while he became quiet and seemed to have forgotten the last events in which he had acted so unlike himself. Exhausted in mind he began to commune with himself when suddenly his eye caught sight of Meta lying upon a couch like one asleep.

"Meta, my child!" he exclaimed with joy, stooping to kiss the girl.

At the touch of her lips he was shocked by their icy rigidity and he quickly felt her hands and body to test whether he had not possibly been deceived.

"My Meta! He has killed my Meta!" cried the outraged father, "Villain, murderous villain! Fiend! Oh wretch! How could he live and walk in human form!"

Agony, despair, rage, fury, all howled and thundered in the tempest that had risen in the atmosphere of his mind.

It seemed as if sorrow upon sorrow, affliction upon affliction had been poured into his cup. What had he done that heaven should strike him so!

Once more he fell into a series of hysterical outbreaks in which he reasoned wildly and terrifically scored the mockeries of life. Empty indeed was its mission—a vast and wholesale deception. To him its very light was becoming chaos; it was a vast procession of masked spectres whose open arms held daggers in their sleeves, whose holy books were prisons to the mind, whose feasts were orgies over mankind overcome and left to grope through poverty's dismal death ditch; a horrible dream, and yet a real life.

In a spell of violent frenzy he threw himself upon the corpse lying on the floor; once more he grasped it by the throat and lying over the lifeless body he shook its head and dug his fingers deeper into its flesh in a vain effort to exact more vengeance upon the author of all his afflictions.

CHAPTER XXI.

Tsor was still sleeping 'neath the broad mantle of night. The giant city felt secure in her strength. The undisturbed peace of centuries was the pillow upon which she rested her head. Her eyes were closed to danger and her future was unbiased by mistrust. Little did she dream of the metamorphosis she was about to undergo; of the violent convulsions into which she was to be thrown; of the impotent writhing and struggles into which, like a headless body, she was to be plunged.

An inky darkness shrouded the city and its circular yims were alive with moving figures. A hundred squads were pushing on through darkness, bent on a hundred missions. A great movement was on foot. Darkness was being used to conquer darkness. A theft of power was to be met with a counter theft. Abuse was to face its own offspring. The threatening monster rising in the dark was but the image of abuse. Father and child were one being and the clash threatened was to be a self-castigation.

The black walls of the Kar Tuki rose high in the darkness, its massive towers reaching into the sky like so many uplifted arms in protest at the outrage of its present use.

In the foreground, fronting along the yim, a score of pitch barrels blazed up like so many huge bonfires, and farther up above the tall, hissing flames rose dense columns of smoke whose crests mingled with the darkness of the sky.

In the weird light thus shed were gathered throngs of men waiting for the dawn which was expected every moment. A brilliant luster was cast upon their faces, as they looked upward, exhibiting an array of features painful to contemplate. Hunger and care had stamped their seal there in language unmistakable. Every one of these faces had been pressed in the mold of fate's antipathies. The hollow, furrowed cheek; the wrinkled brow; the languid, hopeless eye; the bowed head and the pinched, thin lips were common to them all. These were scars of battle; battle with hunger, care, anxiety—all sharp instruments that inflicted pain and left deadened the sensibilities wherever they touched. The scars were outward marks of a change these men had undergone—of an abnormal condition that had been built up. They were a dead crust upon the outer surface. Deeper down raged the pent fire of a volcanic life—the primal seed of growth, the power creative which, suppressed for good, breaks at last all bounds, turning to destruction.

Squad after squad came trooping through the yim, leading their captives, the officials of the city, into the mouth of the now almost empty prison. Steadily the Kar Tuki was filling with a new class of inmates and steadily the throngs were being augmented with returning squads. Reports to the commanders indicated a complete success and when the mist of night had vanished all was ready for the new course of proceedings to be inaugurated.

In the yim the great throngs were exultant over the success of the night's work. They were now divided into companies after the original prison sub-divisions and after being formed into separate squares, were drawn into line prepared to march at any moment to the order of their leaders. A store of provisions was also secured from the Kar Tuki and rations were distributed.

Ortro, who had full command, was looking for the arrival of his brother whom he expected to appear any instant, and he hoped that by the time the men had dispatched their morning repast his brother would be on hand. Much to his disappointment, however, Zuzo did not make an appearance, and it was not long before the multitude began to betray signs of impatience, made more conspicuously apparent in loud, demurring remarks.

Ortro had never in his life known his brother to fail in any trust imposed in him, and he did not in the least worry over Zuzo's non-appearance until after the sun had risen far above the hill-tops and its rays had begun to grow quite intense in their warmth, when a feeling of uneasiness began to grow steadily upon him.

In this frame of mind he called the leaders into a council during which it was decided that, in order to quiet the restless multitude in the yim, a number of stands would be improvised from which the vast body could be addressed. Five men volunteered to speak, among them Ortro, all agreeing to carefully avoid urging violence in any form, and to do their utmost toward holding the attention of their auditors until the arrival of Zuzo, when a new conference would very likely be held and the real work of the day begun.

Ortro opened up with a review of the progress already made congratulating his hearers on their good work. He then continued:

"We've no roof certain
But the sky overhead;
And helpless, through tribute,
At each step we are bled.

"There's no hoard for tomorrow.
Let work be denied
And we've only twixt begging
And death to decide.

"Well, indeed, may our children repeat the words,

While our fathers are helpless
To earn daily bread
We are nobody's children;
We're worse than the dead !

"Until we are no longer borrowers of home and shop and warehouse and store—of all the implements needed in order to make and distribute what we require—we will forever be slaves; for we will only be able to enjoy shelter or work by the grace and good will of the lender, and can be denied the right to live if we do not make such terms as permit the lender to net the tribute he expects.

"If it be asked why we do not acquire these borrowed necessaries (called under one name capital) the answer is that the lenders evade permitting us to pay back the loans. They refuse to part with capital. They sell, it is true, by transferring from one form of capital to another, as from houses to money and from money to lands, but they in the aggregate seek to retain and enlarge capital. We perpetuate the capital for them in the terms of borrowing, paying for wear and tear and in addition interest or a form of tribute, so that the owner can live out of a part of the tributes or profits without relinquishing his ownership of capital itself.

"We can only purchase this capital through SURPLUS MEANS, but in order to obtain SURPLUS MEANS we must first be able to sell our SURPLUS SERVICE, which now is taken from us as the price of the privilege to work.

"Men of Tsor! The issue is plain. Whose wealth is entitled to the protecting arm of the law—the capital that is loaned and held perpetual to enslave for tribute, or the wealth in your arms as it comes fresh from your maker?

"Shall the excess of the master or the deficiency of the slave be first served? Shall need or surplus get the ear of state?

"O comrades, as men, as fathers, as patriots, there is but one answer and but one choice.

"You MUST have your own property or you shall remain slaves today, tomorrow and through all eternity.

"If you wish to end the kneeling farce, the cruel lash, the dark Kar Tuki, if you wish to march to the polls like freemen who dare to show their faces, if you wish to save your minds from gnawing anxiety, if you wish to save your sons from dissolute idleness, if you wish to save your daughters from shame, then speak today for freedom!

"Let no man in all Tsor hereafter prey upon the labor of others, and let no man depend upon others for the privilege to work!"

Cheers and applause followed this statement amid cries of "Down with capital!" "We'll recover our own or die!"

When silence was restored Ortro resumed:

"Two years ago I had a home of my own—a little paradise to me. I had worked hard to get my title clear, but since that day, through family sickness, funeral costs and my own lack of employment, misfortune has driven me step by step out of possession and down into debt until I found myself in your midst yonder in the Kar Tuki. There was no other way!

"I had spoken to my employers and implored them to buy my services as they had sold their own. I show-ed them how my home was melting from my grasp, how I had been using the services of others much more than I had sold my own, and how of right it was due me in order to make some semblance of exchange. I begged their aid to help restore a clear home to me!

"The employers scorned my appeal and scoffed my claims as if I'd been a madman! They declared they would buy only by price, and buy just where and when and how they pleased. "Down on your knees! Go, take your place upon the platform and get out of here!" This was the answer I received.

"'Down on your knees! Down upon your knees!' Think of such words! As well have said 'Starve, dog! or into your kennel — into the Kar Tuki!'

"As sure as fate, I did at last creep into that kennel and met you there, my friends — for the poor of Tsor have been *dogs* and the Kar Tuki *was* their kennel!

"The Lukkan past has been a dark and gloomy night. That night is now gone forever. In the light of the glorious future before us, let us forget that night! Let us forgive the past! Let our eyes, ever upon the future bent, live for the future. Let our sole ambition be for peace and liberty!

"We are prompted in our course, O men of Tsor, by the holiest of motives — a duty we owe to our children and ourselves. We seek neither charity nor to deprive a living person of aught that rightfully be-longs to him!

"All we demand is the recovery of our lost birth-right, from which we have been blindly and wrong-fully divorced! We even accuse no man of intentional wrong. We ask no redress. We merely seek to cor-rect for the future the error of the past.

"In the repurchase of capital we and our children shall be righted and the dread word "poverty" will in the days to come live but a memory! Then, as the ages roll, shall we look back with glowing pride upon this, our victory!

"Let not our children blush to read a tale of cowardice in these our doings; let us not pluck liberty with cruel instruments! Let us appeal to sweat and brain rack, patience and endurance, but not to bloodshed!

"The strength of righteousness, the love of peace, the almighty power of right, and a religious trust in these — let these, O men of Tsor, be our true weapons of conquest. Let us give justice, even as we demand justice; justice for justice!"

The last words, "justice for justice," were taken up by the men in the yim and repeated lustily by the vast throng.

In the midst of the tumult the figure of Zuzo was seen moving through the crowd, welcomed on every side with shouts and greetings whose noise was lost in the general uproar, for the speakers had recognized him in the distance and his coming was a signal for their withdrawal.

Soon Zuzo was ascending the rostrum. All eyes were upon him as he stepped forward, his tall form erect and an apparently calm but defiant look upon his face. He paused a moment; then began speaking, slow and deliberate:

"Justice for justice; aye, and blood for blood!"

His deep voice seemed charged with an almost unearthly intensity. A perfect silence prevailed, each man in that audience standing with head bent forward and with excited gaze, as if spell-bound — as if there had been some magic in those words, "blood for blood!"

Zuzo paused long; then he continued, in calm, deep, impressive tones:

"Blood calls for blood! You may not see her, but there she lies, my wife—she who had been to me more than all the world, butchered—butchered by a hireling—a beast hired by another beast—one of Tsor's proud nobles!"

"Where is she?" "Who did the deed?" "Who was the man?" "We'll avenge her death!" were among the loud exclamations coming from the throng.

"At my home she lies! Poor, poor wreck of life! Distorted image! Horrible sight!

"Pardon, men, that I speak of that you do not know! My wife was such an angel—her murdered form will rise before my eyes to the last day! O, to be bitten by a loathsome reptile and sent to death in such a cruel way!

"The human serpents, the hireling and his master, will nevermore return, but the ring of serpents live and feed my heart with hate unquenchable! I have but sipped of vengeance to make an appetite!"

A long pause ensued after which he again continued.

"Under the very roof of this pompous lord, O men of Tsor, I found my only child. She, too, bore marks of violence! They had not spared even her!

"O, men, you have not felt, perhaps, the bite of ugly wrong which in the dark of Tsor gnaws down into the heart! You have not seen your little ones stretched out in the cold slumber as I have seen my child, and traced the murder to Tsor's pretentious lords."

"Down with the lords!" "Hang the nabobs!" "We will be avenged!" "We've all been wronged!" and many other denunciations were heard amidst a babel of raving which quieted as soon as the speaker resumed.

"I know not why the fates have done all this, but they are wiser than our cold spirits are! O, friends, my girl, my Meta, was purity itself! Dead! Dead!

"When I looked upon that precious remnant of dear life and gazed into that face of innocence, I saw therein a host of babes like angels, robed in white. They formed around my child singing a sad melody of untimely death. They sang of life, when they were Tsor's unfortunates — ill-fed, ill-clad, ill-nursed, dwarfed and distorted with disease, swept to their graves as if by pestilence, beaten by angry parents made angry by the burdens of the State! They sang of fathers exiled in the Kar Tuki! They sang of mothers weeping in empty homes and of brothers and sisters wandering through the yims, living the lives of wretches—growing hardened and cold like the beasts!

"They pointed to blood on their garments and they wept, crying: "We've been stricken and maimed and murdered; we've been murdered by slow degrees! O, Zuzo of Tsor, stand up! Stand up and lead the men of Tsor! Let them wipe away in blood our blood, the blood of the years!"

"Blood!" "Blood!" "We'll have blood!" "We've been treated like dogs!" "They've killed our children!" "We'll be revenged!" and other fierce outcries went up from a thousand throats indicating the rapidity with which the flame of excitement was gaining among the multitude.

"Then we will have blood;" the speaker continued, "aye, in the name of all the persecutions; in the name of the long hours we have been kept degraded on our knees; in the name of the unmerciful lash; in the name of the soulless rack of killing anxiety on which our lives have been stretched; in the name of the foul air and cruel floggings of the Kar Tuki; O, friends, in the name of murder unavenged, we'll dip our hands this day in tyrant blood and consecrate Tsor's yims to vengeance!

"Aye, blood for blood, and all the lords of Tsor cannot half fill the hungry cup of vengeance! Swear with me then, for each and every hour of sacred life torn from our souls, we'll ask a drop of blood — a law for misrule and an eternal mark for tyrants! Swear, men of Tsor, as you are fathers! Swear as you are husbands! Swear as you are sons!"

The men by this time were furious with passion and as of one accord spears, maces and swords rose glistening in the sun, the men following the movement of the speaker's arms and repeating from his lips the words "we swear!"

It was a terrible oath, and the intense earnestness with which it was taken by the vast multitude made it doubly threatening. Well might the lords of Tsor have trembled at the sound!

The throng was really excited to a pitch of frenzy, and with determined threats and loud cries for vengeance broke ranks, rushing confusedly from place to place in their tumultuous fury.

A cry of "Down with the Kar Tuki" was started and was repeated from mouth to mouth until the entire body was animated with this single purpose. Active steps toward accomplishing this end were at once taken, the men entering upon the work like so many fiends.

Huge casks of pitch were rolled in front of the prison, and with the aid of buckets the walls were rapidly being coated with the black liquid so that in less than an hour the entire surface was enveloped.

Torches were then applied and fierce flames began to shoot upward, sending forth a massive cloud of smoke.

The infuriated men raised a wild cry of exultation as the flames rose, many of the mob fairly dancing with delight. Shouts of "Down with the Kar Tuki!" "Out with the debt scourge!" "Down with the black hole!" "To the ground with the home ravisher!" "Flames wipe it from the earth!" and many similar cries went up from the madmen.

In vain did Ortro and some of the cooler heads ex-·postulate and endeavor to calm the men. The fire-brand had been cast among them and that tinder in their breasts, passion, was one fierce blaze. If quenched in one man's breast it would be immediately re-kindled by the blaze of passion all around. It was a conflagration of passion and no single stream of cool reason could hope to quench it. No calm deliberation could gain hearing now.

*
*
*

While Zuzo, in his blind paroxysm of rage, was seeking to vent his passion for revenge, still lying over the dead body of Prince Urg, a procession of ser-pents, who had escaped from the chamber above, were gliding slowly forward, moving toward the dead man. The presence of Zuzo did not deter them in the least in their forward march. Onward they crept till they reached the body which they began to lick with their tongues. Some climbed over it, some coiled round its limbs, some climbed over the living man, who lay there in his fierce passion unmoved by his sur-roundings. His mind was transfixed and his body lay like an immovable statue. The serpents became more bold and coiled around the living body; but Zuzo was dead — a madman lived in that frame.

Presently the madman relaxed his grip on the dead

man's throat, and slowly, as if waking from a slumber, he gave evidences of coming back to an approach to sense. He did not move a muscle at sight of the loathsome reptiles, and changing his attitude he sat up playing with them as a child would play with toys. He did not realize the slightest touch of fear. He conversed with them: "Ye have the true wisdom of life, wee pets, with no heart in the breast and in the tongue the venom of death! Your souls are free from the anguish heaven inflicts upon our kind. You are cold and yourselves hold the sting that death holds over men. You are kings over death! Proud man is a slave; the sooner he's dead the better for all the race!"

While speaking he fondled and kissed the serpents with the utmost impunity.

In his mind the whole world had changed. In his deadly passion the world had become a battle field in which treachery masqueraded in the guise of peace to more readily strike her blows for vengeance and ruin and blood. It was a battle field from beginning to end — kill and murder first and kill and murder last; kill for gain and kill again for revenge. He was in the midst of a carnival of blood. The world had proven to him a treacherous friend whom he had trusted unwisely, and now revenge alone was all that he had left. It had been a delusion from the start—a snare to entrap men—a mere instrument of abuse. It was a cold, indifferent, venomous thing, to whose character the serpents around him were saintly creatures. They did not masquerade; they did not assume a false attitude; men knew what they were and were warned. But the world denied its venom, invited confidence and then struck down its victims. What bond was there between him and such a world? None!

Borne on by a flood of mad reasoning the world lost all ties that had hitherto been sacred to him. In his whirlwind of passion, cut loose from wife and children — his closest ties, all else was lost to recognition and madness reigned supreme.

Suddenly, as if animated by a new thought, he disengaged the coil of serpents wound around him and rushed down the stairway and out into the air.

His faculties were not absent, but were closed to every impulse other than blood-spilling and vengeance. He thirsted for blood as a miser thirsts for gold, as men hunger for bread. The religious fervor and the heroic spirit that had heretofore been strong, active forces within him were still there. It was the world that had changed. It had proven a terrible deception—a capricious, fitful thing, unworthy treatment through calculation or restraint. His madness was the reflex of the world's disorder.

The god-power within him had not lost its force but had changed its direction and had become a power demoniac. The stalwart mountain that had maintained thousands upon its grassy slopes had been suddenly converted into a volcano — an intense energy devoted alone to destruction.

Into the camera of this man's mind Satan had entered and on the plate of consciousness impressed his evil image. Satan was king, and from the throne of will issued his mandates to the body state whose functions he usurped. The great fortress reason and all the powerful cannon of passion had fallen into the hands of the evil one and had been converted into an engine of evil purpose.

Flourishing a dagger over his head, Zuzo departed. The work of death did not in the least seem unusual. On the contrary, it seemed perfectly natural;

it pleased him as if it had been a successful move in the ambition of his life. Had riches been his aim he could not have acquired his first fortune with greater zest. He was only vengeance-mad as other men are riches-mad.

By some instinctive recollection he moved on toward the Kar Tuki. The plans of the previous night had been entirely forgotten, but as he saw the throng of men in the distance they came back to him in a vague form. He realized that these were his former companions in imprisonment and his natural impulse for vengeance impelled him to seize upon this opportunity. They must become an implement for vengeance. A few well-directed words connecting his own wrongs with their sufferings would change the restless multitude to a mob of destruction. He heard the shouts of "justice for justice" and seizing them as a theme for vengeance, added the words "blood for blood!"

His was not the voice of the self-seeking demagogue bent only on his own aggrandizement; it was not a human orator seeking to stir men's souls; it was a messenger from the god of destruction whose words were thunderbolts, whose passions were the lightnings. It penetrated every being; it burned the soul; it roused the sleeping demon from his depths and crowned him in the hearts of these people. All the dead wrongs that slumbered in the past came back to life howling for vengeance.

The words of Zuzo, like a somnambulist's footsteps, went to their purpose home, unconscious of all aim. All the power of his madness was concentrated in these words; all the fire of his soul went into them. They fairly tingled the ear and made the blood boil.

To his brother Ortro these utterances were bewildering. He was astonished and shocked. He could not realize the strange tale of murder and the change that had come over Zuzo seemed past comprehension. This terrible being was no more like Zuzo than a child's voice is like a cannon's roar. He listened to the speech, paralyzed and dumbfounded.

He was thoroughly alarmed, and completely at a loss what to do. He had never seen his brother so violent before—a violence that appeared grand and superhuman but fearful viewed in the light of reason. He had never seen his brother animated by a passion so fierce and bloodthirsty; he had never seen him so beastly, so like a demon. Zuzo, the patient; the calm philosopher; the loving philanthropist; the cool-headed man of reason; the man of religious fervor and passion—it could not be that Zuzo. He was a paradox. He was Zuzo in every way, but in all the grandest and highest phases of his being he was not Zuzo.

This was surely another being; this was Zuzo the destroyer.

In vain did Ortro beseech him to return to reason and quiet the multitude. In vain did he implore him to desist from urging violence and in vain alike were all his own attempts to gain a hearing before the multitude. The flood was on. The stream of abuse that had started centuries back had been withheld only by artificial power, by the dam of civil authority, and that dam had burst. A perfect cloudburst of vengeance was being hurled against the old prison. As well bid Niagara stop as seek to repress the irresistible deluge that threatened e'er long to bathe the yims of Tsor in blood.

Anathemas of every description were being hurled against the lords of Tsor.

"They've stolen even our flesh and blood!" piped a small weazen-faced fellow in the foreground, who looked as if the accusation might have literally referred to his own body.

"They would steal our souls, too, if they could only lay hands on them," bellowed a stentorian voice from a globular specimen of obesity.

"By all the fiery devils," squeaked another, "we'll have their blood till all the yams and yims are crimsoned!"

Ortro made another attempt to address the men in the midst of the tumult and uproar. He exhausted himself in efforts to gain attention. He seized a huge bell and rang furiously to get their ears. He begged the men to maintain order as they hoped to succeed. He besought them to abstain from bloodshed and violence, but in response was confronted with shouts of "Down with the traitor!" "Hang him!" "Kill him!" "Kill the traitor!"

A crowd of angry men surged to the platform and climbed toward him. He held his ground, calmly asking what they would have.

"Your blood," responded a tall, lank Tsoran, advancing to seize him. Ortro struck the man down with a well-aimed blow, but the next moment he was seized hand and foot by the mob and hurled against one of the walls of the prison. He struck a projection on the flaming wall, breaking his spine, and before the body reached the ground life was already extinct.

Near by Zuzo, who but yesterday would have died for his brother, looked on with utter indifference, absorbed in urging on the work of destruction.

The poor madmen of revolution, blood-hungry, callous and insensible in their frenzy, do all their murderous work in a few hours. The money-hungry madmen of the world are no less callous and insensible to the subtle murder they slowly and unceasingly commit, daily, hourly and yearly, from age to age. They, too, labor under a delusion, a dream of pillage and murder in which they revel by the side of untold suffering — in which they, too, look on indifferently, living in their revels while the flesh of their flesh is being smitten to the earth. The dream of madness in which they live seems natural also, to them perfectly natural. To them, things should be so. Let us not disturb their carnival.

Soon after a thundering cry went up from the yim, followed by repeated huzzas. The glass in the tall towers over the prison was beginning to melt and was running down along the walls in ruby streams. Striking the cold earth the hot liquid burst into a spray of brilliant globules, shooting into the air and piercing the upper smoke, through which they sank again like so many falling stars upon a summer night. All the walls were soon running with sheets of liquid glass, whose varied colors mingled with the frequent rising sprays of crystal globules formed a gorgeous panorama.

For awhile the men forgot their dark mission and stood gazing breathlessly at the display. Suddenly a loud crash announced the falling of the northern tower. This time a tremendous spray of globules rose, many of the fiery little balls falling upon the heads of the men in the yim, who howled with pain while their companions hooted and jeered. All the inflammable material in the ruins added to the intensity of the heat, and soon there formed underneath a small lake of molten glass that worked its way downward wherever an avenue was open.

One by one the walls came crashing into the pool of liquid glass, receiving fresh material as fast as it ran off into the lower floors, the yim being all the while one continuous roar of tumultuous delight. The triumph of the mob was complete. The Kar Tuki was a heap of ruins. The curse of centuries was completely blotted out.

What became of the officials confined within its lower cells no one will ever know. Whether they found a safe refuge on the lowest floor or whether, in the midst of the confusion, they managed to escape from the building; or whether they had possibly been suffocated in the cells may only be conjectured. That they were never again heard from is all that can be said, and it may only be hoped that they succeeded in escaping unnoticed.

The news of the revolt spread rapidly. All over Tsor it traveled from lip to lip. Two hours after sunrise it was the theme in every household in that city of a million souls.

On the Tok Yim the idle kneelers hailed the news with delight, and when they heard of the burning of the Kar Tuki they became wild with exultation. They hurried in large crowds to the scenes of tumult where they helped to swell the throng and soon became infused with the spirit of violence that prevailed.

As the news was authenticated the factories closed and more than a hundred thousand persons poured out into the yim, the majority at once departing for their homes, where they remained in readiness for any danger that might threaten the household.

Thousands, however, joined the crowds going towards the Kar Tuki, all driven by a curiosity to see what was going on—an anxiety to be present in case anything unusual transpired, without the least definite aim or motive to guide them.

From the Kar Tuki the center of attraction was

now shifted to the Kar Yuk.   All told, there must now have been a hundred thousand persons converging toward the center of Tsor, toward the great Kar Yuk.

Zuzo meanwhile was not idle.   The Kar Yuk must also be destroyed.   The heart of this democratic despotism of wealth, containing the royal temple with its upper halls all filled with records upon whose entries rested all the titles to property in Tsor—this practical key to the vaults of despotism—this vital organ of the monster—must be destroyed; the Kar Yuk must be leveled to the ground!   He aimed to destroy order and he struck at its root here.   He aimed no further. What greater victory could madness ask?

The Kar Tuki was already a mass of ruins, and now all attention was centered upon the towering Yuk.   Within its chambers were confined a whole legion of priests.   In imposing majesty they were assembled among the minor temples on the lower floor, gathered in worship around their favorite idols.

The upper floors were all vacated, and now before their god-idols the priests chanted in slow and measured cadence while marching in a circle around the sombre images.   Their chiefs stood directly in front of the massive idols going through a weird dance, in the course of which they narrated in woeful manner the tales of their sin and wrong-doing.   Into their huge incense vats they poured a mixture of sacred barks and roots from which pale, thin pillars of odorous smoke arose.   Then they decked their idols with rich garments dotted with rarest jewels.

Meanwhile the priests had ranged themselves in lines as in military drill.   A long silence reigned, and at the stroke of a gong the priests, as if acting by a single impulse, fell flat upon their faces in the dark halls and lay there like dead.

The chief priests, still erect, began reciting short stanzas of a strange, musical gibberish between each stanza going through a series of odd antics in the way of leaping and dancing upon the bodies of the prostrate subordinates.

Not a muscle moved to indicate a sign of life among the priests lying upon the floor. The chiefs proceeded with their rites, later on using whips and sharp instruments upon the fallen idolators, pricking and hewing their flesh yet provoking no token of life in these determined penitents who sought thus to appease the wrath of their gods.

In the meantime the outer path that wound upward around the great tower was filled far up with fierce Tsorans who had formed in a double line extending many miles in length. Between these lines hundreds of buckets filled with pitch were being passed up to be poured on the walls and handed down again to be re-filled and kept in continuous circuit.

Steadily the work was progressing. All day long great casks of pitch were being rolled through the yims to the foot of the Kar Yuk. All day long the buckets were kept in motion until the walls of the monster building, to a height of more than four hundred feet, were thickly coated with the purple liquid. Thousands of casks were consumed in covering the sides of this colossal tower and it was coated scarce half way to the top.

Within, the priests were still lying prostrate engaged in their harsh rite of penance. They lay like logs of wood, their minds by the force of long acquired habit, conquering the rebellious senses. They felt within a blind faith that there could be no danger if only their gods were with them.

The chief priests finally withdrew to a secluded

corner where they held a council as a result of which
they prepared to go forth to test their power over the
multitude by invoking the Curse of Kodor, an influence that in past years had been very potent.

They went forth upon this mission with solemn
mien, proudly confident that the presence of so many
high dignitaries in their sacerdotal garments before
the temple would be infallible in pacifying the maddened masses. They were not out very long, however,
before they returned in terrible discomfiture and
minus several of their number. They had been
hooted and jeered by the crowd who sent the Curse
of Kodor back as a boomerang upon the heads of the
priests. They pelted the latter with stones, tore their
garments and bore several of them off as prisoners
whom they permitted to escape only after passing
through a fearful gauntlet of abuse.

All beliefs sustained largely by social force suffer
a reaction whenever this power is suddenly withdrawn, and the influence of the religion of Zmun
with its Curse of Kodor seemed to have vanished
marvelously quick—something almost incredible, but
for the fact that the religion which was outside of the
heart in the shape of an institution wrapped in a
thousand folds of form and ceremony and literal
beliefs had long ago crumbled and had been for centuries held in place by the guys of social force and
social needs. That the creed from the beginning had
carried in its structure much of temporal as well as
spiritual power was overlooked. By its very central
position in social life it was clad with vast power
which it appropriated to aggrandize the institution of
religion while repudiating the social obligations involved in its power. Religion could die in the human
heart but the institution of religion, like its idols, was

to be glorified. The multitude came to its shrines because these practically exclusive speaking organs of the public frightened them with tales of horrid punishments buzzed constantly in their ears—tales cuningly wrought so that no one could disprove them, coming from assumed sources beyond human reach. Even the more intelligent came because it could damn their social happiness by ostracism and a host of contingent evils, and this whip of blackmail drove thousands to crouch in the corners of the temples—not through fear for themselves but fearing evil to their daughters, brothers or sisters if placed under the ban of Zmun's frown. This arrogant creed that sought to make the beliefs of one age bind all the generations to come— that had been the mainstay of the commerce of Tsor, now so flagrantly exposed—stood for once unmasked, its power consumed, like a huge idol burned and turned to ashes.

Poor deluded wretches; deceived by their own blindness! They thought the men of Tsor came to them of their religion when they came driven by worldly dependence. They thought the religion of Zmun was rooted in their hearts, but they found they had made hypocrites and the callousness they had nourished with the Curse of Kodor and the Kar Tuki had grown to roaring evils that threatened now to destroy their temple and crush them in its ruins.

When night came the torch was applied to the pitch-covered walls. Gradually a circle of flames began to ascend from the base of the Yuk and was hissing and crackling with fierce vigor while a savage shout went up from the sea of living forms extending far out in the dark as if to the very outskirts of Tsor. A crazed and rampant mob occupied the foreground and their deeds of lawlessness added to the horrors of the scene.

The lower half of the Kar Yuk was now trans·
formed into a colossal drum of fire, while all above was
hidden in a dense pillar of smoke towering to the sky.
It formed a stupendous image whose dark frown was
full of ominous significance.   Millions of flaming
tongues hissed 'round its glowing sides, which now
and then flashed like a wall of gems.   Higher up, above
the flames, a series of glowing streaks played like rain·
bow bands half hidden in the smoke.   Mirrored sec
tions reflected and multiplied the lights until the great
walls appeared a monster kaleidoscopic belt, high up
in air — a perfect marvel of magnificence!

The mass of humanity below gazed aloft in wonder
at the imposing grandeur of this colossal panorama.
Far off, to the very outskirts of Tsor, the light was
clearly visible and for miles around the housetops
were peopled — men, women and children gazing upon
the terrible but wonderfully fascinating picture.
The roofs on the Kar Yim, the innermost yim that
circled 'round the Yuk, shone like surfaces of silver on
which all shades of color played and danced.   Colors
and combinations of hues and shades whose richness
defied description, feasted the eyes; and now and
then, as some extraordinarily beautiful flashes greeted
their view, loud, ringing shouts of applause burst on
the still atmosphere of night and were echoed and re·
echoed from yim to yim, like a grand peal of thunder
rolling o'er the heavens.

Wonder and amazement held Tsor spellbound.   Beneath this passion welled a dark ocean of awe.   The
unparalled brilliance of this show of splendor measur·
ed the depths of the darkness underneath.

In the halls of the great temple the prostrate priests
still lay immovable.   Their garments had been hacked
into bloody shreds that lay scattered over the floor.

The chief priests carried the work of mutilation to the extreme of torture and one priest had already bled to death. Still their gods were unappeased. The chiefs held another council. The gods must be appeased at all hazards.

A huge bonfire was built at the feet of each of the greater idols and when the flames were blazing in full fury they dragged from the floor a number of the prostrate priests and into each fire they cast a victim. Then, standing before these human sacrifices each of the chiefs repeated a solemn invocation and fell down clinging to the feet of his idol.

The victims met their death without a cry—without a murmur. The heroism of their faith was almost superhuman. By this sacrifice they believed they were to be absolved from all their sins and an eternity of bliss would open up to them. Was this courage or cowardice? Was it the warm and sensitive—the sympathetic, or the cold and callous in man? Were these living beings or were they already dead?

To the chief priests, faith-mad, superstitious men, these murders seemed natural also, perfectly natural. They too were totally indifferent to the real active world—the true life—worshipping apart a cold creed of words.

Against the threatening evils of the unknown future the miser piles his wall of glittering gold; the plutocrat a tower of dazzling figures, while the bigot builds mountains of dead prayers out of cold words, each being in his own way deaf to the cries of those they trample under foot in the real life—the life they live today.

While these horrible rites were being performed within the Yuk and all Tsor was entranced with the burning temple, the Yam Yim was being converted into a theater of carnage. Among the homes of its stately lords raged a reign of vandalism. Bands of lawless men and furious women ransacked and pillaged houses, killing and outraging with a brutality worse than that of beasts. The dagger and the torch were in the hands of fiends. Entire families were butchered and thousands fled in haste, leaving behind all they had. The most revolting orgies ensued and madness became truly epidemic.

Drugs were indulged in such as plunge the mind into terrific fury in which judgment and will, the brakes that check our over-hasty movements, were paralyzed, and the energies within went spinning on with resistless speed. All the latent forces of the mind that are ordinarily held in balance were let loose to exhaust themselves in a day—a chaotic mass of cruel, aimless force. Even on the pet animals of the household they wreaked their vengeance.

Meanwhile the Tsorans were still gazing from the housetops upon the burning Yuk. While they were watching, a wonderfully beautiful series of stripes, alternately emerald and ruby, flashed across the walls, half way up and lingered before their eyes, a very paragon of splendor. The thundering outburst of applause that followed this vision was repeated in widening circles from yim to yim. The noise of the uproar had not yet died away when a sharp and intense crackling sound startled the million lookers-on. From the north side of that beautiful belt shot forth a dozen silvery streams of molten liquid, and a moment later the upper portion of the Yuk slid forward with an oblique downward lurch toward the north side where it had first weakened. Before the vast audience could realize this shift the entire upper portion of the Yuk toppled over, striking the ground with a terrific crash. It was followed by a fearful suspense in which the host of spectators waited breathless, brought to a sudden realization of the awful calamity that was to spread from the darkness in the wreck below.

The Pride of Tsor was in ruins. Its towering head that had for centuries inspired only wonder and admiration was leveled to the ground. Its grand walls pictured with historic life were degraded into a formless liquid. As if in the terrible throes of a death-struggle; as if resisting to the utmost the dull obloquy to which it was being doomed, and as if animated with an undying hunger for admiration, it sent up from its ruins a hundred fiery fountains; it rose in the dark like a vast bouquet of stars aglow in every color and then it sank slowly from view in the deep bosom of night.

The awe inspired by the crash was lightened by the glitter that came after. The true significance of events was strongly reflected in the fitful splendor of the show and the deep gloom that filled the intervals between.

Before long the lower walls of the Yuk began giving way—at times crashing in, and then again dwindling away into the molten pool at their base. Slowly all was turning into one mass below. Slower and feebler the flames flickered. The variegated colors merged gradually into a dull, silvery sheet and the great field of ruins took on a ghastly look in the gloom that was deepening around it.

The outer multitude had scattered; some to their homes and some to the Yam Yim. The inner mob, composed mainly of the least intellectual of the semi-naked ex-prisoners, now also began to break up, but only to renew in other quarters its work of destruction. It had only begun its carnival of crime.

It would be useless to follow them further. Enough to say that the same lawlessness and dreadful orgies that had thus far only been enacted in the Yam Yim were now repeated in the Tekya, the Oksh and the Oz yims where the merchants' stores and warehouses and the residences of the well-to-do classes were.

The terrible reign of inhumanity that darkened the city for many days thereafter was but the extension of the rule that had preceded. It was the outgrowth of a society cemented only by force and forced beliefs—a mock realm whose rocks were tinsel and whose truths refused to face scrutiny.

Zuzo, the scourge of Tsor, that unfortunate man, was never seen again. He had been observed on the north side of the Kar Yuk just before the crash. The ghastly ruins over his head became a fit monument to the emptiness of revenge, to madness and to his sad career.

The spirit of destruction that was carried beyond his life was still an active force, but would soon be expended. Was not the seed of eternal truth which had been cast upon Tsor's soil also left after him? Surely a new life was dawning upon Tsor ; the foundation of a new temple was already built, the seed of a higher brotherhood already planted. A fairer temple was soon to rise—one truly reaching the skies, bringing them nearer to God.

Let us carry his grave in our memory and lighten the darker side of his life with those wreath-words of forgiveness, "More sinned against than sinning!"

Freedom Day was being celebrated for the first time in Utopia. The great city of Tismoul was one vast flutter of excitement. All attention was centered on the ancient Royal avenue, her grandest thoroughfare, now thick-lined with enthusiastic spectators upon either side of the broad slopes leading to the roadway. It was a new holiday, the first anniversary of a miraculous transformation in her government and in her welfare. This was not a mere bread and butter victory; it was a spiritual triumph — a triumph of the the soul. The soul could now expand and grow upon the manna of liberty, for liberty is the bread of the soul.

Such a celebration taught the many to realize that they are one. They were moved by one impulse, by one infatuation, by one worship. The whole city was one church, the whole people had one soul and in that soul was God.

A soothing music, sad but thrilling, varying from the most plaintive wails to the liveliest and most joy-inspiring peals besieged the ear — the very air overhead seeming to teem with floating strains. It was intended to betoken the triumph of the ages and aimed to express regret over the fallen in the trail of victories, yet throbbing with joy that the battles were over and a holier life had begun.

A procession was advancing in the distance headed by a colossal vehicle on which stood the heroic figure of a woman shielding her two children from the onslaught of a five-headed beast, representing liberty shielding her children, Peace and Progress, from the demon of tyranny, whose heads represented cannibalism, slavery, feudalism, aristocracy and capitalism.

Following this group was its mate showing liberty triumphant, her armor scattered on the floor, the dead monster at her feet and by her side her children Peace and Progress looking up in an attitude of worship. On a pennant waving over all were the words "Liberty Triumphant; Now and Forever!"

Following this were legion upon legion of marching citizens in the regular uniform of their craft, every craft having its distinctive uniform. Thousands of banners and pennants related the triumphs of the year and communicated to the spectators instructive lessons, teaching in brief the varied truths belonging to this new epoch.

Choruses of children paraded in the procession singing songs of liberty and waving the flag of Utopia on which was a white star in a blue field, a large number of variously colored beams meeting in the star which typified perfect exchange, the beams symbolizing the varied services that united in the new Industrial Union of Utopia.

All in all it was a glorious gala day and the universal happiness pointed to an overwhelming confidence in the new State. There were no poorly-dressed people to be seen; and throughout the city there was not at this time a single home but was a healthy, spacious, clean and comfortable abode. Hundreds of old rookeries had been torn down and filthy streets had disappeared, literally wiped from the face of the earth.

The sorry looking tramp was likewise almost entirely relegated to the realm of myths and museums; but a mere handful of incorrigibles remained kept in a special district under greater restriction of liberty because lacking the ability to move at large without tampering with the liberty of others. They were the product of the past, incapable in the short space of two years of adapting themselves to the wider opportunities thrown open to them.

When I reached home that day a sealed letter was handed me. I knew at once it was from Arda. I hastily tore it open and as I unfolded the leaves a beautiful pressed violet was exposed to view. It was the symbol of constancy and it doubly brought to mind my almost forgotten Violet over the sea. Alas, poor unhappy girl! In the Old World it must have been past 1960 and surely we would never meet again unless beyond the grave.

In spite of everything I could not refrain from reproaching myself as I had done many times before. The picture Violet invariably bore in my mind was the very figure of Arda. Her voice and her every move was a reflection of Arda. Could it be, as I had often thought, her entire personality, lost in memory, had been supplanted y Arda? Was Violet any longer more than a name? She answered no distinct being to my mind; she was a mere shadow, a dream.

I read the letter, which ran as follows;

To Ross, Now of Tismoul:

With keenest pleasure I hasten to greet my other soul, my truest friend in this sad world. Oh Ross, if you could only imagine the happiness your treasured lines brought to my heart I fear you would do nothing but write every blessed hour. I am delighted to hear such good news concerning the prosperity of the great city in which you are making your home. The fathers of Utopia have acted with almost divine wisdom in fitting their laws to human needs and I wish you would thank Ministers Aggra and Tasha in my behalf for the many kindnesses so generously extended you. Papa Jurgo has just recovered from an injury he had received to his ankle. It kept him in the house over two weeks during which time I have been attending him and assisting in the dispatch of important business communications. We are going to drive over to our friend Velva's today. She has been distracted ever since her husband's arrest, and besides she has not heard a word from Meta since that day. It seems so strange! Papa has written to the Chief Guardian of the Peace and offered a special reward for her restoration but nothing has thus far been heard and I am praying that we may meet her on calling today.

After reading your description of affairs in Utopia Papa is reconciled to our removal, particularly since the Curse of Kodor has been done away with, and he says the sooner we go the better. He is going to make a calculation and if his means permit intends to purchase the release of Zuzo and his unfortunate' brother. It will depend some on his success in disposing of his present business which he will have to sell at a sacrifice. He says it is wiser to sell at a loss than conduct a losing business with constant danger of ruin before him. He is thoroughly sick of business in Tsor; merchants seem to have nothing left to do now but stand in their stalls and grumble at fate.

As I am writing I hear that the prisoners in the Kar Tuki have burned that structure to the ground. I hope they have not attempted so revolutionary a measure, yet I long to see the day when there will be no Kar Tuki on earth.

The violet you will find enclosed was plucked yesterday and was pressed in the volume of poems you left me, even at the page of your favorite verse about the king of the leaves whose empire girdled the earth and who was the warden of all the great secrets of life.

I fancy your new world must be as near like paradise as present ideals will admit. We are not to expect a painless eternity unless we wish to become painted dummies, or nonentities. War is a perpetual necessity; it only changes its fields to the mental and moral world, leaving bodily butchery for beasts.

Tell Dr. Giniwig I love him as much as ever and do not be jealous yourself. I have just been comparing the Bible of the Colonists with our Book of Zmun and find both contain great truths, and I am convinced all truth is sacred and is God's word and it is sinful to deny or belittle any of it. The paper, cover and the words—in fact all the literal meanings of these books are like the dust of our idols—they are far from the ideal conveyed by the idol and such worship is vulgar and degrading. The Book of Zmun has no doubt been a great constructive factor in the development of the Lukkan mind, but I am inclined to think that its literalism has always been an obstructive element. To become a constructive force its truths must be detached and held above the literal. The book is a spiritual reflex and not a literal budget.

A messenger is waiting to bear this to the station so I bid you a hasty but not less loving farewell. Do you expect to visit us soon? Write early and don't forget to let me know more about those merry bachelor quarters Dr. Giniwig and you have been assigned.

Sincerely and affectionately,

ARDA.

Tsor, 1st day, 1st moon. Tsoran year III.

Putting aside the epistle, I sat up in my chair and was soon lost in reverie. Strange, thought I, how the church that once contained all the higher truth has been slowly deserted; art, healing, law, literature, all had left her door and each had established a shrine of its own with its own spiritual side inseparable from it, so that the voice of the remaining tenants is but a faint echo of its former self. How like my Violet who had vanished from me all but in name, whose real being I have inherited in an outer world — in my Arda, her true ideal! Is not the church also an ideal that oft remains behind in life's fitful voyage and when we are driven hopelessly apart must we each time deny our newer love and break another heart without being able to mend the old that's dead to us forever? Must we withhold our love from the new beings that enter life's arena because they are not akin in bodily identity with our friends who have passed away? We revere the memory but do not love the bones of the departed. We may also revere a creed that's dead without being deterred from our loving a new and living creed. Reverence is for the dead but love is for the living only.

That evening a band of refugees from Tsor arrived bringing news of the revolution that was in progress in that city. On hearing of it I at once recalled the rumor Arda had mentioned and I then realized that it was only too true.

Without a moment's delay I packed a valise, engaged an elphy, and without more ceremony than leaving an explanatory note for the Doctor and my host, I started on the way to Tsor.

Passing through a village the next morning I took breakfast at the only public house in the place. My host no sooner ascertained the direction of my journey than he advised me to remain where I was or else retrace my steps.

"You'll be killed, man, if you enter Tsor!" he insisted. "Why, friend, they are all mad in that city! No one ever heard of such doings! They have burned the entire place!"

"Not the entire city!" I exclaimed in amazement.

"So the tale goes; they are killing each other off so fast there won't be a soul left! The almighty Zmun has at last overtaken the wicked city. I always knew they would sometime be punished for their unrighteousness. For nigh ten years, I remember, no infidel has been punished with the Curse of Kodor, and now the wrath of the gods has come upon them at last."

"It is too horrible to be true," I answered, inwardly doubting this evidently overcredulous fellow.

"It is true as the Book of Zmun!" my host reiterated, "for did not three men from Tsor tell me so of their own lips yesterday! It is a visitation from heaven! If the priests have no heart to castigate the wicked the great Zmun will castigate them from heaven, and they will be thrice castigated. Thus it is written in the Book of Zmun and it is just; for, see you, the infidelity has been of the people first; of the priests second, and all being guilty they deserve to be thrice punished!"

Of course I did see, not deeming myself well enough versed in the Book of Zmun to discuss the merits of the case.

Before leaving, being sore from the bareback riding

of the previous night, I engaged a roja to take me to the city, but I could not persuade the frightened Tsoran to permit his property to be hazarded any nearer than within an hour's drive of the riotous city. His son therefore accompanied me until within view of Tsor when we parted and I continued on the back of my elphy.

Entering the city I found instead of meeting with turbulent mobs the yims were unusually quiet.

That my host's tale was a gross exaggeration was very soon apparent. Crossing the city on my way to my old home I happened to pass the ruins of the great Kar Yuk, and I almost shudder to this day as I recall the dismal and hideous sight. Human skeletons from which the flesh had been picked by dogs and buzzards were lying scattered about and here and there in the colossal mass of molten glass I could see the blackened figure of a human body that must have been suddenly engulfed by a flood of the liquid and had been later on covered with layer after layer until it lay encased far down in its deep transparent tomb. These bodies appeared like huge giants—an optical illusion produced by their covering of glass.

The whole formed a wonderful mound, a glittering epitome of the glory and of the sin of human vanity. Acres and acres of glass rose in varying heights and in fantastic shapes, twisted and twirled—here blackened with smoke, there aglow like a field of diamonds. There were mountains of ruby and vales of ashy darkness, spires of purple and silver seas; there were crimson crags rising up like monster crystals; there were lakes of red that looked like frozen blood, and in their bosoms clasped were blackened bodies lying stark and stiff like huge logs sunk there forever. There were bridges and arches and pillars; there were clumps of trees with trunks of gold and there were grottos in which all the gems of the earth seemed to have been set together to blend in rival brilliance. What a grand spectacle and hideous recollection!

The very ruins of the Yuk clung to the splendor of its ancient fame with an unyielding tenacity. Its wonderful beauty retained a charm even in the smoke and dust and shapelessness to which it had been doomed—even in that sadder sphere of sepulcher to the dead. The scene was so vivid and weird, so striking and impressive, that it appears before me to this day in all the distinctness of the original.

Midday was approaching and the heat had already become very oppressive, so that by the time I reached the house of Jurgo I was completely exhausted.

Arda met me with tears in her eyes and I then for the first time was informed of the tragedy that had so sadly ended the career of a family of nature's true nobility. I could neither weep nor speak, I was so shocked by the news.

For a while neither of us spoke a word.

"I am so glad you have come, Ross!" Arda began at length, taking my hand. "You cannot imagine how lonesome I have been since this misfortune."

"It is a fearful blow, Arda;" I said, "as long as I shall live some sadness from my heart will find expression in recollection of these friends."

"Within my heart," Arda added, "each one of them shall have a chosen spot and each shall be an inspiration living again in me. They shall live in your heart, too, Ross?"

"Yes," I answered, touched more and more, "their souls shall join my own; their's were souls too great to perish and be lost. My being will take new root in memories of their lives and carry on their being."

CHAPTER XXIII.

THE REVELATION.

The evening after my return to Tsor Jurgo and I were conversing quietly about the probable outcome of the revolution.

He was delighted that Utopia was so happily situated and being very much interested in the subject, drew me on, by degrees, until I had described almost every prominent phase of Utopian life. I even mentioned all the details of my trip to Tsor and was just engaged in attempting to describe the scene of the ruined Kar Yuk when a most peculiar sensation came over me. I seemed transfixed, while Jurgo sat in his place immovable as a statue. The room began to darken, slowly expanding into a weird, indescribable mist. Overhead a dark sky was cast, lit by a single star of inexpressible brilliance. Then before my eyes, as if to mock my puerile attempt at description, rose through the misty veil the very mound of the ruined Kar Yuk.

I was held as in a trance. I could neither move nor speak. There it was; exactly as I had seen it during the day—all its brilliance heightened by the black robe of night in which it was set. Even the huge charred bodies lay visible in their tomb.

The air around me seemed pregnant with a mysterious magnetism defying the senses. I almost felt myself drawn to the scene. I felt as if my whole body were transparent and airy matter and I, aside from conscious sense and feeling, had really no bodily existence. I was lost—mysteriously lost indeed, for I was lost to myself; and between the atmosphere, the mound and my own body I could not on my life distinguish where one began and the other ended. All was one sea, and while distinctions still existed I would have utterly failed in bounding them.

In this strange condition my vision became riveted to a charred figure rocking slightly within the tremulous sea of glass in which it was imbedded.

The figure appeared of gigantic stature. As it lay there I could see the cinders cracking and falling away, as if the body were undergoing a tangible expansion. I could see the face recover its color becoming a swarthy hue. The man had jet-black, shaggy eyebrows meeting in the center and overlooking a pair of intensely black eye-lashes. His nose was prominent and his face was marked with many wrinkles. My whole attention was absorbed in this figure. His strange transformation and the awful expression of sadness in his countenance transfixed my mind completely.

The man in the glass rose slowly to his feet, stooping slightly. A huge, black gown hung to his feet. On his forehead I could detect the pale figure of a cross. He stared vacantly around and then gave vent to a most agonizing cry. His form was dreadfully bent; he trembled in every limb; his dark, wrinkled visage bespeaking an age in strange contrast with his raven locks, and pleading for pity with an eloquence pen cannot convey. Bowing his head as he sank upon his knees, he began speaking in a deep, imploring tone:

"I had hoped at last to die forever here, and I must live again! Can I never rest—never lay down this dreadful burden—life! O God, am I doomed to wander an endless, aimless journey—drifting through all the years, forever homeless! No shelter here, no rest! O God, look down upon the path my wanderings have made—exiled from love, a picture that is dark for all the seeds of light I've strewn along its desert course! Is this to be forever, this wandering in the dark? Will that promised day ne'er come when Thou, as the Messiah, shalt reveal Thyself again on earth? I pray for Thy kingdom, God; for in my wanderings now, even in the shadow of Thy church—covering all the earth, I hear but tales of woe and sounds of agony! Darkness and doubt sit lurking in men's souls and sighs and groans grow deeper and more desponding day by day. Our load of trial outweighs our human strength! All around is sin, and even for the righteous no avenue seems clear. Faith in ourselves is sinking and men are breaking ranks, wading through sin, declaring there is no other way! O God, Thou hast not left Thy children! Thou'lt come again, Thou'lt come! O Master, I long for Thy arrival and Thy Kingdom! Master, grant my prayer!"

The whole vision seemed miraculous and when I recognized in this person the traditional Wandering Jew there was not the slightest doubt in my mind as to the correct identity. It could have been no other than that mysterious personage.

A dead silence followed, lasting I know not how long. In the sky above a dim form became faintly visible in the dark and steadily grew more clear. It looked like a grey mist aggregating and shaping itself into the figure of a huge cross whose arms spanned the heavens. I gazed upon it in breathless suspense. Then a voice, clear and calm, spoke out of the impenetrable darkness overhead, saying:

"Thou sufferest not alone. Thou art free to wander at thy will. Here, pinioned to my cross, I linger still —awaiting the eternal dawn."

The brilliant star that before had lit up the sky,

now returned and as the heavens brightened under its
rays I could see a great cross and there, suspended by
thorns which pierced His flesh, I recognized our Savior. It was my God!

A cheering light shone in the luster of His eyes,
and though His wan face hung sad upon His breast
and from His thorn-pierced limbs ran streams of blood,
He struggled with His suffering like a God who knew
the end and looked down upon the swarthy Hebrew
with compassion as to say "For thee, too, I feel!"

A cry of surprise broke from the lips of the kneeling man at sight of the vision before him. Tears
welled from his eyes and his whole being seemed to
be moved.

"Pardon, O pardon Master; that I should ask de-
liverance ere Thou art free! Ever in my wanderings
hath it been made known Thy sufferings had ended
upon earth! In all my journeyings, even in the remotest corners of the earth have I found Thy cross,
Thy church, Thy people, and Thou wert ever hailed
as the Redeemer who from the cross had saved mankind!"

As he was uttering the last words the sky again
darkened and the brilliant star disappeared. Only
the dim outline of the kneeling man was visible, his
pallid face turned upward to the grey cross that rested
in the heavens.

After a pause the voice continued:

"I am the God Almighty. I am the God that lived
in fetish form, in that of dreaded beasts, in the fiery
orbs of heaven, in thunder's voice and in the frowning idols that filled your temples once. In all these
forms I lived as the Ideal to which thy mind looked up
in worship. I was the great Ideal, the All-powerful
Creator, under whose image, looking up, thou'st ever

grown to higher being and been created unto higher spheres. I am that Jehova under whose all-creative name was born the reign of law, binding all into concordant life in the first great brotherhood. I am that Jehova who came down as Christ and suffered to teach a broader sympathy. The true, living Christ was the patient, God-like suffering that looked on wrong as erring. Into your hearts the high ideal came of God-like strength wedded to infinite love—the seed of higher unity and truer brotherhood! In this ideal I again did live, and in its worship—in looking up to this Ideal, ye have grown nearer to my being. This is creation!

"In the lowliest forms—in plants, in beasts, in infant races, in every stage of life—my creation lies in worship, in upward looking, in striving toward the highest! Therefore, my child, look ever up and in true reverence worship thy Ideal, seeking it in the highest!

"I am the Ideal in the Highest, the God who rules over heaven and earth, the one and only God — God of the Universe.

"Not in the word alone is worship; nor in walled temples only, for everywhere my temple is where thou canst upward look, or upward strive—in every sphere that lifts thy being higher, drawing soul to soul and all thy being nearer unto me. I live in poesy and art, in fiction, music, drama, painting, science, in all fields that kindle with warmth the human heart.

"My church is broader than temples of mere creed or worship of mere words. I live in law and teaching and my favorite temple is the common school—open to all. I live in all work well done or earnestly projected—in sports and pastimes even where all in all there's looking upward.

"All sincere worship and all devotion, all kindness

and all mercy—all these are prayers. Each throb for
human suffering is a prayer I hear, heeding no dress of
language or of creed!"

In the long silence that followed I was carried away
in a series of strange reflections such as never before
had entered mortal mind. All aspects of life under-
went a change as if brought under an enchanter's
wand. I felt in my being it was the voice of God I
had heard. Surely this was God. Who could deny
this subtle but all-powerful being? Who could deny
the existence and potency of the Ideal?

Who would not go through the forge of sacrifice in
worship of his God, to taste the being of a God—to
rise and grow and be created in the everlasting march
that makes the music of the spheres? Who would not
worship the Ideal and make sacrifice for being?

Who will deny the Ideal? None have yet denied
him; none ever will. Words may speak denial, but
action denying is the death eternal.

I also thought of those who worshiped God as first
creator and the thought came to me that "the first"
God was also like the dull stone of which men once
built their idols; in the word "first" it proved a vain
dream like heaven-reaching Babel through which men
sought to enclose expansion within its own derivative
—the finite distance. They sought to embrace being
—the finite-infinite with a finite unit, its own derivative or part. They saw not God *in being* and sought to
make Him an exterior cause—a final starting point
for continuity—such a vanity as even was Babel's
tower. Yet these were all ideals once and though
once conveying to the mind a great ideal—God, must
not forbid our looking farther, to seek Him in the
highest, in the Continuous Creator—a part of being,
the living God. Man and God are inseparable and

man will forever depend on the recognition and worship of God.

Again I heard the voice from above:

"My child, gaze upon the horizon of thy present view as far as thou canst see, tracing thy source creative to germs in chaos hidden; low as these specks of life appear to thee, so low even is thy present being to what thou art to be!

"Look not with dread upon thy infancy but draw therefrom the prophecy and inspiration of thy future grandeur in the true worship of My being, the Ideal in the Highest.

"Living in Me ye live the life eternal—living beyond the self, seeking the life of Humanity-as-One. In that grand life thy noblest being is carried on forever, though death engulf the self viewed absolute by itself. The self that lives in Me—the self living in My imperishable world of Humanity-as-One—that self shall rise again borne higher on the rising tide of life's wavering sea; and there again identities will appear, enlarged, expanded, broadened, more beautiful and loftier than before, and all the cherished loves ye sadly part with now shall return in lovelier aspect—affection, passion, glory, hope, and the fond dreams in which ye look beyond—all, all shall re-appear! The mother shall hold her infant to her bosom, sister and brother shall clasp hands, husband and wife embrace, friend shall meet friend, the victor's brow again be crowned with wreaths—all, all shall be repeated in infinite variety upon life's stage.

"Come then, into My temple of the Ideal! There worship! There look up! Then shalt thou come nearer unto My being—Humanity-as-One. I am thy God and the God of all, of the lowly and the high, of pagan and Christian, believer and unbeliever, of the righteous and the wicked, man and beast, of all that come toward My throne, all that bow down to Me, of all that bend in the sweat of their brows, the rack of their brains or the pangs of sacrifice, of all that righteously strive, all that look upward.

"I am thy God, the God of all Gods—the God that in all gods lives as the Ideal—Humanity in the Highest and Humanity-as-One."

"Ah," whispered my soul to me when silence again reigned, "our Jehova was Creator though the creation we interpreted was not true. God was not false but our feeble minds sought for all time to interpret what belonged alone to their finite day!"

Once more the stillness was broken and the kneeling man spoke:

"O Father, speak to me! Tell me, is there to be no day of reckoning—no day of judgment when good shall be rewarded and evil punished? Must we live forever dragging our load of suffering through all the ages along time's endless shore?"

From the darkness above once more I heard the voice of the Invisible in tones as clear and sweet as music, seeming possessed of an indescribable ring, cheering to the soul yet incomparably solemn and impressive.

"All time is one continuous judgment. O, son of man—forever in thy childhood! Hast thou ne'er weighed thy life by feeling measured? Hast thou not seen the gloomy chambers of the prison made bright with a single ray when the gilt palace, open to the sun, was dark and dim within? Hast thou not watched the lurking moods that oppose all outward cause? Find not the ill-provided great joy in little things? Doth not abundance dull the edge of appetite? O, man, the savage—ill-guarded from My warring elements finds in his native air a palace! The strong is burdened with impatience till he assume his part; the weak is blessed with endurance, casting off the cares that others bear along.

"Have not My prophets in poesy proclaimed the everlasting truth in every shape and form? Verily, God tempers the winds to the shorn lamb!

"Thy outer experience is like to the winds that rave and fret; thy inner moods are great tides welling in the bosom of the deep, and thy joys and sorrows are the waves that dash, now high, now low, forever to one level.

"Judge not the heart by the winds that rant and strike their shoulders 'gainst the frightened stars, nor by the deep hollows of the roaring sea that scrapes the very bowels of the earth—all madly ranging, to no measure bound. Upon the surface, where the forces meet—in consciousness—a fretting like the sea's broad face tells an eternal tale of even measure.

"O my child, look within thyself and in thy feelings read thy other life of promised recompense—the judgment. On faith still hangs thy destiny—on looking up to Me. Look up to Me, and thou shalt read in every cloud My word of heavenly light.

"Have faith in this, My word, as thou hast faith in sleep; for every morn thou wakst to new identity and in thy span of life more change ensues than that between successive countertypes that through all time pursue their course beyond the gulf of death. In these countertypes humanity re-appears refreshed, restored by transfer through life's clearing-house—the grave— after the longer sleep; yet sleep and only sleep! Out of the whole again the whole appears—a round continuous—a growth perpetual—the constant resurrection—the unmistaken immortality in which true beings find unfailing recognition and naught but dross and names, the flesh of life, is faded out complete. The truer life is love, and love finds love by the pure light of love alone—unaided by the label of the flesh. The good can never perish; the wicked are but the lesser good.

"Living beyond the narrow self, living nearer to My being, living in humanity — the God-life that is thine to realize, thou shalt inherit the promised immortality—the life imperishable!

"Soul in being am I even as thy soul is in thy being —not apart from it, but OF IT. The action of the flesh co-operative gives to thy soul its being—an existence inseparate from the flesh, yet not like flesh. More subtle is the soul but not less existent than the vivid flesh. Thus am I unto all being co-operative, living in the highest in the co-operative unity of varied being. In the highest I am the soul of all collective being as part of one grand life in which all being lives. I am the Ideal of Humanity-as-One in the Highest, and of Being in the Highest."

Once more the solitary star came forth in full brilliance and the figure of the Savior was again visible, the sad, pale face reflecting an infinite sorrow.

The kneeling man looked up, his face the picture of deepest reverence, mingled with a touch of awe.

"O, God," he cried, "how far have I wandered from Thee! O, Father, help me that I return! Help Thy feeble, erring child! Father, it was dark where I did wander and in Thy church Thou wert held up to me in form of flesh idolatrous. I sought to repel idolatry; I turned away and closing my eyes to Thee I lost Thy light. It was my sin, my blindness, my idolatry. That grossness was my own—casting away the flesh to lose the spirit. I fought against a gross idolatry blind to the Ideal it embodied and thus myself became idolatrous. Yea, the untutored pagan was wiser than was I; and under the broad mantle of Thy temple — in the open school, he has at last imparted to my soul Thy light, bringing my being nearer to brotherhood and nearer unto Thee."

The last words had hardly died on the air when I seemed to realize a change in the atmosphere which began to lose its magnetic influence. The vision and all its surroundings returned to mist while my own body began to resume its form and substance.

Looking around the first sight I beheld was Arda coming toward me pale and like a faded figure — the mere outlines of a living being. She seemed like a ghost—like a phantom. She appeared to be sinking from view like a resolving mist. I could not bear the sight! I made an effort to rise, but I could not move. I grew impatient and desperate and summoning all my power of will in one tremendous effort — I awoke.

My wonderful vision had after all only been a dream. Worn out from my exertions on the journey to Tsor I had fallen asleep in the course of our conversation.

Sleep and dreams, however, are real life — its more discordant phase, but not unreal, and truth even in a dream is *still the truth*.

I was overjoyed when Arda came to my side, for in the dream I had a sudden notion that I was about to lose her for ever and I really believed as I saw her form fading from view she was leaving me never to return. It was a strange illusion but it made a lasting impression in my mind.

CHAPTER XXIV.

"LONG LIVE LUKKA."

Four days had passed since the burning of the Kar Yuk and the city of Tsor was still under the reign of the mob. Men durst not leave their homes for fear of meeting with violence, and already famine was beginning its cruel work. Factories, stores and warehouses were closed and all doors were barred alike against friend and foe. There had only been one quiet day since—that immediately following the burning. The mobs that day were concentrated in the yim of the warehouses. After that they scattered in broken squads whose riotous cries were frequently heard to the terror of the household. Only when pressed by extreme necessity would the wife consent to the husband's going forth in quest of food, and many a man left his home thus never to be heard from again.

While darkness reigned in the homes of Tsor the Lukkan sun shed its violet rays over the glistening roofs, the birds sang in the golden trees and the soft breezes stirred the gilded leaves undisturbed by the city's inner gloom. The little elphies, spry dogs, the horn-backed cattle and wandering flocks of geese filled the streets with bellowing and barking and cackling in an almost continuous strain as if to let the world know they were enjoying a freedom picnic of their own and having a lively time.

The clear sky looked brighter and more cheering than ever and under its broad wing Tsor was nestled like an eaglet in the parental nest.

The sky communicated its smile to all the outer world, but from the minds of the million Tsorans were projected a million worlds, each clouded with awful darkness, and all the outer ocean of sunlight was devoured and lost in the gloom that shadowed their hearts.

On the morning of the fifth day news spread to the effect that an army from Utopia was nearing the city. The Tsorans scarcely knew what an army was and, without leaders, no difinite steps were taken to meet the dread object. By noon a corps of Utopians were stationed upon every yim of Tsor. Silently they had entered, with neither flourish nor ostentation. No one had opposed their advance and they had already taken possession of the city.

It proved fortunately to be an army of peace. The Utopians, on hearing of the calamity that had befallen their sister city, at once responded.

This was an army organized to fight famine and they brought with them a large store of provisions. Booths were set up along the main intersecting lines crossing the yims, one at each yim, and food was freely dispensed.

Wherever violence or plunder was encountered it was checked and the marauders placed under arrest.

A proclamation soon after was posted at conspicuous points throughout the city placing Tsor under a Utopian dictatorship until it should be re-organized into a settled government. Until such time the Utopians agreed to maintain order and peace; to feed and shelter the helpless and to supply employment to all persons willing to work. The factories were placed under the managment of receivers and were in no instance to be allowed to remain idle.

Rapid communication was maintained between

Tsor and Tismoul and all special supplies disabling a
factory from operating were advanced by Utopia so
that no further destruction of property through unnecessary idleness would recur.

The factories were not to stand in the way to production.   They were declared a public highway to be
controlled for no private purposes.

The responsibility for idleness was to be borne by
capital not by the working classes.   At least, thus
was it to be under the Utopian protectorate and the
cost of this protectorate was to be levied on capital.
They further offered to assist in organizing trade and
in other ways to use the governing power so as to
make their burden as light as possible—becoming for
the time being if anything a source of profit rather
than a tax on the owners of capital.

The proclamation also announced a time when the
Tsorans were to determine what immediate steps they
would take toward the formation of a new government.   A choice was suggested between four propositions, as follows:

1—Return to the former Tsoran government.

2—Forming an entirely new government.

3—Adopting the constitution and form ruling in
Utopia—a representative industrial and civil government.

4—Amalgamation into one body with Utopia under
the Utopian government, thereby forming a united
Lukka once more.

An outline of the existing government in Utopia,
with a brief review of its principal merits was circulated.

The Utopian was pre-eminently a conservative government, both educational and distributive; but above
all it was a man-developing government treating the

wealth of human culture as the highest and regarding all accumulation of property as of value only in so far as it operated to advance human development. It was particularly a conservative government, provided with a distinct bureau for conservation and enlargement of property in all forms—material and immaterial.

It provided also a bureau of progress in which new ideas, methods and systems were devised, considered and promoted and original thinkers in every department of life were rewarded according to their achievements determined by the most approved methods available. The highest reasonable inducements to encourage such work were given and everything was done to prevent long delays and uncertain results, the bane of the old order of society. There were to be no capitalists here to steal from the inventor or swindle him out of his property or to blackmail him by mock legal contests into sacrificing his well-earned rights.

Instead of being governed on all subjects at once through local sub-divisions and by representatives characteristic more for what they do not know of the multifarious matters for them to act on, the government here begins along lines of occupation, in guilds of labor, each guild being provided with a constitution and every member having equal representation in its action.

These are operated each according to its own choice in internal matters, working under equality of wages, piecework or with graded pay according to quantity and quality of service, as each guild finds more suitable to its work or otherwise prefers.

Each guild is again represented in the grand guild in which their relations to each other are determined and their general affairs administered.

These guilds cover all fields of industry from miscellaneous or unclassified forms of labor to the highest professions, arts, literature and invention and other originative and projective work.

There are also educational, religious, social and clearing or financial guilds. Distributive bureaus are made a branch of the co-operative union of factory guilds.

In the regulation of pay the worker is given the equivalent of the full product of his labor after deducting a pro rata assessed by the guild of conservation. This assessment deducted is for the perpetuation of home, factory, apparatus, machinery, etc.; support of the helpless, the aged, mothers and children, widows, the school funds, and expense of general government. In any industrial change of conditions by which a person is rendered incapable of work losses are made good so that each has a reliable, permanent income and his family likewise is always assured of support. Then, be he personally a financier or not, he is always secure.*

The pre-Utopian captains of industry had used gold as the Roman generals had used swords, to subjugate their own people. The latter caused strife and destruction, in which craft and greed supplanted courage and honor. They arrayed army against army until competition for power produced general insecurity and forced the civilian to join the ranks of the contesting leaders. The army of production was absorbed into the army of plunder; the noblest virtues

---

* Few people are by nature gifted as financiers, and the security of the future is practically uncertain in the hands of the best financier where amounts are small and the income capricious, coming from unreliable and irregular sources. It is ridiculous to assume that though one man be a better financier than his neighbor the latter should become his prey. As well assume that the physician act as a dictator over us because he can cause illness often to terminate life if he choose to misuse his power. He has no right to misuse his power; neither has the financier such a right.

we converted into the most hideous vices. Competition made neither better soldiers nor better men, but the worst of both and Rome fell at last by the hand of free competition. Competition is the sword of industry being used against ourselves. It puts robbery on a level with production; villany on a par with virtue and honesty, and it is creating constantly non-productive pursuits and increasing the army of non-producers. It says every dollar acquired is as good as a dollar earned. It was a lie in Rome and it is a lie in modern civilization. In Rome military power finally tore down the civil rule and the sword of gold had threatened to do the same here in Lukka.

The revolution and the ideas emanating from the Kar Tuki were discussed on every side and the same ideas were expounded at meetings where the proposals of the proclamation were also considered. A constant agitation and excitement kept Tsor alive with feverish anticipation of great things in store.

The old rule under the law of Zmun was bitterly attacked and its operation condemned in severe terms. The indictment against the old system was terrific. Its robberies, such as land rents, interest on capital in all sorts of forms, its wastes from bad distribution of population and its extravagant conduct of trade through wars for supremacy, all its vast destruction and tributes and its vicious restriction of productive capacity were estimated to cost much more than half the true product of labor, a tax on production no political party could question. No one had to discuss whether it was a tax or not a tax, as has been done over the question of tariff in the Old World. No one had to ignore off-setting benefits to make men believe it was a tax.

Aside from this its moral iniquities, its despotism,

its irresponsibility, its utter insecurity, its depraving effects on humanity, its vicious obstruction of progressive reform, its despotic usurpation of law in the bribery and shaping of legislative bodies and of courts, its constant invitation to crime for the sake of wealth coveted, its ghastly influence in family life, vitiating the institution of marriage and hinging the welfare of members upon the death of parents—a ghoulish barbarism; its mean, cringing dependence that impressed itself upon all, high and low—forcing its way into the pulpit; on the bench; on the stage; on the rostrum; in the press; in literature; in art; in short, insinuating itself into the holiest precincts with its character-killing blight; its continuous resort to force, creating mobs and then suppressing them again; the persistent clash in struggles between rival districts; the very insecurity under which it dominated the government, all these things conspired to condemn it as utterly worthless to base Tsor's future on. For this rule the average Tsoran had no further use.

Of the four propositions that of amalgamation with Utopia was most popular and it was agreed to publicly ratify it on a day set, through proper representatives of both Tsora and Utopia.

All Tsor was gathered in the Tok Yim not long after—not on their knees, begging for work, but jubilant over the approaching crown of liberty. The ratification was to take place in this yim than which no more fitting place in all Lukka could have been selected.

The yim was bridged with triumphal arches gaily decorated with millions of roses and wreaths and the flag of the new Lukka with a double star waved aloft inspiring a strong and hearty enthusiasm at the expected re-union and rejuvenation. Holiday attire and holiday cheerfulness stirred the air with a distinct music of its own and fluttering hearts beat as joyfully as if marching to the altar—there to consummate a great bond for future weal; and so they were—they were all marching to the altar of their country, where their future weal was soon to be sealed to a new and glorious age of active, prosperous peace.

More than half a million spectators were thronged along the yim upon which a hundred stands had been erected, from which to address the waiting sea of humanity. From these stands the constitution of Utopia was read, followed by elaborate speeches intended to further expound and more clearly elucidate its various features.

It was late in the day when a prolonged ringing of bells all around the yim announced the time designated for signing the declaration of union. One by one, the names of representatives were called, in response to which they advanced and entered their signatures upon the document.

After each signature a chime of bells rang, followed by a shout of applause from the entire multitude. One signature after the other swelled the list; peal after peal of the bells rang on the yim; shout after shout went up and the army of spectators grew more and more enthusiastic, and as the last signature was being attached the vast throng stood waiting in breathless suspense.

The last representative had not yet laid down his pen before from all Tsor went up a tremendous ringing from thousands of bells, great and small, announcing the glorious news of final union. Tsora and Utopia were one.

A new Lukka had been born!

Then from the vast throng spread miles around

the yim came a cry of "Long live Lukka!" repeated over and over again like one prolonged shout.

It was a thundering cry—such a cry as I shall never forget!

It deafened my ears and as it was being repeated and repeated the noise became actually painful.

To escape the terrible sound, in sheer desperation, I held my hands over my ears, when ——

What was it?

"In the name of heaven, Ross, do not move!" I heard some one speak, as I felt a strong hand laid against my shoulder.

I tried to look around, but all was dark. I had never in all my life been in such a predicament. I could not imagine where in the world I was. In the dark I could not tell who my companion was. I seemed to be carried away.

What could it mean?

If ever a man was puzzled I was at that instant. I really began to be so befogged and mystified that I almost questioned my reasoning power. I tried hard to collect my senses. Fortunately a cool breeze just then struck my face, and suddenly it all came to me like a flash.

"Is that you, Doctor?" I cried.

There was such an air of uncertainty in the tone in which I addressed my companion that he was astonished.

"You don't take me for a spirit, I hope!" was the response, "but if you wish to finish your nap I believe I can hold watch for the rest of the night."

I now realized the fact that I was on a balloon, though I could not resist the impression that the world of glass had been real, and that world seemed tenaciously rooted in my mind. I must be deranged, thought

I; that alone could account for all the strange events
that had transpired since I had left Paris in that fool's
flight in a balloon. Only with the force of the
most sustained effort could I bring myself to realize
my present situation ; for I was at that moment floating over two thousand feet high in the air, suspended
from a balloon, in the company of Dr. Giniwig.

"If possible," I answered, "I wish you *would* hold
the watch till morning, Doc ; I declare, I have had such
a dream that its impressions hover in my mind to my
utter bewilderment!"

"If I thought you were joking," replied the Doctor,
convinced by my tone that I was in dead earnest, "I
would go to sleep and leave you to care for the balloon,
but—I'll see the voyage through to terra firma. A good
thud when we alight may shake things up in your
mind and bring it down to a more solid footing, eh?"

"What's that?" I asked, suddenly seeing a strange
light ahead.

"That's Old Sol on a morning stroll. He's a little
earlier than usual this morning because we're up so
high. He's just rolling out of bed. Now, I'll pull the
escape valve and by the time we get down Sol will be
entirely out of bed ; and wont he be surprised to see us
coming down so early!"

"For my part, I'm glad he came ;" I said, "for to
tell the truth, I've been shaken altogether too much
to relish any further adventure, and I shall prefer
hereafter to rest my feet upon solid earth. Catch me
in a balloon again!"

"You don't call this an adventure!" retorted my
companion in a mocking tone, "I declare ; that sounds
well from a man who has done nothing but sleep every
blessed hour ! If you feel any soreness, my friend, or
if you discover any blue marks on your person, please

accept them as a testimonial of my earnest endeavors to wake you. They may also help to elucidate some of the brilliant incidents of your dream. It will no doubt puzzle you all your life more than anything else to determine between the respective merits of your talent for sleeping and your genius for dreaming!"

"You've a right to banter all you please," I responded, "after I have kept you awake all night; but I assure you I had not the slightest intention of imposing on your good nature, Doctor. I hav'nt the slightest doubt but you'll forgive me when I tell you the story of my life in another world; for in reality it will always remain another world to me and this world will be its parody!"

In a few moments it was broad daylight and our balloon was nearing the ground in a country district near by a village, from which a number of peasants ran toward us arriving in time to render material assistance in landing. To our astonishment we found ourselves less than twenty miles from the spot at which we had started in Paris.

The shampoo had done its work most effectually, for by the time I leaped out of the car I felt as chipper as a ten-year-old boy.

"We're in good time for my wedding yet," I exclaimed, feeling jolly.

"Your wedding has been postponed, I am sorry to say;" the Doctor retorted. "Don't be provoked now, for it was absolutely necessary during your illness and I couldn't inform you then!"

That evening I was seated in the parlor of the Hotel Lafayette in Paris reading *Le Petit Journal* when the garcon politely presented me with a note neatly folded, which I hastily opened wondering from whom it could be — for I was a stranger at this place.

What was my astonishment on reading these lines:

My Dear Ross: Have just arrived this minute. Surprised to find you registered here; suppose that you will be as much astonished at my appearance. I never had a more agreeable surprise. Come up at once, love; I have so much to tell you. I'll be looking for you every moment.
VIOLET.

This was an astonishing coincidence indeed, for until four o'clock I had not the remotest idea of stopping at this hotel.

I was at first overjoyed at the news, but as it immediately after brought to mind visions of Arda, a strange feeling came over me. I can scarcely describe the emotion. Would it be the same Violet I had left? Would she inspire my love as before or would she appear like that fading phantom of Arda that had impressed me so like an evil omen, and had at last come true — alas only too true.

My God, the Arda of my heart still claimed possession and left my long lost Violet a memory—a mere fading outline of her past!

Almost against my inclination and trembling with a strange sense of dread I knocked later at her door. The door opened and there stood—Arda. It was the very image of Arda in form, figure and features but lacking her warmth and life; still I could not resist the mental impression that it was Arda. In fact, so thoroughly was I thus impressed that I greeted her in that name.

"Arda!" she exclaimed, after we had embraced, "what do you mean, Ross; have you coined a new pet name for me?"

"No! no!" I stammered in confusion. What could I say? Should I explain my wonderful experience and confide to her my love for that shadow, Arda—the ideal of a dream? What if she should reject the new

ideals I had become attached to in that world of glass
and through this the main channels of our lives were
from now on to diverge? Could I love her then as
before? In this doubt there was something that re-
strained me. Who could tell! The Violet of the past
might be dead to my heart, since other faith had
entered. In this doubt I suffered terribly.

There was only one course to pursue; I must tell
her all. And so I did. We were up very late that
evening—for it was a long, long story I had to tell,
and as I proceeded to unfold its details I could see
Violet becoming more and more intensely interested.
The strange doctrines of exchange, of capital and labor, and the restoration of the poor to their true
estate, seemed to captivate her soul, and I saw her
more and more as the Arda of my dream. Her eyes
began to sparkle with new life, her cheeks assumed a
ruddier warmth, and her whole being assumed its
original vivacity. I became more and more inspired
by the keen enthusiasm of my listener and spoke with
a marvelous mastery of words, my thoughts flowing
clear as crystal, and when I explained the dream
within the dream and the words spoken from the great
cross all came to my lips with miraculous and unaccountable precision. I fairly took Violet to the very
scene of the ruined Kar Yuk and brought it to her
mind in all its original force and grandeur.

Violet was charmed and delighted with these views
of life and the revelation of God in this new light
won her heart.

"Ah, Ross," said she, "you are an angel; you must
have brought this new world down to me from heaven.
You are a true angel, Ross!"

"You exaggerate, my dear;" I answered, "I am
only a wingless goose that treads the earth like other

bipeds—but I did bring this world to you from a lofty place, I admit, even if it was only a mental balloon from whose high altitude I used the telescope of mind and read the astronomy of our personal universe."

"So your balloon story is all a fib?" she asked.

"Yes, and no. It was only a mental balloon but not an unreal one. Its body was drawn from the solid matter of our earth and earth's career; its soul was in the harmony of those parts. Is not our earth and life itself a vast balloon that carries us through newer worlds as the ages roll? Is not life itself a mental balloon floating away from the solid base of matter, yet bound thereto forever?

It is not in that world but in this—in our world, that the kneeling and the lash and the Kar Tuki exist, and men go to the polls behind their masks; it is in our world that all this dependence is felt! It is our world that is darkened by the rule of the Koofim who have planted themselves upon the highways of legislation—at village councils and in the halls of state! It is in our world that the Koofim dictate who shall administer justice! In our world are those Koofim who wield serpents of gold that murder conscience. It is our world that is being crushed in vast pythonic folds; it is in our world that the moral health is being poisoned by the nauseous breath of this monster serpent—capital. It is we who must strike ere conscience sleeps, benumbed under the chilling gaze of this hideous reptile! It is we who must rouse from our lethargy ere the maddened multitude add horror to the horrors already here! Even in our land we have had warnings—at Chicago and Homestead, at Cincinnati and Pittsburg and Buffalo. The cry has been loud and long—awake! awake!

*
*
*

Two months after the events just narrated my better half and I were the two happiest mortals in the world. There had been a wedding at a snug little cottage on a quiet street in Chicago, and Violarda Murdock Allison is the way my wife's name is registered in our family bible.

One cloud still lingers in the horizon of my life. I have another Violet—another better half, another love to win. That other part of me—my world, still seems to me like faded—like Arda's dwindling image in my dream. Will she revive? Will she be wooed like Violet and change from that weak phantom to the sweet picture of my dream?

Will my world retain its gloom and make life's journey a dismal march, an endless wilderness, or will it borrow light and warmth from the ideal world, and like my Violet grow ruddier, brighter, fairer than my dream?

Will it be to me a truly better half — a living, cheering, soul-inspiring mate?

I know the answer; this world is not to perish, but to grow.